PRAISE FOR

The World Beyond the Redbud Tree

"Madison Brightwell has constructed a story about a sixteen-year-old girl and her journey to adulthood in a world with parallel universes and challenges no one could imagine in this lifetime. She's created a world in which parallel universes exist. It's a world where people have telepathic powers. It's a story of the survival of a young girl managing to meet challenges that are very real in some senses—after all, she survives a world where people have lost faith, she writes, 'in institutions and governments, other people, and the nature of truth itself.'

The novel offers us the story of a struggling young girl making her way through both dystopian and utopian futures. A very thought-provoking tale for readers of all ages. I highly recommend *The World Beyond the Redbud Tree*."

> —**David Silverman**, Hollywood screenwriter; writing credits
> include *The Flintstones*, *The Wild Thornberrys*,
> and *Life with Louie*

"This is an inspiring adventure story about a determined yet fallible 16-year old girl, Charli, in danger of being overwhelmed by what she faces in her everyday life, being given a second chance by her exposure to a compelling alternative world, accessed via a magical portal. Her journey is full of twists and turns, obstacles, a whole tribe of people, the Q'ehazi, with a super-holistic and egalitarian lifestyle. The story is full to the brim with positivity and, dare one say it, a blueprint for a different way of living. The design for such a Utopian society is woven into the fabric of the story via an informative set of rules, which are expanded upon in an appendix. There's also a board game. Buy the book and experience the world of Q'ehazi".

> —**Simon J. Williamson**, London literary agent
> specializing in television and film screenplays

"Author Madison C. Brightwell travels deep into the well of her imagination in this enthralling coming-of-age novel about sixteen-year-old Charli, who uncovers the keys to a parallel world where peace and love prevail. At a time when the girl's known world is in turmoil—there's a pandemic, her cat is killed, her grandfather is ill and her relationship with her mother is unravelling, due largely to the destructive influence of her mother's abusive boyfriend—Charli entranced by the utopian world of Q'ehazi and is eager to move there permanently. There are, however, conditions that force Charli to look far within herself and examine her life through a different lens. The realizations are unexpected. Brightwell's storytelling is vivid and rich and her writing compelling. *The World Beyond the Redbud Tree* is a fascinatingly adventurous and original examination of life, grief, forgiveness and com-passion. It's unlike anything I've read before: captivating, touching, gently magical and ultimately uplifting."

—**Penny Haw**, author of *The Wilderness Between Us* and *The Invincible Miss Cust*

The
World
Beyond
the
Redbud Tree

Madison C. Brightwell

VIRGINIA BEACH
CAPE CHARLES

The World Beyond the Redbud Tree

by Madison C. Brightwell

© Copyright 2023 Madison C. Brightwell

ISBN 978-1-64663-937-3

This is a work of fiction.
All the characters in this book are fictitious,
and any resemblance to actual persons, living or dead,
is purely coincidental. The names, incidents, dialogue,
and opinions expressed are products
of the author's imagination and
are not to be construed as real.

Published by

◄ köehlerbooks™

3705 Shore Drive
Virginia Beach, VA 23455
800-435-4811

For my husband, Ray, who is king of my heart.

AUTHOR'S NOTE

I would like to acknowledge that this book was written, and I reside, on lands that were once the indigenous homeland of Turtle Island, the ancestral name for what is now called North America. Moreover, I wish to acknowledge the Cherokee peoples, who were the original inhabitants of the land we now call North Carolina.

What if another world existed just out of reach
and yet as close as your heartbeat?
A world that looks almost exactly like this one
and yet is fundamentally different?
A parallel world, where different decisions
made over time completely changed the trajectory
of the human experience?
Could that world be utopia?
And if we could reach it, would we embrace it,
or destroy it?

Tears streamed down her face, warm and comforting on her skin. She let them fall. Waves of grief passed through her and then were released to the earth below. Sitting cross-legged on the moist grass, she felt strong hands clutching hers on either side. Her eyes were closed, and all she heard was the soft chanting of the group around her, and a mellow voice intoning:

"We send our dear little Belilly across the Rainbow Bridge for the last time, where all is peace and comfort. And we will miss her, for she brought joy to everyone she met, and now her time has come, and she can remain with us no more."

The girl's body swayed back and forth in rhythm to the soft flute music playing a tune she knew well because she had heard it many times before. There were no words, but she hummed a sweet harmony to the notes.

The smell of jasmine permeated the air. She remembered how Belilly had loved to sniff the scented air on her morning amble. She remembered the way the breeze would ruffle Belilly's beautiful white fur and how her whiskers twitched in anticipation of the events of the day ahead. The memories were bittersweet: bitter because she knew she would never again experience them, and sweet because she had experienced them so many times before and they would always exist in her memory.

Gradually, the tears on her face dried. She felt the stroke of a burdock leaf on her cheek, and she turned her head and opened her eyes to see her mother smiling at her and passing the leaf gently over the dried tears in a soothing ritual. Tenderness emanated from her mother's face as she made this gesture, and the girl felt a sense of relief at the knowledge that Belilly's passing was done and all suffering was over.

As the girl allowed her gaze to traverse the scene, she took in this group of about twenty people, all known to her, all seated on the ground and clasping hands in a circle, and all swaying to the music around them. Behind them, the beautiful rays of crimson light cast by the huge stone on its ceremonial plinth were enhanced by the stream running behind it. The tinkling of the water cascading over rocks in the stream harmonized with the flute.

Belilly was gone and would never be here again. She knew there was nowhere else she'd rather be than in this place at this time with these people. An intense gratitude swept over her, casting out the grief and replacing it with joy and contentment.

harli hated herself at that moment. She felt weak for letting them see how upset she was, these strangers. She swept the tears angrily from her face and sniffed.

"Can I take him?"

"Yes, honey," said the animal control lady in her soft Southern drawl. She was obviously trying to be sympathetic, but her pitying look only increased Charli's resentment. "Are you okay, dear?"

"I'm fine," Charli declared with a defiant thrust of her chin. She held the little body in its black plastic bag, angry tears flowing at the thought of Casper being unceremoniously dumped in that bag as if he were trash.

"I gotta go. Mom's outside." Charli rushed out of the office, trying to ignore the unwelcome stares in the waiting room, and stumbled over to the car where her mother sat in the driver's seat, using the car mirror to put on lipstick. Angela failed to notice the tear stains on her daughter's face and couldn't help a twinge of disgust at the thought of a dead animal possibly staining the upholstery, but she popped the passenger door open.

"Oh, my dear God!" she exclaimed at the sight of the bag in Charli's arms.

"Yeah."

Angela sighed and started the engine, speaking to her daughter with her face averted. "Did they tell you what happened?"

"They said he was run over by a car."

"Where at?"

"They don't know exactly, but . . ." Charli's voice faltered a bit. "Whoever did it had left him by the side of the road. It was on Weaverton Road, close to our house."

"How did he get there?" Angela shook her head and gave a tut of disapproval.

"I don't know, Mom," Charli grumbled, sensing her mother was trying to somehow shift the blame for her pet's demise onto her. "He was a careful cat. He never strayed far."

"Well, he sure did this time."

"Maybe something else happened." Charli was too tired and upset to argue. Her gaze drifted out the window to the familiar trees and hedges along the road as she contemplated Casper's untimely passing. It being April, spring had seemingly come overnight, and the tall, spindly trees that had been devoid of leaves only a few days before were now springing to life, with their various shades of green decorating the highway. But the beauty of her natural surroundings only served to sharpen the contrast with Charli's mood and increase her sadness and frustration.

"Like what?" asked Angela, insisting on continuing the conversation.

"Maybe, I dunno, maybe it was . . . on purpose."

"Oh, because he was black you mean?"

"What difference does that make?" Charli demanded. Why did her mother always have to leap to those kinds of conclusions?

"None, really, but some people don't like black cats—think they bring them bad luck or something."

"That's dumb." Charli hesitated for a moment as another thought struck her. "Do you think Sean thinks that?"

"What?" Angela's attention was on the road and only half on the conversation.

"That black cats are bad luck?"

"I don't know, honey. I shouldn't think so."

"He didn't like Casper. I know that much." As usual, Charli

reflected, her mother wasn't taking her ideas seriously, but she was going to tell what she knew.

"What are you talking about?" Angela's tone was predictably dismissive.

"I *saw* him kick Casper," Charli responded with passion. "I *told* you about that before."

"I really don't think he'd kick a helpless animal, honey."

Charli opened her mouth to say, "I knew you'd say that," then decided against beginning the usual argument and sat in stubborn silence the rest of the journey. She had some ideas about her mother's boyfriend that she kept to herself for the time being.

They pulled into the driveway of their house. The sight of the pink redbud trees and the white dogwoods in the front yard comforted Charli for a moment. In LA she had always loved this time of year for the jacarandas that blossomed along the city streets, and here the presence of spring was similarly announced by nature as if it didn't have a care in the world. Sometimes Charli wished she could be the same. But in her experience, life was too complicated and full of unexpected twists and turns that she felt unable or unwilling to navigate.

Charli brushed her feet dutifully on the front mat before entering the house, then kicked off her shoes with difficulty because of the burden she was still carrying.

"You're not bringing it in the house, are you?" Angela admonished.

"What am I supposed to do with him?" Charli demanded sulkily.

"It'll smell if we leave it inside before we get it cremated."

"He's not an it!" Charli retorted. "And I'm not having him cremated. I'm going to bury him."

Angela didn't respond to this statement, simply showing in her expression that she didn't believe her daughter would carry out this intention, then vanishing into the kitchen. Charli placed the package carefully on the front porch steps, just outside the front door, whispering gently to its contents as if Casper could hear her: "I'll come back for you, little guy."

"I'm making veggie lasagna for dinner," called Angela from the kitchen as Charli reentered the house.

"Okay." Charli flung herself on the couch in the living room and picked up a copy of the *Mountain Express*, leafing distractedly through the "What's On" section, wondering how many venues would be open now since the governor had introduced limits on social gatherings. The black leather couch was not particularly comfortable, seeming more suited to a bachelor pad than their suburban home, but since the house was rented fully furnished, they had no choice.

Angela came into the living room briefly, drying her hands on a kitchen towel that had a picture of the Biltmore on it. "I thought you loved veggie lasagna," she said with an aggrieved air. "You said it was your favorite."

"I like it fine. It's not my total favorite or anything; I'm just glad you're not doing meat and stuff every night."

"I don't do 'meat and stuff' every night," Angela responded, aping her daughter's tone, "But I want to make things Sean likes as well."

"Yeah, right. Gotta make sure Sean likes it." Charli kept her head lowered, knowing that her sarcasm would aggravate her mother. She looked up and saw Angela giving her a look she'd seen before. "What?"

"He's not my first priority in this family. *You* are."

"It sure doesn't feel that way."

"You're an only child, and you're just not used to sharing."

"I don't want to share you with *him*, no. I don't see why I should—"

Angela overlapped her: "You see, you've never had to think of anybody but yourself. When I was a kid, my parents had so many other mouths to feed, I knew I had no choice in anything for myself—"

"Yeah, yeah, I know. I didn't mind sharing you with dad. He was my family—*our* family. This guy is nothing to do with us. He's just a guy. And not a great guy." Charli muttered the last sentence, wanting to make her protest known without entirely upsetting her mother.

Angela moved closer to her daughter and put a soapy hand on her young shoulder: "I know you adored your dad, and nobody will be as good as him in your eyes," she began.

"Not nobody. Anybody but *that* guy. Why couldn't you pick somebody more—I don't know—less . . . Oh, whatever. I guess you'll do what you want."

"Look, I know he's not Chuck. But your dad wasn't perfect either." Angela gave her daughter a meaningful look, but Charli didn't notice it, so caught up was she in her own feelings.

Charli's words started to tumble out of her mouth, and her voice rose with every sentence. "I wish we'd never left California. You said things would be better here, but they're not."

"I know you're upset right now about Casper, but . . ." Another thought struck her: "It'll be better when you can go to school. You can probably go back in the fall and start making some new friends."

"I liked my *old* friends. I was happy in LA."

Angela raised her eyebrows: "What, even when those boys attacked you in chemistry class?"

"I fought those boys off, *if* you remember! Four of them against just one of me. Thought I was pretty bad-ass, to be honest," Charli retorted defiantly.

"Yes, well, it's not really anything to be proud of."

"Maybe you don't believe in fighting back, but I do." Charli was going to continue, but something about the look on her mother's face halted her. She snappily changed the subject. "I don't know anybody here, and that's the problem. How in the hell do I make new friends when it's a pandemic and I have to be home-schooled?"

"I know you liked your friends in LA. But they were not *all* the greatest friends. Especially the ones in rehab."

"I know you don't like Shashawna, but she's an amazing person."

"It's not that I don't like her, dear. It's just that, well, she's older than you, and I don't think she makes good choices."

"You don't like her because she's Black."

"That's got nothing to do with it."

"It does, underneath. You might not think it does, but you've always been down on me whenever I have Black friends."

"That's ridiculous, and you know it." Angela's face grew red, as it always did in the midst of an argument, especially one with her daughter, who was always so convinced of her moral superiority in any debate.

"I know you can't help it. Your parents are racists—" Charli began.

"Now, you quit that talk right now, young lady. My parents have been very good to us. Taking us in when we had nowhere else to go and no money. They didn't have to do that. I was the one that left home to marry Chuck, after all, and go live thousands of miles away."

Charli kept her mouth shut now, but her face was burning in a tell-tale fashion similar to her mother's. Although she was smart and capable of besting Angela in any argument, Charli was also kindhearted and didn't like to see her mother discomfited, as she was now. She backed down for the time being and stored all her pent-up resentment and hurt for another time.

Angela, sensing an opening, continued: "You should be grateful."

"Yeah, I know. I am."

"By the way, they want us to visit for Memorial Day."

Charli gave a barely audible "Ugh" of disgust at this revelation, which Angela decided to ignore, preferring to return to the kitchen and the dinner preparation that was a lot easier to deal with than her daughter's emotions.

Charli, meanwhile, stared back at the pages in her hand without seeing the writing on it, too engrossed in the swirl of words and emotions trapped inside her head, unable to be articulated. She wished she were able to explain how much the loss of her father had hurt her, in those deep places that cannot be healed; how alone she'd felt ever since; how all of her drug use and "acting out" was inextricably linked to that—not a cry for attention or a selfish desire to have everything her own way, but a cry of pain that knew no outlet and no bounds.

⊙ ⊙ ⊙

The alarm went off at 9 a.m. the next morning, and Charli moaned, remembering glumly that she'd set it the night before even though it wasn't a school day. She wondered vaguely what had produced this optimism, then recalled: *Oh yeah, I'm sixteen today.*

Sixteen was supposed to be a wonderful age, and Charli had anticipated reaching her sixteenth birthday for months with such hope and optimism, but now that it was finally here, the only thing motivating her to rise from her bed and grab her phone from the desk was the anticipation of all the "likes" she might have gotten from last night's TikTok posting.

When she opened up the app, to her dismay there were only five responses, most of them neutral or from people whose opinions she didn't care about. Only one person gave a thumbs-up and a "wink wink" emoji, and Charli smiled when she saw that it was her friend Shashawna, who was the only person who really understood her. She immediately texted Shashawna, forgetting the three-hour time-zone difference in her haste to reach out: "Hey, girl, nobody else got it but you. Happy sixteenth to me, lol."

Charli waited for the response, her fingers trembling over the phone as she listened to the many insistent birdsongs drifting through her open window.

Pretty soon the answer came back: "Hey there, birthday queen! Yeah, your video was the bomb."

Charli had posted a short video on TikTok of herself doing the "movements" from the TV series *The OA* (a show she was currently obsessed with). Charli knew that only certain people would have any idea what she was doing, and most would find it odd. Predictably, the only person who understood the reference was Shashawna, who was also a huge fan of the show.

Charli suspected that Shashawna was probably pulling one of those cocaine-induced all-nighters she often employed to get through taxing exam season; otherwise, she wouldn't have responded to a text at 6 a.m. Pacific time. And while Charli herself was committed to staying clean and knew that her use of spice and dabbling in other substances had been more a temporary aberration than a predilection for using drugs, she knew that Shashawna's drive caused her to do whatever it took to succeed. Charli loved her best friend and typically accepted without judgment other people's decisions about their lives, even if she didn't herself agree.

Charli was relieved that her mother didn't use TikTok and had never watched *The OA*, as Angela's strict religious upbringing made her very narrow-minded about other spiritual beliefs and practices. Angela would be even more disapproving of the ongoing text conversation between her daughter and this girl, who she considered to be a "bad influence." Charli felt this was just one more example of Angela's "closet racism." In Charli's idealistic world of right and wrong, there was no excuse for putting people into categories based on their race.

Charli stared glumly at the range of birthday wishes on her Facebook page, with their standardized emojis and icons representing cakes and balloons and the usual birthday paraphernalia. She wondered why she felt nothing, none of the joy she'd been expecting or the thrill of being almost an adult, able to drive at last.

She knew her mother had bought her a car for her birthday, and she wasn't at all upset that it wasn't a new car but rather an old, beat-up Hyundai—all her mother could afford from the car dealership in town. She had been relishing the idea of her newfound independence and ability to go wherever she wanted, whenever she wanted, up to a point. Yet now, despite the fact that she was overall grateful to her mother, the excitement seemed to pall.

Charli felt disgusted with herself for not enjoying her special day, even though she knew the reasons why. What was the point of having a sixteenth birthday party on Zoom, as her mother had suggested for her, when she couldn't see any of her friends in person? Charli had texted several of her old high school friends in California the day before, and a smattering of them had replied, but it all seemed rather desultory and pointless.

Charli cared passionately about the things that were important to her, and her friends knew her dislike for frivolities, even if they didn't share her idealism. The pandemic and resulting social isolation had only exacerbated Charli's natural tendency towards introversion and reflection, along with the fact that she was a recent transplant from California to North Carolina, with no chance of making actual friends now that all of the schooling was happening online.

If Charli was honest with herself, she didn't at all miss shopping at crowded malls or visiting friends for noisy parties in their homes.

She did miss living in a society where her fervent desire to make a positive contribution to the world might be more readily received, and she was therefore annoyed with her mother for forcing her to live in this "backwater" part of North Carolina.

Another reason why Charli was not in the best of moods today was held in the black plastic bag currently on the front steps where she'd left it the day before. The previous day's events had been pretty terrible, and even the delight of a sixteenth birthday couldn't uplift her spirits this morning.

Her mother called her down for breakfast, and Charli dutifully complied, knowing that at least Mom would have prepared something special for her. Charli wished that it weren't just herself, her mother, and her mother's boyfriend, Sean, enjoying the meal, sitting in the sunroom and watching the trees sway in the wind. But nobody else was allowed to visit because of the current isolation rules.

Mom and Sean seemed to be in a good mood this morning, affectionately teasing each other with Mom shooting conspiratorial smiles at Sean from time to time as if they held a secret they didn't wish to share and Sean slapping her playfully on the butt as he made some suggestive remark. Charli wondered if that was the result of them having sex that morning or the night before. She'd seen these sorts of things in movies, even if she hadn't experienced it herself.

Mom and Sean were making cute conversation together and kind of ignoring her, and that irritated Charli. Wasn't this supposed to be *her* day? Charli sighed and fingered the little necklace with her name on it that her mother had given her. It was a pretty object, with its little glass diamonds spelling out her name—Charlotte Grace—in old-fashioned letters.

"Hey, don't forget, we're going to talk to Nonno at 3:30 today." Her mother's voice brought Charli out of her reverie.

"Oh yeah, right." Charli brightened at the thought of talking to her grandfather. At least she knew he'd pay her more attention than Mom did. Since learning that he had contracted the virus while resident in the nursing home in Los Angeles where he'd lived for the past few months, Charli had been even more vigilant about maintaining contact with her grandfather on a regular basis. There was no telling if or when he might recover.

"What do you want to do this afternoon? We could see a movie."

Charli was surprised by her mother's suggestion. "I thought the theaters were closed."

"No, at home, stupid." Charli turned to see Sean smirking at her. "Don't you remember your mom told you? I got you guys a subscription for Starz so we can see all the new stuff. There's a new Harry Potter—"

"I don't like Harry Potter."

"Well, whatever." Sean threw himself down on the couch and lit up a cigarette.

"Please," began Charli's mother with a nod to her boyfriend that he recognized.

"Shit, okay." Sean gave a look between annoyance and resignation and took himself outside on the front porch to smoke.

Angela turned her attention to her daughter. "I'm sorry there isn't much fun stuff to do today, honey."

"That's okay."

"By the summer, this virus thing will all be over, and we can take a fun trip somewhere and celebrate for real, okay?"

"Yeah, sure." Charli welcomed her mother's attempts to cheer her up, even though they weren't enough to drag her out of her current funk. "Do we have a spade?"

Charli's question seemed to startle her mother. "A what?"

"I want to bury Casper."

"Oh, I see. Where do you want to do that?"

"I think he'd like to be by the creek."

Angela now understood both the implications of the request

and the underlying reason for her daughter's sadness. She wanted to say something to make it better, but she knew there was nothing she could say. She went to fetch the spade from the shed, leaving her daughter in the sunroom, staring out at the garden, lost in thought.

The sun was shining, and it was becoming a beautiful spring day. Charli couldn't imagine why anybody would wish to spend such a day inside, watching a television or computer screen. She had a sudden longing to feel her feet in the grass and the wind on her face. She imagined Casper would want to do the same thing. It would be an appropriate homage to him if she could spend the rest of the day in the open air while she laid him to his final rest.

Charli went up to her room to put on her outdoor shoes, then traveled to the front patio steps, where she collected the black plastic bag, holding it to her chest like the precious object it was.

From the front patio, Charli could hear through the open door a familiar argument raging between her mother and Sean as they stood in the backyard, and her heart sank. Couldn't they give it a rest for once, at least on her special day?

"You don't get to tell me what to do." Charli recognized the belligerent tone Sean employed when he was starting to get riled up, usually after his first few beers of the day.

"This is my house," began Angela plaintively.

"No, it's not your house, stupid. You're renting this place."

"I don't want my daughter exposed."

"Give me a break. Your daughter's already 'exposed' every time she steps out of the house. I bet you she's already using drugs. Get real. Everybody's a crackhead in LA."

"Charli's been sober since she got back from rehab."

"Oh yeah? Like nobody ever relapsed."

"Not my girl."

"Guess what? She's sixteen. It's normal."

"Not in my family it's not."

"Always with the 'family.' You're no saint, Angie. Your dad may be a priest, but he's as much a sinner as the rest of us. They're the biggest hypocrites."

"How dare you insult my father!"

"Trust me, darlin', ain't nothing special about your dad."

Charli heard the familiar sound of an opening can and the ensuing fizz.

"Don't you dare open another beer."

"I'll do what I damn well please."

"No, you won't."

"Get the fuck off me, woman!"

When Charli heard a scream from her mother's lips, she could stand it no longer and hurtled down the steps to the back of the house where the argument was raging. When she got there, she saw her mother cowering and on her knees, her cheeks red as if she had just been slapped.

"Leave my mom alone, you bully," Charli yelled in righteous rage. "You're not worth one ounce of her!"

"Shut up, you little bitch," Sean growled, now stumbling away across the grass, still clutching the beer in his hand. At least he seemed momentarily humbled by recent events.

Charli tried to comfort her mother and helped her to her feet.

"I'm fine. I'm okay," Angela protested. "You go and do your . . . thing, honey."

"Did he hurt you?"

"No, no, really. I'm good."

With a sigh, Charli told her mother she'd be back soon. She wasn't sure exactly where she'd bury her beloved pet, but she knew it was something she had to do today.

☉ ☉ ☉

All Charli wanted was to finish digging the hole.

She had gotten maybe six inches down, but the work was much harder than she'd anticipated, and she was already exhausted. Little rivulets of sweat formed between her breasts and ran down her forehead, and she was breathing heavily. Charli castigated herself for being such a wimp. She'd always regarded herself as so strong and tough, and yet this damn hole, just a small hole and a seemingly simple operation, threatened to defeat her.

Her frustration with the situation gave her a new burst of energy, and she dug more forcefully. She had imagined soil to be loose and crumbly, kind of like the soy crumbles that looked like meat when you cooked them—not this hard, impacted, stubborn ground. The truth was, the teenager knew very little about real soil, having never encountered it before in this intimate way. Every time the spade hit the ground, it had to be shoved in with her foot, as if the soil were rebelling against her attempts to disrupt it. The hardness of the earth felt like stone or clay, and yet as soon as it was dislodged, it did actually crumble and look a little like soil was supposed to look, although it was deep red in color, nowhere near brown.

Charli glanced behind her at the small black plastic bag containing the creature for whom the hole was being dug. Her feelings of frustration turned instantly to a painful sadness. She had to bury Casper. Her little black cat, who was such a fearless soul in life, and who had been with her his entire four years on the planet, accompanying her from the busy streets of LA to these forested slopes, and somehow always adapting to his environment without any fuss.

Casper had seemed at times like her only friend, especially in the first days of moving to this alien place. And now he was gone. Just a young cat, so healthy and strong and independent. Tears of frustration pinched at Charli's eyelids, and she sniffed them back, using the extra energy of her anger at the unfairness of it all to push through the remaining hard soil.

Her efforts finally produced something resembling a hole, although it was probably only about a foot deep. Every inch of that had cost more sweat and tears than she had ever produced, but Casper was worth it.

Charli stopped to catch her breath and bask in the air for a moment. She noticed the smells around her, which seemed particular to this spot on the earth. They were not smells she was familiar with, but she didn't find them unpleasant, just a little strange. She wasn't sure how to describe them, but they made her feel oddly comforted, as if the earth below her feet were all the more real and present because it was giving off this powerful odor.

Then there were the sounds around her—a little less insistent than the ones she heard at night, but still very much a part of this place. Sounds of many different birds, some in chorus and some independent and singing solo; sounds of the rushing waters of the creek a few feet distant; faint sounds of agricultural machines going about their business on the farm next door; a low hum of crickets just beginning their concert in the middle of the afternoon. The air around her was neither hot nor cold but pleasantly lukewarm, with a thick humidity to it that hung around her like fog.

Charli enjoyed all these relatively new sensations. She wondered if she was the only person in the world who even paid them much attention. Charli was very much a person who paid attention to her surroundings. She was hypersensitive to noises, sights, and smells—a character trait that had gotten her into trouble in the past and caused her some distress, but not anything she could change, or even wished to change.

Her mother called Charli stubborn and willful, just like her father. Charli didn't mind at all being compared to her adored dad.

Plus, she knew that her stubbornness had helped her to survive the vagaries of the sixteen years she'd been on the planet so far, and for that she was grateful. If she hadn't been stubborn, she wouldn't have volunteered to dig a hole for Casper, which was a responsibility only she was prepared to take on. Stubbornness had caused her to start digging, and pride was what drove her to complete the job. She could hardly go back to the house with her tail between her legs, having not finished the job she'd set out to do. That would only make Sean happy.

A few more stabs to the ground, and Charli felt something beneath her spade that was even harder than the tough clay soil she'd been digging through. Perhaps it was a rock, perhaps even gold. *Do people dig for gold in this state?* she wondered. Throwing down the spade, she got down on her hands and knees to investigate. She scratched away at the earth with her bare fingers, not minding that the soil was dirtying her fingernails. Since Charli bit her nails, they were always in a state of disarray anyway, with the cuticles in various stages of rawness.

Something glinted under the soil, giving Charli a twinge of excitement. Even if not gold, she knew that some rocks could contain gemstones or at least bright, shiny fragments that were a joy to look at and which she could claim as a prize to take home. But when she dug deeper, she realized she had not uncovered a rock at all. In fact, the item appeared to be made of glass. Obviously man made, perhaps somebody had deliberately buried it, so it was possibly precious in another way.

After some sustained and determined digging, Charli managed to uncover the object enough to recognize what it was. It was a large, heavy glass bottle with a wide glass lid, the whole thing about two feet long and six inches in diameter. Charli managed to dislodge the bottle from the ground, and she heaved it up above the soil so she could take a closer look.

The good news was that now there was a substantial hole into which Charli could easily deposit the black plastic bag containing the body of her deceased pet. She picked up the little carcass and laid it carefully into the ground. She wanted to say something relevant and special, but she couldn't think of anything beyond "Goodbye, Casper, little sweetie. I'll miss you."

A lonely tear welled up in her eye and dripped down her cheek at the memory of collecting this bag the day before. Charli had been told that Casper's body was "mangled," and she preferred to remember him as a lively little black cat, full of energy and sauce and a zest for life that few humans displayed.

"You were a special guy, Casper," she added as she replaced the soil on top of the plastic bag with her hands. "At least you had four years of a fun life." Her voice came out small and girlish, and she wished she could be more profound or sound worthier of the occasion. She felt Casper deserved a proper ceremony, yet all he had was a young girl shoving his body into a hole.

Now that she'd completed her task, she returned her attention to the glass bottle she'd unearthed. It looked pretty plain for something that had been buried so deeply and deliberately. There were no markings or writing on it of any kind. Though it was more opaque than transparent, Charli saw that something had been stuffed inside. Charli couldn't tell exactly what it was, and she felt another glimmer of excitement.

Charli considered taking the bottle back to the house before trying to open it. But Sean would be at the house still, and her mother had probably retired to her bedroom after their fight. Charli did not relish the idea of encountering Sean without her mother there to mediate between them. She knew from experience how badly that would end.

Charli ran the scenario through her mind. There probably would be an argument with shouting and yelling or even the threat of a physical altercation. Charli knew that her breasts were starting to form in ways that were attractive to men, and she often felt uncomfortable around Sean when she was alone with him for reasons she couldn't quite put her finger on—something to do with the way he looked at her with a sly and cunning smile. Mom would arrive in the middle of their argument, and Charli would take the opportunity to flee to her room and lock the door, leaving Sean to give his side of the story to her mother and convince her of Charli's wrongdoing, after which Mom would knock gently on her door and explain in mournful tones how Charli had to try to be nicer to Sean because she cared about them both so much. Charli would protest and plead with her mother to recognize how Sean was abusing both of them, but her protestations would fall on deaf ears, after which Charli would cry herself to sleep, vowing never to confide in her mother about anything and feeling betrayed and without an ally.

Obviously, the best thing to do was to open the bottle here. Maybe the thing inside would be uninteresting anyway—or maybe it would be very interesting. The only thing to do was to look.

Charli gently pried the lid open. Even though the lid was a little tight, it was relatively easy to remove. Inside was tissue paper that was old and brown with age and crackled when she touched it. It was so thin that it largely disintegrated into dust as Charli removed the top layer to see what lay underneath. And inside the tissue paper was another surprise.

It was some kind of clothing, made of wool and either knitted or crocheted. The most surprising thing about it was the colors—red, blue, purple, yellow, green, and all so vibrant, as if the article had been made yesterday! Charli let out an exclamation of delighted surprise as she drew it out of the bottle. When she opened it out fully, she could see it was a shawl. The pattern of the shawl was very intricate, unlike anything Charli had ever seen.

She stood and held up the fabric. It was maybe three or four feet in diameter, and she couldn't resist throwing it over her shoulders. With a young girl's vanity, she wished there were a mirror so she could see how she looked in the shawl. She wondered if the water in the creek was still enough to show her reflection, and she thought about walking over there, since it was close by.

But all of a sudden, Charli was overcome with the strangest sensation. The feeling was hard to describe because she'd never felt anything like that before. She felt light, almost dizzy, and slightly breathless. An elation bubbling up from her stomach caused a smile to gradually spread over her face.

Then she saw the line. She felt quite certain it hadn't been there before, and yet it most certainly was there now. A hazy line—dark brown in color, as thick as a piece of string, and a foot or so long—hovered in the air a few feet from Charli. She blinked a couple of times, wondering if something in her eye was causing a visual illusion, but the line persisted. It stayed in the same place, suspended in midair and pulsating slightly as if it were alive or had some energy about it. Charli was intrigued, excited, and afraid, all at the same time. Despite her trepidation, her curiosity got the better of her, compelling her to reach out and touch the line.

To her amazement, when Charli placed her fingers on the brown surface, she perceived its slightly rough and scratchy texture, like the zipper on the back of a dress. Charli moved her head to peer behind the line, and suddenly it wasn't visible at all, although she could still feel it. When her head resumed its original position, the line became clearly visible once again.

Then it seemed to slightly separate in her fingers, opening to reveal a very small hole. It was like a tear . . . in the air? It was the most peculiar thing, as if the air all around Charli weren't open space at all but a thin screen with the world painted on it. Charli tried to stop from trembling, and she felt obliged to reach further into the aperture and see what would happen. She continued to pull apart the two edges of the opening that she'd created in this painted screen of her world. She peered through the rent, wondering what it would reveal.

And through this split in her world, she saw something that amazed her even further.

harli saw another world that was the exact replica of this one—or perhaps it was the real world behind the painted one.

She tugged the tear larger and larger, until it was about five feet tall. Charli realized that she could now easily step through the hole.

She wanted to go through, but she hesitated. Would it be dangerous? Was she even allowed to go through? Part of her wished that her mother were here to advise her. She never heeded Mom's advice anyway, but Charli would have taken advice from just about anybody right now.

While she pondered her decision, Charli stepped back from the hole she'd created and breathed deeply, trying to calm herself enough to think. She tried to recall anybody whose advice she trusted and imagined what they would say in this situation. Her mom, of course, would say she shouldn't even go there, should never have started this in the first place, should have just walked away. Her best friend Shashawna would probably have already barreled through the hole and be enjoying herself at a crazy party right now. Her grandmother in Saluda would give her dire warnings about how it was against the scriptures, or some such religious fanatical talk. Her old teacher in junior high, Mr. Henry, who gave her straight As and regarded her as his best pupil, would say something encouraging like "Whatever happens, I'm sure you can handle it." Sean would call her names and say she was selfish and tell on her to her mom.

And what would Casper do? Casper would go for it. He was a cat, of course, but he was the most fearless creature Charli had ever known. Casper would have confidence and curiosity. And even though those were the traits that had gotten him killed while he was still young, he'd always enjoyed life and done what he pleased. That was who Charli wanted to be—a person who enjoyed life and didn't shy away from things because they were scary or unfamiliar or difficult. Through the hole there could be dangers, and she would overcome them; or there could be nothing, and she'd get over the disappointment. After all, how great were things for her right now, with a crazy mom and her mom's sleazy boyfriend and no friends here in this new place they'd moved to, and no money and no way of escaping?

Charli stepped up to the hole again with renewed determination. This time, she pushed through before she had time to change her mind.

Glancing back briefly, she noted that the tear was not visible from the other side. All she saw were the trees and the forest she'd just left behind. They were all in the same locations, and yet they were different. The pink blossoms of the redbud tree next to the creek had morphed into the flame-colored leaves signaling the start of spring, and Charli knew she could recognize this tree again if she needed to find her place, even without the benefit of a dark-brown, hovering line to guide her.

She faced forward and began a totally new adventure.

◉ ◉ ◉

Meanwhile, Angela was at home, wondering when her daughter would return. Whenever she felt a little stressed and wasn't quite sure why, she would calm and distract herself by doing some cooking. The kitchen was her domain and the place where she felt the safest and most in control. Her current creation was key lime pie, made with fresh limes and graham cracker crust made from scratch. She hummed to herself as she worked—"The Rock of Ages," an old hymn she remembered singing in church with her parents when she was a kid.

Sean was sitting on the couch in his underwear, watching reruns of the World Series from 2019 on Fox Sports, shouting encouragement to the Atlanta Braves and bitching about the fact that there were no current sporting events to watch because of "that stupid virus hoax thing." Angela didn't enjoy sports herself, but she understood it was an activity that men were compulsively addicted to and therefore tolerated it in her partner.

Her mind often strayed to memories. Her mother had said that Angela lived in the past, and perhaps she did, although for her it felt normal because the past was more comfortable. It had already happened and was therefore a known quantity. The future was a scary place, and the present was potentially threatening, but happy memories from her past, mixed with a sanitized and idealized portrait of her childhood, were a safe haven from which to view the world.

Angela had first met Sean a few months ago, at a church function that friends of her parents had invited her to as a way of welcoming the young woman to the neighborhood and their parish. Angela had difficulty making friends due to her reticence in unfamiliar situations, so a social event at church seemed like a good way to meet new people in a nonthreatening environment. She'd tried to persuade Charli to accompany her, but her daughter was strangely resistant to all forms of religious ceremony, much to Angela's disappointment.

Angela had been immediately attracted to what she perceived as Sean's confidence and strength. His personality was larger than life and seemed to complement her own quiet and passive nature. She liked that he was proactive in approaching her and offering to walk her to her car, opening the way for conversation, which she sometimes found awkward with strangers. His ebullience comforted her. She didn't have to make any effort because he did all the talking, and she could therefore hide behind her mask of politeness. He made frequent remarks about her physical attractiveness, praising her long blond hair, large, baby-blue eyes, and hourglass figure. Angela had initially assumed that he, being a Christian, would be respectful of her wishes and "not too pushy," as she liked to call men who were overtly flattering—though she secretly enjoyed his compliments.

Sean never made any attempt to discover what she was thinking or feeling, and that was fine by Angela because she was secretive about these things anyway, always preferring to wait for others to express their opinions before she dared express her own, lest it diverge from the norm.

With other men, and most notably with Charli's dad, Angela had felt some shame about her lack of education and aimless attitude towards her career. But with this man, who worked in construction and who was more interested in money than education or career goals, she didn't feel any embarrassment. He was "her type," as most people who knew her well would agree, and they certainly would never have said that about Chuck Speranza, who had been from a far more sophisticated background than Angela could have dreamed of.

Angela liked the way Sean took charge, even the manner in which he had made the decision to move in with her after only knowing her for a couple of months. Angela enjoyed feeling wanted by somebody, and Sean's physical attentions were flattering and validating. For that reason, she put up with the fact that he could be aggressive and mean-spirited at times. She put up with his drinking, even though it often led to arguments and fights between them and she disapproved of drugs and alcohol, as she had been raised in a religious environment where these things were frowned upon, with Mother not allowing any of the "Devil's drink" into their house and her father railing against the "sins of the flesh" every Sunday in his church sermons (although everybody turned a blind eye to what was going on in his own household).

Even though three months had elapsed since Sean had moved in officially and he and Charli still had a relationship that could most tactfully be described as strained, Angela felt certain that Charli would like him better as she got to know him. Her daughter could be stubborn and opinionated, but she hoped that one day their relationship would improve. Perhaps some sort of magic happened when one's child reached a certain age, and they started to understand things better and have more sympathy for their parents. That was what she'd been told, anyway, and she kept praying to God to make it so.

Thinking of Charli brought the tense feeling to her chest again, so she went into the living room to distract herself.

"Hi, honey, the pie is almost ready," she opened in a cheerful tone.

"Oh, for fuck's sake, did you see that?" As usual, Sean spoke to her without turning his eyes away from the television and then proceeded to give a blow-by-blow description of the baseball game he was watching, which Angela feigned interest in as she fetched him another beer.

"Here you go."

"Thanks, babe." She liked it when he called her "babe." It made her feel young and desirable, and she ignored the fact that he used this moniker with almost every woman he spoke to, including complete strangers.

"I wonder when Charli will be back."

Sean turned to look at her. "Jesus, you don't know where your own daughter is?"

"Well, she said she was going to bury Casper by the creek."

"And you let her just do that?" He was glowering, but only a little bit. He didn't look as dangerous as on those evenings when he'd been at the bar with his cronies for hours and his eyes held an evil glint to them that showed a potential for violence.

"Well, I didn't see the harm—"

"Jesus." The expletive cut off her explanation, and she decided not to pursue this line of conversation, fearing that it might end badly. She had secretly hoped that Sean might take the opportunity to go after Charli and find her, but he didn't seem in the mood for moving from the television set.

"I'll get you some pie." Angela knew from experience that the best way to deal with Sean was to surf the waves of his moods and gently disengage whenever things started to escalate. She'd perfected this technique following years of experience with her own father, although she didn't recognize that she was doing the exact same thing; it was second nature to her by now.

This time, to her surprise, however, Sean followed her into the kitchen and continued the conversation about her daughter.

"That daughter of yours is plain selfish and ungrateful. That's what I think."

"It's not easy for her, you know. She was so close to her dad, and then she had to leave all her friends and everything she knew."

"That kid has got it made. With you doting on her all the time. It's not like she's got to go out to work and support her little ass, now, is it?"

"She's a bit young for that."

"I started working construction with my dad when I was just fifteen. It was hard work in them days. Hard," Sean stressed, with a quick blow to the table to emphasize his point. "But I didn't have no choice."

"I want my daughter to have an education, like I didn't get."

"Oh jeez, what is the point of giving your girl an education?

She's never going to use it anyway. You know she'll throw it all away soon as she meets some boy she likes and shacks up with him."

"You sound like my father."

"Well, I'd like to meet your dad. He sounds like my kind of guy."

Sean had insulted her father in the abstract earlier that morning, but she pushed away the thought in favor of believing that her boyfriend and her father might get along well in person. "Yes, maybe you will. We do have to go visit for Memorial Day weekend."

"I'm surprised you ain't got better standards of parenting. After all, you were raised in the church. What would your dad and mom say about your daughter wandering all about the hills and streets with no supervision?"

Angela opened her mouth to give the retort that was in her mind (*Why are you the expert on parenting when you've never actually raised a child yourself?*) but thought better of it, especially as Sean's eyes were darkening and his mood was becoming more irascible by the minute. Her silence encouraged him to continue his diatribe.

"With those teeny-weeny short skirts and the makeup and you letting her run around like she does, ain't gonna be long before she's in the family way, just like you yourself."

This last comment stung. Angela recognized the truth in it that she didn't wish to face: that she had fallen into the trap herself of being a teenage mother, and she didn't want the same fate for her daughter.

"If she wants to be a little slut, that's her business, but it's your job to put some discipline into that girl before it's too late."

Angela held her tongue and bit her cheeks. Springing to Charli's defense wouldn't help, especially as she half believed Sean's words.

Angela regretted bringing up this subject, while recognizing that she had a habit of sabotaging herself in this way, almost as if she was driven by a compulsion to talk about the very things she knew would aggravate Sean most.

Angela remembered the last time she had tried to take her daughter's side during an argument with Sean. These arguments were often cyclical and focused on Angela's attempts to allow her daughter more independence, feeling as she did a sadness that nobody had allowed that for her when she was a girl. Sean, on the other hand, hated Charli's self-reliance and wished to quash her rebellious spirit. Angela had learned more recently that if she wanted to approach Sean with anything out of the ordinary, she had to pick her moment very carefully, usually during that "sweet spot" in the midafternoon when he'd had enough beers to overcome his hangover from the night before but hadn't quite reached the aggressiveness he displayed when he made the switch to hard liquor, usually just before dinnertime.

If she chose the wrong moment, the outcome was predictable. Yelling and insults would lead to physical manifestations of Sean's anger. Sometimes it resulted in bruises that were embarrassing to acknowledge and took some creativity to explain away to others. Often it led to Angela retiring to her bedroom for a few hours until he cooled off. Occasionally, she took a day off work because her emotional and physical state was too troubled to hide.

"Do you want me to go after her?" Sean suggested, knocking Angela out of her reverie.

Angela was surprised and relieved at this sudden offer, and she smiled her approval. "That's a good idea. But please, be nice to her, Sean. Casper meant a lot to her, and she's still grieving. And it's her birthday."

"By the creek, huh? Pretty stupid to feel bad about a damn cat."

Angela pressed her lips together and said nothing more as Sean grumpily put on his shoes and headed out the front door.

⊙ ⊙ ⊙

Charli was at first disappointed when she realized that the world she had just entered looked exactly the same as the world she had left behind. In fact, standing in the spot where she'd entered, she wondered if she'd stepped into a new world at all. The sky was still blue and flecked with clouds; the trees and grass around her were still several shades of green; the distant sound of the creek still burbled in her ears; the lazy sound of birds and crickets still permeated the background noise; the air still felt warm and still on her skin. And yet, somehow, even though everything looked the same, it felt different.

The truth was, her surroundings seemed the same and at the same time more so. The colors were heightened and more intense, as if she'd up till now been looking at the world through a foggy glass that had just been cleaned so that everything sparkled with a shiny light. It was like that with the sounds, too; they confronted her ears as if they were meant not to fade into the background but to be listened to. The birdsong was sweeter, higher, and more piercing and ethereal. The water rushing in the creek sounded clearer, as if she could hear the individual drops and notes of each cascade tumbling over the rocks beneath.

The smell in the air was a living, breathing thing as it entered her nostrils, tenderly caressing her nose with an odor of fresh earth. All senses combined created a fertile tapestry of colors, sights, and sounds operating in harmony together. The parts of life that she normally ignored or that passed her by, even with her tendency to notice things others didn't, she could now recognize as if able to experience each little part, both independently and together.

Perhaps this was the real world after all, and her entire life had been the illusion. Or perhaps this was a dream, but like a lucid dream, where everything was incredibly vivid and intense. Charli's brief flirtation with hallucinogenic drugs at Shashawna's urging during those weeks after rehab when the two girls had still lived close to each other in LA had resulted in some intense and vivid experiences such as this—pleasant, yet with an aura of danger and unpredictability about them. But this was different. Her senses were heightened and sharpened, but she herself didn't feel unreal. In fact, she felt more real than ever before.

Because of the newness of this situation, Charli felt disoriented but also excited, as if she were on the precipice of fundamental change for the better. She took a few steps forward, tentatively exploring this new place as a blind man might navigate an unfamiliar room, unsure of the obstacles. After a few steps, she gained confidence and strode across the grass.

It wasn't until she had gotten about a hundred yards ahead, taking the usual path that led back to her house, that she realized some things were objectively different about this place. The six-acre vegetable farm that usually lay to the right of the path, where she could see the white plastic hoops covering rows of corn and beets and tomatoes freshly planted, was still there, but it had changed its aspect in a number of ways. There were no white bubbles covering the crops and no residence at the edge of the field where the farmer lived; there were also no other dwellings in the distance. There was no noise of machinery from faraway tractors or the hum of fans in the largest greenhouses.

Off to the left, a carpet of green covered the fields, trees, and meadows. No buildings dotted the hillsides. The sky above her was an unbroken sea of blue, lacking any trace of white airplane trails high above. She heard no traffic. Behind her, the mountains still rose high above the foreground and dominated the horizon, and she recognized that the creek was still positioned behind the tall trees. But this whole landscape had an eerie, primitive quality to it. It looked like land that had not been carved and manipulated by generations of humans.

Charli wondered if she had stepped back in time, to a period in history when the land was still occupied by humans but without the devastation she was accustomed to, and where the animals and plants still thrived.

harli suddenly spotted an individual walking towards her. She was in large part relieved to see somebody she could maybe converse with, but she was also afraid at the thought that this person could be unfriendly or downright hostile, or not speak her language, or any number of alarming possibilities.

As Charli moved closer, she realized that the approaching stranger was a young woman, perhaps in her early twenties, with a very pleasant face and a smile that beamed as she encountered Charli.

When the two girls were a few feet apart, Charli halted and stood shyly, wondering if she should attempt a salutation. The girl stopped also and opened her arms in a gesture that seemed welcoming, particularly as she continued to smile broadly. Charli was now even more confused as to how to respond. She opened her mouth to speak, but then the oddest thing happened. Though she didn't hear any words, and the girl's mouth remained in its smile, Charli could hear in her mind what the girl was saying to her—not in words, exactly. More like someone else's thought entering her head. At first, she was completely baffled by the sensation and gaped at the girl, who stood with a quizzical expression. The girl repeated her unspoken words—"I'm pleased to meet you"—and smiled again, even more warmly.

Then the girl did something that Charli found quite incredible, albeit not unpleasant. The girl reached out and hugged her. And it was a genuine, friendly, warm hug, as one might hug a beloved friend or family member.

"Hello, and welcome to our land. Where are you from?"

Charli attempted to speak aloud, but her voice came out in breathless gasps, almost like a little scream and certainly nothing resembling the confident yet friendly way she wished to sound.

"I see you are afraid. It's fine; there's nothing to be afraid of. I understand you are a stranger. And strangers are always welcome here. We hope they will become friends in time." Now the girl had a sympathetic expression.

She wore a many-hued, brightly colored dress of fine, shimmery material that glinted in the sunlight. It came down to the girl's knees, where it flowed out from her body. Slim and lithe, she had the body of a dancer or somebody who enjoyed movement. Her active face conveyed energy and a zest for life. On her feet she wore soft, flat shoes that looked more comfortable than decorative. She wore no makeup, but her eyes sparkled with infectious vivacity, and her smile was wide and broad.

Charli started to breathe more freely and deeply. She allowed herself to look into the girl's eyes and saw a kindness there that reassured her. Charli had been trained to put on a façade of confidence and relaxation, but she had an idea that this was neither necessary nor capable of fooling this girl, who projected an authenticity and naturalness that was both refreshing and unfamiliar.

The girl stretched out her right hand with the palm up and open.

"Are we supposed to shake hands?" These words popped into Charli's head, and though she made no effort to project them or communicate them to the girl, her companion seemed to instantly receive the information as if Charli had spoken aloud.

The girl giggled. "Shake? You can if you like. Although we usually just join hands for a minute and feel each other's energy. Do you want to do this?"

Charli briefly thought of the trite phrase "You just read my mind," but even that didn't express what had just happened here. This was some two-way form of communication that was not audible—not to the ear, at least—but still just as clear and precise as if the words had been spoken aloud. Since Charli couldn't find a way to articulate this phenomenon, even to herself, she decided to call it mind language, as it somewhat resembled sign language, in that a whole thought could be conveyed wordlessly but at the same time completely.

Now Charli did as the stranger had suggested. As soon as their palms touched, a warm buzzing sensation came from the girl's hand, a strong force that energized and relaxed Charli at the same time. She became aware that the girl's hand was a lot darker than her own, and long, straight, black hair fell to her waist, matching large black eyes.

As Charli took note of all these things, the girl remarked: "It's true, you have very pale skin compared to me. But don't worry. I know some people say that darker skin is better, but I don't believe that at all. I think light-skinned people are just as attractive as dark-skinned people. We can be friends, if you like." She laughed again, this time heartily, as if she'd made the greatest joke.

Charli smiled and thought, "Yes, I'd like that very much." The girl said in mind language: "My name is Abyssinthe, but everybody calls me Abbe for short. If we're going to be friends, what do you call yourself?"

"I call myself Charli. My whole name is Charlotte Grace Speranza." Charli was more amused by than proud of her whole name, so she was not disconcerted when Abbe had a similar reaction.

"Three names. Good for you." There was no irony or sarcasm in this statement, just a genuine sense of enjoyment. "Where are you from?"

"I'm not quite sure. I'm kind of . . . from here, I guess. The house where I live is just over there." Charli pointed to where her house should have been but which now was just a grove of trees in the distance.

"House?" Abbe's reaction was not at all what Charli had expected. She put her hands to her mouth as if utterly shocked, and her eyes became even larger than usual. "I've heard of houses," she continued. "Centuries ago, when our forebears came here from the Old World, they spoke of houses. I heard tell that they had one house for one family only. We have treehouses for individuals and small families to use and the buildings we call longhouses for meetings and communal gatherings."

Both girls were silent for a moment. Abbe regarded Charli with an expression of intense curiosity. "How did you get here?" Abbe asked.

"I just . . . walked." That explanation fell a little flat. "First, I found this shawl and put it on. And then this sort of . . . thing appeared in front of me." Charli waved her hands in a futile attempt to describe the tear she'd seen in the air. "And when I touched it, it opened up a bit more, and I was able to walk through it. And now I'm here."

Abbe's face registered a mix of confusion and astonishment. "How can that be? I don't understand." She thoughtfully fingered the shawl still draped around Charli's shoulders. "This shawl is from here. It has our colors and our handiwork. And it is done in a style of many centuries ago."

"That's weird, and I just found it."

"Where did you find it?"

"It was buried in the ground, in a glass bottle. Somebody wanted to keep it safe, I guess."

Abbe eyed Charli with an amazement that held no hostility and no distrust, for which Charli felt grateful. She had initially wondered if this girl she'd only just met might accuse her of stealing the shawl.

Charli suddenly felt overwhelmed by a mix of emotions as she realized the enormity of the situation. "This is like home, only it's not. It's really confusing. I don't get it. Where am I? Who am I now? Am I another person? Is this another time? Another world?" Charli felt so disoriented now that she almost fainted but instead found herself sinking to the moist grass.

Recognizing Charli's distress, Abbe sat beside her and put a comforting arm around her new friend. "I'm sorry. I didn't mean to upset you. It was a big surprise; that's all."

Charli looked into Abbe's kind, dark eyes. "It's okay. You must be just as confused as me. Tell me about the shawl. When was it made? You say it's from the past?"

Abbe responded, "This was woven on one of our looms. It's a familiar design—from the old days."

"You use looms?" It was such an old-fashioned word that Charli wasn't even sure what it meant. She stifled a giggle behind her hand and wondered if she'd stumbled into an Amish village. "I thought this was knitted or crocheted." She gazed at the shawl and stroked it with her fingers. The design was very unusual and intricate and, now that she thought about it, nothing like anything she'd seen before in her world. The fact that it had been buried in an old-fashioned glass bottle suggested that it was special—that the person who buried it wanted to keep it hidden away.

The two girls sat on the ground and mused together over the strange circumstances of their meeting. Charli described to her new friend how things appeared to her in her world, what her house looked like, what the year was, giving all the place names and local highlights she could remember. Abbe took it all in with an air of acceptance that Charli found reassuring, knowing that her tale must sound very strange and to a different person might even seem suspicious.

"I have heard tell that there are different worlds. What they call parallel universes." Abbe offered this thought in mind language and then hesitated, as if she couldn't believe the veracity of what she had just suggested.

Charli was immediately reminded of a show she'd watched on television recently: "Oh my God, you're right! I saw a documentary on PBS about that. There was this scientist guy saying that every time something new happens or we make a decision or a choice, the world splits into two separate universes. There might be, like, trillions and gazillions of other parallel worlds out there, and we just don't know it. So freaky. Is that what this is? You are kidding me!"

"Well, you say that you're from here, and yet you're not, so that's the only explanation I can think of."

Charli jumped up with a burst of energy and gave a whoop of excitement: "Woo-hoo! I discovered another world! And one *so* much better than the one I left." She had never before felt so enthused or elated. Her whole world had just altered for the better. Abbe laughed gaily when she saw Charli's delight and couldn't resist joining her. The two girls jumped up and down, laughing and squealing until they collapsed again, breathless and worn out from celebrating.

"I don't care what world you're from, anyway. You're here now, and I can tell we're going to have lots of fun together," Abbe concluded, giving Charli a playful nudge on the shoulder.

"You're right," Charli agreed. She decided to accept what was happening and go with the flow for now. With no facts to work with, they weren't going to think their way to the explanation. Perhaps the shawl had transported her or created the tear in the fabric between worlds through which she had come. Or was it something else? Filling her mind was a tide of unanswered questions that couldn't be stemmed. But none of that mattered too much. It turned out she was having the most extraordinary sixteenth birthday ever!

However, one question seemed answerable. "So, when you're

in a parallel universe, are you in a different time or the same time?"

"I'm not sure. Are you in the second decade of the twenty-first century?" Abbe asked.

"Yes."

"So, we are not in a different time."

"Am I in a different place?"

"I can't tell. What place are you from?"

"Weaverton, North Carolina."

"I think we are in the same place because you said the landscape looks the same, although we have a different name for it. The name we give to our world is Q'ehazi. Right now, we are in the E3 Province in the Northeast Mountains Coastal Area."

"You said you have scientists?"

"Of course. We have very advanced scientists. They have helped us travel to other planets, and even to control the weather." Abbe's smile was one of quiet pride.

The feeling of being overwhelmed returned in force. Charli remained on the ground and breathed deeply for a few moments, unsure what to say—or to think—next. Abbe gently guided her to her feet and stroked her hand warmly.

"It must be a lot for you to take in. It is for me too, but at least I'm home. I think you'll feel better once you get to know our world. Come with me. I want to show you something I think you'll enjoy." Her smile was playful now, like that of a little girl about to show a secret to her friend. In fact, a lot of Abbe's demeanor was childlike—not in the sense of being immature or selfish, but like a person who found joy in everything she experienced.

After a moment of hesitation based on her usual distrust of strangers, Charli felt a flutter in her stomach and impulsively decided to jump into this new adventure and let her feelings of ease and comfort with this new friend guide her. Charli felt energized by Abbe's uplifting presence. She nodded and followed Abbe across the fields of tall grass that waved and undulated in the gentle wind, and through the many trees and wooded areas.

It was quite a long journey, and as they meandered in this way, the two girls were silent, both in words and thoughts. Charli concentrated on taking in the sights and sounds and sensations around her: the huge oaks and pine trees; the abundance of plant and animal life, such as squirrels scampering up branches and rabbits occasionally hopping across their path or even a shy deer poking its head around a bush. These experiences were like a heightened version of reality. In her own body she recognized the sense of inspiration she felt when listening to a piece of music she particularly enjoyed. Every leaf crackling beneath her feet sounded distinct; the buzzing of crickets and tiny insects in the trees created a musical chorus, like many different instruments being played at once and in harmony; the sunlight shined in dappled shades through the tree branches, creating colors that were distinct and vivid, yet all of a piece.

As Charli took in these incredible sensations, she felt absolute trust in the person walking alongside her. Abbe had such a buoyancy about her that she practically danced along, her gait light and vivacious like her personality. Sometimes Charli felt an impulse to laugh out loud, reminded of watching Casper's antics with a ball of string when he was a kitten.

The two girls eventually ascended a small rise in the landscape where several people were engaged in different activities. Charli was surprised to see so many different people gathered together and active outside or under rough-hewn canopies.

A tall, older woman with light-brown skin and flowing gray hair was seated on a wooden bench, using a handloom to weave a large and intricate carpet or wall hanging. She made a high-pitched wailing noise halfway between a tune and a drone, which persisted without wavering or flagging. The sound was neither loud nor unpleasant, and it bestowed an ethereal quality upon the woman. Like Indian flute music, the haunting melodies flowed into each other as seamlessly as the threads of the carpet she crafted. At first sight of this extraordinary woman, Charli felt like she had entered a place of infinite possibilities. She had no idea what would happen next.

The woman looked up and smiled as Charli approached. Charli expected the woman to cease her river of sound and offer some greeting, but the woman continued the same tune, still smiling and weaving her colored threads in and out of the cloth with deft fingers. Now, though, far from ignoring her visitor, she seemed to be singing directly at Charli, as if using her music to project what was in her head.

In another part of the grounds, under a large white canopy made of a heavy, cotton-like material and mounted on large poles crafted from tree trunks, several men sat hunched over swathes of silk, painting them with delicate strokes of the brush. All the workers glanced up and smiled upon noticing Charli but, as the woman had done, continued with their art. She approached one man and gazed with interest at his picture, which was an elaborate and skillfully executed mandala. The man appeared to be in his fifties, and his impressive head of curly gray hair was tied back in a ponytail. Earrings gave him a slightly feminine appearance, although his arms were quite masculine in their definition.

"That's beautiful," Charli thought/said with sincerity, hoping to stir some reaction from the artist with her compliment. The man smiled with evident pleasure and inclined his head in acknowledgement of her appreciation. He placed his brush on the paper beside him—which, being covered with tiny scratches of color, Charli imagined he used as a sort of practice pad before committing himself to the silk—and made a couple of strokes downwards and upwards. He peered up at Charli, and she realized he expected her to reply. His quizzical expression and upturned mouth gave the impression that he was amused by Charli's obvious confusion.

Charli hovered in embarrassment, uncertain what to say or think, and he made the strokes again—the same strokes, which resembled a sort of wide tick symbol—before looking up at Charli and smiling expectantly. Suddenly it dawned on her that the painter was talking to her with the strokes, as the woman outside had communicated with her singing.

Smiling in relief and new comprehension, Charli essayed further dialogue with the man: "How long did it take you to paint your picture?" she asked in thought.

This time the artist furrowed his brow in concentration before dipping his brush into one of the nearby tubes of paint and applying it to the paper. Running from the top of the page to the bottom and executed slowly and laboriously, a long green line appeared. Charli was taken aback, having expected a more recognizable symbol such as a number to represent hours or days, but recognized that this mark said everything about the length of completion time for the mandala and the painter's attitude about it. A man such as this in Charli's own world might have made some joke meant to tease the young girl for her naivete, but this man simply smiled and continued his work.

Charli thought it would be inconsiderate to keep the man from his work any longer and waved a hand goodbye, to which he responded with wavy blue lines across the top of the page, done fluently and with a facility that suggested they were a frequently repeated emblem.

The ground was covered in lush green grass daubed with ribbons of gold by the afternoon sunlight. On the grass, some men and women appeared to be dancing, although they moved without the routine or repetition of a formal dance. Both sexes wore long, billowing trousers and wide cotton shirts, which gave them great ease of movement. The only difference between them was that the women were slighter. There were about twenty people in all, moving in a circle and ranging in age from teenagers to people who could have been quite old based on their wizened faces but who still moved with relative effortlessness, grace, and energy.

Charli had never viewed anything similar to this dance, which was at once comic (with strange movements that likely imitated the motions of animals, such as flapping arms to symbolize wings) and sinuous, performed sometimes carefully and sometimes with abandon. They used their entire bodies in the movements, and their torsos contained a powerful strength balanced by the elegance and harmony of ballet dancers. The gestures were at times quick and staccato and then slow and relaxed—all enacted with no music to accompany them, yet synchronized.

For some time, Charli stood watching. One of the dancers spotted her, and all smiled but continued with their movements, ultimately forming a circle around Charli and enveloping her in motion.

It was an extraordinary routine, obviously well known and often repeated. Again, she felt as if the dancers were speaking directly to her with the dance, that it was their form of language, and they could communicate more easily with this performance than with words. After a minute or two, the circle disbanded and tailed off into a regular line of dancers, all facing Charli but still executing their individual movements, some almost still and some more energetic.

Charli realized that she had always been obsessed with words. But here was a place where words didn't need to exist, and where language was neither a barrier nor a defense but simply a means of expression. And she was filled with joy.

bbe appeared delighted at Charli's reaction. "If you enjoyed that, I have something even better to show you!"

She drew Charli by the arm, and the two girls left the gathering, walking slowly and linking their arms together as if they had known each other all their lives. This slow, ambling walk across the grass allowed for deep contemplation, as did the fact that they continued to communicate more with thoughts than words spoken aloud. Abbe seemed pleased to have a new friend with whom to share the wonders of her world.

"You asked me what my profession was, and I told you I'm a musician. It is the thing I love most in all the world. Here, we encourage everybody to do what they really want to do, what they have a gift or talent to do."

"Is that really possible, though? What if everybody wanted to do the same thing?"

"But they don't. Some people want to be scientists, some people cooks, some farmers; some people want to be artists, others doctors, and some people want to be mechanical engineers—"

"And some people want to be cleaners or pick up the trash?" Charli regretted her sarcasm but found it hard to believe that everybody truly could do what they loved. The idea was alien and idealistic to her. She had always been told that she couldn't do what she loved, because she had to worry about making enough money to support herself. Charli had watched her mother struggle with this all her life, and it was a common theme in discussions with friends. Charli was still young enough to be idealistic in certain respects, but she was also born of a generation that was remarkably cynical in their view of the world and what possibilities were offered to them.

As usual, Abbe picked up on the underlying meaning behind Charli's words. "It seems there's a lot of pain in your world. It may be hard for you to believe, and perhaps you'll believe it more when you've seen it, but a lot of that pain can be avoided when everybody works together for the good of the whole. And yes, some people enjoy cleaning. And when we all care about keeping things clean and harmonious for everybody, we all do our part willingly."

The notion of explaining the huge contrast this presented with her own world was almost more than Charli could handle. Was it possible that such a world could exist, where people were kind to each other, and caring? Was it possible to live in a world where greed and ego and power were *not* the only things society valued or appreciated?

Charli focused on one specific aspect of her own life that she could at least partially convey to another sympathetic person. "I don't think my mom is a happy person. And I wish I could help her. But she makes mistakes, and I can't stop her. Like this new guy she's with, Sean."

"What's wrong with him?"

"He's an unbelievable asshole!"

Abbe giggled. "I guess you really don't like him."

"I mean, what's to like about this guy? He mooches off Mom, who works all the time to try and support us. He treats her like dirt. I don't know why she puts up with it. She's such a victim. He drinks like a fish, even though she asked him to quit. I've seen him hit her, more than once." Charli looked at her friend with her eyes wide. She had never admitted that to anyone before.

"Hit her? That's not good." Abbe's eyebrows rose in shock. "Did you tell anybody about this?"

"I tried to. Nobody believed me. They think I'm a hysterical teen. Mom had this big bruise on her face for days, and she tried to pretend she'd walked into a door or something. She makes excuses for him. I told her she should leave him, but she won't listen."

Talking to someone else for the first time about the circumstances in her household made tears well up and prick at her eyes. She hadn't realized before just how upset and agitated she was. Now that she had someone to confide in, the emotions sensed a potential outlet and threatened to engulf her. Charli turned her face away and focused on the beauty around them, biting her lip and screwing up her eyes, pretending to stare at a nearby bird on a tree branch.

Abbe squeezed her arm in a gesture of compassion. "I am glad you are here, Charli."

Charli smiled at her friend and felt a weight lift away as she remembered where she was. "I'm glad I'm here too. It's amazing that I found this place."

"Perhaps it was meant to be."

"I hope so. I never felt like I really belonged there, anyway," Charli reflected sadly.

"It's all about choices, the choices you make. Sometimes, one little choice can change the course of history, for everybody. We in Q'ehazi chose to have a society founded on peace and harmony, and we have always adhered to that." There was pride in Abbe's words, but her demeanor was matter-of-fact.

Charli felt the need to defend her world a little. "We had some great ideals too, you know. The Founding Fathers made a constitution that we all should abide by. But I guess not everybody sees it the same way." Charli had another thought. "Are all other countries like this one?"

"No, there are countries that have made different choices. But many countries wish to emulate what we are doing when they see how peaceful and harmonious we are, and we welcome that. We are always happy to educate others. We are a large country and very influential, and that is what gives us power, not our military might. We operate through persuasion and role modeling, and never through force or occupation."

"Does that really work?" Charli was dubious. Even though it sounded wonderful, she'd learned that human nature usually sabotaged such attempts at universal brotherly love.

"When you've been here a while, tell me what you think," Abbe replied with a knowing twinkle in her eye.

Charli sighed with longing. So many things were possible in this world that were virtually impossible in her world, which had strayed so far from these ideals that it felt as if there were no way back.

Her mood could not remain dark for long, though, in Abbe's company.

"We need to hurry. I don't want to be late." Abbe's gait shifted to a half skip and half run, so Charli followed quickly, wondering what further delights lay in store for her.

"Where are we going?"

"There's going to be a concert, and I'm performing in it, playing my violin. Everybody will be gathering there, so it's a great opportunity for you to meet people too. You'll get to meet my mother, Sovereign Aurora, and my brother, Joslyn."

Up ahead, Charli saw a large throng of people assembling in a nearby meadow. They smiled and conversed with each other—silently, for the most part, and without the usual hubbub. The people arranged themselves in a circle around the musicians as they tuned their instruments.

Charli was content now to stop asking questions. It all seemed like a dream, with unbelievable events unfolding very naturally and unforced. Charli ordinarily liked to feel like she was in control of most things, but in this world, though everything lay beyond her comprehension, she felt safe, no matter what happened. She once again determined to go with the flow.

And so, a few minutes later, Charli found herself listening to a beautiful concert played by about twenty musicians, including her newfound friend. To Charli's surprise, no clapping followed the end of each piece. The audience members instead rocked gently back and forth on the grass, as if sending their positive, grateful energy to the performers, and Charli thought she heard the words "Thank you, thank you" emanating from the crowd.

At the end of the concert, Charli was introduced to Abbe's mother and brother. Sovereign Aurora was very tall and slender with a mass of curly black hair resembling her daughter's and glossy black skin that seemed to glow. She also had a huge smile as she welcomed Charli to their land. Even though she was the sovereign, and people treated her with deference, she moved among them as if she were their equal and not in any way superior or deserving of special attention.

Charli was more struck by her meeting with Joslyn, Abbe's brother—not because he had a particularly sparkling personality or was even devastatingly handsome, but more because the feelings he evoked in Charli were things she had never experienced before: a nervousness for no specific reason, a shyness, a catching of her breath that was very unfamiliar to her, and yet not unpleasant. Charli had spent many years witnessing the way her mother acted around men, and she had silently vowed she would never be the same, never marry, never be a victim to a man who abused her, never allow herself to be vulnerable in that way. And so, she had built unseen walls around herself that none of the boys she met at home could ever penetrate. But here, she felt different.

Joslyn looked a little older than Charli and was tall and slender like his mother, with the same glossy black skin and with warm brown eyes that reflected kindness and a tender heart. His smile was less broad but no less genuine. When she met Joslyn, Charli wanted to stay in this place for a long time, perhaps forever.

But Charli became aware that time was passing, and not just in this world but in her own. All of a sudden, the image of Grandpa came to her with a sudden shock of realization and guilt. How could she have forgotten? The family Zoom call with him was at 3:30 p.m., like it was every Sunday, so that they could catch him just after lunchtime in his time zone. He needed those calls so much; he said they were a lifeline to him. How much life he had left Charli didn't know, and she didn't know if she could visit him if he took a turn for the worse, as he was in a hospital back in Los Angeles and it wasn't safe to fly anywhere.

Charli glanced at her smart watch and saw that it was 2:50 p.m. She had enough time to get back to the house for the Zoom call with Grandpa, but only if she could easily find the place with the tear again.

Abbe sensed that her friend was in a state of distress.

"What's the matter?"

"I'm really sorry, but I have to go. I have to get back to my world."

"Why so soon?"

"It's my grandpa. He's the most important person in the world to me, and he's . . . dying of COVID." Charli choked back tears, her sadness compounding the urgency she felt.

Abbe asked no more questions but grasped both of Charli's hands in her own and looked deep into her eyes. "Then go, little sister. I hope I'll see you again, soon."

"Oh yes, oh yes, oh yes." The unspoken words tumbled over in Charli's mind as she tried to convey how genuinely she wanted to come back. "Can I come back here? How do I do that?"

"Make sure to take the shawl." Abbe gestured to the article of clothing still draped around Charli's shoulders. "You may need to use it again in order for the tear to open up for you. But be very, very careful." Abbe's eyes became serious and even darker than usual. "The shawl may be your way back here, but it probably works for anyone else who uses it too. Hide it well so we don't have any unintended visitors."

"Yes, yes, of course." Charli didn't want to seem impolite, but she couldn't bear the thought of missing Grandpa, and that was uppermost in her thoughts right now.

The two girls briefly hugged. Even though she was in a rush, Charli reveled in the love and warmth coursing through her body as Abbe hugged her. With the pandemic, hugging anybody other than immediate family was taboo, and Charli hadn't felt like hugging her own mother for a long time now.

Then Charli sped off down the path, attempting to retrace the steps she had taken a couple of hours before, back to where she originally found the tear in the fabric that connected the two worlds. She wasn't sure if or how she would find the exact spot, but she had faith that she would work it out. Already, she felt the atmosphere of the Q'ehazi world had changed her, had subtly altered her thinking. Having encountered the buoyant spirits in the Q'ehazi world, she too had a spirit that was light and buoyant, bright and happy, full of a zest for life she hadn't felt in many months.

As Charli thought these things, a smile formed on her face, and despite her hurry, she enjoyed herself as she sped down the path, faster and faster, almost dancing with a sense of energy, strength, and grace. *Grace, just like my name*, she thought. *What a kick that I have a name like that; it's pretty cool, actually.* And that thought made her even happier, and her steps became even faster. Glancing at her watch again, she saw that it was now 3 p.m., so she still had time.

At first, she didn't feel the heavy plops of rain, but then they came faster and faster and harder and heavier until a sheet of rain pounded around her. Still she raced down the path. The grass beneath her feet grew moist and slippery. A number of times she almost fell, and she cursed as she lost her footing on the slick ground.

Despite all of that, she managed to get back to the creek by 3:10, and she soon found the redbud tree she had been standing next to when the tear first appeared. She placed her left hand on the tree and hunched over to steady herself and catch her breath. When she looked up again, the vista before her seemed hazy and indistinct, as if the particles in the air were moving in strange and unexpected ways. Blinking, Charli reached out as if to brush away a thick fog and took a few steps. Gradually the haziness cleared. She felt a mixture of relief and profound sadness when she realized she must have come back through the portal and into her own world again.

A sense of dullness overcame her. When she looked around, the colors were less vivid, the sounds less musical, the air less sweet. Everything was just *less*, somehow. When she looked back, no tear was visible; everything looked normal again, as if the adventure in Q'ehazi had never happened.

The next task was of paramount importance. She retrieved the glass bottle that had housed the shawl. She didn't know if time moved at the same speed in the two worlds, but her watch was still working and now read 3:15, so she should have time to quickly replace the shawl and bury the glass bottle before getting back to her house, if she ran all the way.

She had to choose a different burial spot for the glass bottle because the original hole was now occupied by Casper's little body. Knowing she'd always recognize it, Charli chose the base of the redbud tree that had formed her entry point into the other world. She quickly dug past leaves and twigs to form a hole, which could have been a little deeper, but she needed to be quick. She could always bury it deeper later.

As soon as she finished spreading the earth over the hole so that it looked undisturbed, Charli raced all the way back to her house as fast as her young legs could take her. Her heart pounded from the exertion of the run—and with the excitement of the incredible adventure she had just experienced and the thought of all the adventures still to come, now that she had discovered the world of Q'ehazi.

ean reached the dense pocket of trees that hid the creek from view just as Charli stepped through the portal and back into her world. He knew her affinity for this particular spot and figured it was a likely place for Charli to bury her dead cat. As he got closer and spotted a flash of her through the trees, some instinct warned him to stay back and watch her from cover.

Despite the fact that Sean had never served in the military and didn't know anybody who had, he had a reverence for the idea of army combat and everything it represented to him—courage, honor, sacrifice. He had therefore completed some paramilitary training, of which he was inordinately proud, and which allowed him to now hide from Charli's view.

He was determined to catch her doing something wrong so he could report her activities to her mother and disentangle the remaining bond between them. He disliked and was suspicious of this strange girl. In his own way, he initially tried to be nice to her, even offering to take her to Disney World once the pandemic was over. But she had refused him in what he saw as a disdainful manner. Her mother suggested that she was "too old" for Disney World, but in Sean's opinion, you were never too old for the Happiest Place on Earth, and anybody who couldn't enjoy Disney World was un-American.

Un-American was Sean's catch-all word for anybody he distrusted and didn't understand. To him, it summed up a whole category of people who for some reason populated this land but had no right to be here. Although the girl had been born in America and was ostensibly as much a citizen as he was, something about the way she acted and behaved felt alien to him, and he was sure that his feelings were not wrong. He hated the way she looked right through him with that piercing stare, despite his having nothing to be ashamed of as far as he was concerned. She was a lot less passive and compliant than her mother, and her defiance felt like more than normal teenage rebellion.

Charli was dangerous to his worldview. Sean wished to be top dog in every situation, even that between a mother and her only daughter, and was nothing if not persistent. He was accustomed to getting what he wanted in the end. Even the way he had wooed Angela was consistent with his style of never giving up. She was at first reluctant to get involved with him, preferring to move slow in accord with her Christian beliefs, but he had done his level best to make her feel so special that she couldn't resist him.

After years of practice, he was very adept at wooing women, and it only took a few days to wear Angela down with his constant flattery and attention. Once he had her hooked like a fish on the line, he didn't need to make so much effort. A woman's natural tendency to bond emotionally with whatever partner she has chosen would take over, and he could relax. The one fly in that ointment was Charli.

Sean watched the girl crouch beside a large redbud tree growing near the creek. Although he couldn't see her clearly, she was clearly in the process of burying something beneath the tree with the spade. Sean was surprised it had taken her this long to bury the cat. She had left the house more than two hours earlier, and it only took around fifteen minutes to get to the creek by foot. He was even more surprised when he spotted a glint and realized she was burying not a cat but rather a large glass bottle. *Did she put the cat's body in the bottle? What possible purpose could that serve?* The girl was certainly weird, so perhaps this was some bizarre ritual she had cooked up or read about online.

Charli finished what she was doing and rocked back on her heels with a sigh, looking up into the sky as if to say, "My work is done."

Charli rose, and Sean shrank back into the dark trees as she passed by his hiding spot, obviously heading for home.

Even though Sean wanted to get home before Charli so he could talk to Angela about what he'd seen her daughter do, he was overcome with curiosity. He found himself hoping that the glass bottle contained a stash of drugs or something Angela would really castigate her for. Sean was always secretly thrilled when Angela referenced Charli's stay in rehab back in California and hoped fervently for a relapse. He knew this was relatively common in teenage addicts. Most of the time, the girl was curiously committed to her sobriety, but perhaps that was all an act, put on to fool her naively religious-minded mother.

Once Charli had vanished from sight, Sean crept up to the tree and found the area of fresh earth and piled leaves where she had been digging. He dislodged the bottle from the ground with his hands and to his surprise was able to easily open it. But when he removed the lid, Sean was amazed and disappointed to see what was inside: nothing but an old, worn-out shawl! He scratched around with his fingers, in disbelief that this was what all the fuss was about, but there was nothing else but this peculiar and not even very attractive article of clothing.

Sean stuffed the shawl back into its bottle and buried it again, not wanting to alert Charli that her stash had been disturbed. He still felt absolutely sure that she was up to something nefarious, and it was up to him to get to the bottom of it. He hastened back to the house. Hopefully he would get there soon after Charli arrived so that he could further influence her mother not to believe whatever crazy story Charli was cooking up for her.

⊙ ⊙ ⊙

By the time Sean arrived back at the house, he was unable to speak to either Charli or her mother; they were both engaged in the weekly family Zoom call with Grandfather Speranza, to which he was never invited.

Charli held the iPad as she and her mother sat in the sunroom and gazed at Nonno Speranza lying in his hospital bed. His wrinkled visage crinkled often into smiles while he spoke in a faint, raspy voice to his beloved granddaughter:

"How are you, *Tesoro?*"

Charli was out of breath from the run home but managed to control her panting.

"I'm okay, Grandpa. It's great to see you."

"You are looking well," Angela remarked to her father-in-law. He actually looked as pale and sick as she'd ever seen him, but she wanted to hearten and encourage the old man.

In reply, he drew in a deep breath and coughed sporadically, then wheezed his response: "I'm doing my best, Angie dear. Need to stay here so I can take care of you two girls." The wheezing started off as a laugh at his ironic comment and became a full-blown coughing attack.

Charli knew that talking too much was both a danger to him and something he was prone to do, so she tried to do as much of the talking as possible, even though it came less naturally to her.

"Hey, Nonno, guess what? I'll be taking the SATs in a couple of weeks. They're making us do it online."

Angela chimed in, "The kids are doing everything virtually. We don't know how long it's going to last, so they've decided to close down the schools early and reopen them in the fall."

"Which is a good thing because I don't want to have to wear a mask for school," said Charli, finishing her mom's sentence.

"So now I'm forced to basically homeschool her," Angela said, smiling. "It's a good thing she's such a great student."

"Yeah, well, I want to still get good grades so I can get into college."

"Charli said she wants to be an epidemiologist," said Angela proudly, stroking her daughter's back with a tender hand. Angela wasn't quite sure what an epidemiologist was, but she had been hearing about them more recently and was happy that her daughter's aspirations were heading in this kind of direction.

Grandpa Speranza appeared to be trying to say something, but his audio cut out momentarily, so mother and daughter peered closer at the screen to try and read his lips. "What was that, Grandpa? You cut out for a bit."

"I always knew you would do something special, little girl." His breathing was labored and his speech slow, but Charli recognized the pride and tenderness in his voice, and she beamed.

"Oh yes. I raised her to be successful." Angela beamed also, with vicarious pride and reflected glory.

Charli often felt irritated when her mother said things like this, as if trying to take credit for Charli's accomplishments, which Charli felt she had achieved in spite of her mother rather than because of her. But Charli stifled her resentment and kept her mouth dutifully shut. The important thing was that Grandpa was happy. She didn't know how much longer Nonno had to live. In the meantime, their weekly Zoom calls seemed to lift his spirits quite a bit. Being unusually perceptive for her years, Charli realized that this would have an effect on his physical health too, and hopefully enable him to keep going for a while longer.

While she loved talking to her grandfather, Charli also wanted the call to last as long as possible in order to delay the inevitable. Her mother would surely ask her about burying Casper, and she would have to make up some lie about why she had taken so long—without giving away anything about her recent adventures.

Even though nobody in the other world had actually told Charli to keep the existence of Q'ehazi a secret, she knew in the deepest recesses of her being that she should not tell another soul about what had happened to her. As soon as people from her world learned about this other place, they would swarm it like locusts, infecting it with their negative attitudes and habits and trampling the pristine nature of the peaceful Q'ehazi world. Charli would be devastated to be the cause of something like that.

⊙ ⊙ ⊙

There were times when Angela felt she really wasn't cut out to be a mother. In fact, she felt that way most of the time. Not that there was anything she felt she *was* cut out for. Her parents hadn't believed she would amount to much, so she'd internalized their judgment of her as being probably more realistic than her own.

When she'd discovered a couple of years into her marriage to Chuck Speranza that she was unable to conceive any more children, Angela was nowhere near as disappointed as her husband, though of course she had feigned the supreme regret she knew he felt in order to appear more the dutiful wife. In her heart of hearts, although she loved children and enjoyed very much being around them en masse, as when she was an elementary school teaching assistant, she found the responsibility of motherhood daunting.

As a child, the few activities she loved—cooking, sewing, an occasional dabble at painting landscapes—she was allowed to pursue without much interference, and she always managed to land on her feet, usually by utilizing her pretty face, buxom figure, and compliant nature to coast on the coattails of a man who was better equipped to handle life than she. But she had never imagined having to take full responsibility for raising a child, which forced her to make decisions and initiate awkward discussions about difficult subjects—neither of which she relished.

When Angela couldn't avoid one of these intimate discussions with Charli, she turned to cooking or baking. If the recipe was something Charli particularly enjoyed, so much the better; she could kill two birds with one stone and hopefully appease her daughter with homemade brownies or chocolate muffins.

This was the reason for Angela's industrious attention to Charli's favorite muffin recipe immediately after the Zoom call with her father-in-law ended.

Charli was about to retire to her bedroom, but Angela persuaded her to stay a little while longer in the living room by promising that the muffins would be ready soon, knowing that her daughter preferred them warm and straight from the oven.

"So, honey, did you manage okay?"

Charli felt irritated enough to force her mother out into the open. "Manage with what?"

Angela gave her a look.

Charli sighed briefly and gave a small tut of disapproval at her mother's delicacy. "If you're talking about burying Casper, yep, did that okay." Her flippant tone was at once designed to annoy and to hide her more complex feelings.

"You were a pretty long time, so I thought maybe it was difficult or something." Angela carefully slid the muffin tray into the oven and set the temperature, grateful for a task to distract her.

Charli was silent. She stared at her mobile phone, seemingly lost in thought. Angela was so accustomed to having her comments ignored that she soldiered on, refusing to feel slighted. "Nonno was looking well. I'm so glad."

Now Charli looked up, obviously warming to this change of subject. "Yeah. He looks amazing for eighty-two, don't you think?"

"I talked to his doctors at the hospital—"

"Can he go home soon?"

Angela felt a rush of pity for her daughter, who had no idea how close to death her grandfather really was. This knowledge had been kept from Charli out of compassion; everybody knew how much she adored him. "I'm really sorry, honey, I don't think he's gonna get to go home."

"But they said—"

"I know, but I think they were just being nice, you know? They've kept him out of ICU so far, but we don't know about the progress of the disease."

"What if he rallies? He's super tough."

Charli looked on the verge of tears. Angela dusted her hands of flour and sat on the couch next to her daughter, taking her hands in hers. "Honey, I think you and I are gonna have to face up to things now. He doesn't have long." Angela felt Charli's shoulders tremble, and she put an arm around them and tried to hug the slim body close, but Charli kept stubbornly upright. "Nonno asked me to talk to you."

"He did?"

"Yes." Angela stroked her daughter's hair. "He wants you to know that he loves you very much, and he will understand if you can't be there when he . . . when he . . . ." She couldn't bring herself to say it.

Charli understood the genuine nature of her mother's words, and she felt suddenly guilty for her resentment. Now she melted into her mother's arms.

"I wish . . ."

She didn't even know what she wished for, but it was something different than this. She wished she could hold on to the one person who had always been there for her, who seemed to understand her better than anybody. And yet she knew it wasn't possible. In theory she knew that everybody would have to die eventually—and yet it seemed so unfair. She needed him now more than ever.

Angela was grateful that her daughter had dropped her usual mask of invulnerability, at least for the moment. Playing the role of comforter was much easier for her than being the disciplinarian. And there had been such a rift between them these past few weeks she'd been dating Sean that she wondered if it could ever be healed. Perhaps this was at last a window of opportunity for them to bond again, like they had when Charli was a child. Charli's intelligence and her independent spirit and strong personality threatened to overwhelm Angela at times, and she wasn't sure how to handle a daughter who displayed all of the personality characteristics of her father and none of her mother.

Angela gently steered the conversation to more practical matters. She told Charli her grandfather was leaving her a lot of money and that he wanted it to be used wisely, for her education. Although Angela was just scraping by, her former husband came from wealth, and Charli was the adored granddaughter from their union. Charli listened with her eyes widening, having never expected material advantages from her wealthy grandparents.

"Nonno thinks I should invest the money until you come of age, which is when you're eighteen. I agree that's a good idea, but I don't know anything about how to invest money, so I asked Sean about it—"

"You told your boyfriend about my inheritance?!" Charli's tone was one of shock and anger.

Angela felt the need to defend her actions, which she always did when Charli got on her high horse about something. Even though she was the parent and should command respect from a teenage girl, somehow Angela never managed to lay down the law with her daughter. "I told you I don't know anything about investing, and I needed advice—"

"From him?!"

"I know you don't like him, but—"

"He's an asshole."

"Don't use language like that. I've told you before, Charlotte Grace." Charli pursed her lips at the mention of her full name and her mother's sharper voice. "He knows something about investing. He's done real estate investment."

"He works in construction," said Charli as if this were the lowliest occupation in the world.

"He flipped some houses, and he helped to fix them up."

"That's not investment."

"Charli, I'm not going to argue with you about this. Perhaps we don't see eye to eye, but I'm trying to look out for your best interests, and this is the best way I know how."

Charli knew that the debate was over, and she had lost—not because she wasn't good at winning arguments but because she had no power in the situation. Her mother was the one with the power, but unfortunately, Charli believed, her mother did not have the smarts to do the right thing, and there was nothing Charli could do about it.

Charli often veered between compassion for her mother—who she realized made bad decisions more out of ignorance and low self-esteem than innate stupidity or bad intentions—and anger that Angela's bad choices impacted her daughter in negative ways that she seemed to deliberately ignore. Charli saw her mother as a victim, and Charli wanted to be the hero, but she couldn't force her mother to be the person she wished her to be, or the person Charli would have been in similar circumstances.

Part of the reason she hated Sean so much was because her mother had fallen completely under his spell and now was powerless to protect either of them. Charli vowed that if she had a daughter, she would teach her to be strong and empowered and to stand up for herself and know how beautiful and capable she was, without the need for a man to validate her.

Still, Charli obediently dropped the subject and went to her room, clutching one of the warm chocolate muffins and setting the intention to leave home and start an independent life as soon as she possibly could.

⊙ ⊙ ⊙

When Sean realized that the weekly family Zoom call was going to preclude any chance of his talking with Angela about Charli until later that evening, he popped out to the local bar, which was his habit on a Sunday afternoon, or indeed any time he felt a little stressed.

There he bumped into his friend Martin, who he'd been buddies with ever since they went to school together and both flunked out of the eighth grade. Like Sean, Martin was from the South—Raleigh, to be exact—and had had something of a hard-scrabble existence, brought up by a single mother with a father who spent most of his time in prison for drug-related offenses. With his superior street smarts, Sean had managed to succeed in areas where Martin had not done so well; thus, Martin looked up to Sean, although he would never admit to it. Sean enjoyed Martin's company because he liked being the center of attention and enjoyed even more being around somebody who felt themselves inferior to him, as this boosted his ego.

Sean had already explained to Martin that Angela was a great catch—and not just because of her ample breasts and blond, girlish fragility. Since money was the ultimate driving force in Sean's life, his nose could sniff out money in the unlikeliest of places, and he had picked up very early on that Angela had a source of money.

Although Angela worked shifts at Ingles as a checkout girl (her job as an elementary school teaching assistant having been put indefinitely on hold due to the pandemic) and was for all intents and purposes a single mother barely scratching a living to pay for her only kid, he could tell by the style and newness of Charli's shoes and iPhone that she had a rich benefactor somewhere.

He'd managed to worm out of Angela that her former husband, who had been killed five years earlier, was from a wealthy Italian American family, the head of which still lived in Los Angeles and totally doted on Charli. Sean was also well aware that Charli's grandfather was not long for this earth and would leave a huge sum of money for Charli to inherit. He hoped the old guy would kick the bucket before Charli turned eighteen and had full control of her inheritance. That way Sean could finagle his way into at least some of it if he played his cards right and became indispensable to her mother.

Sean had not had to explain much of this to Martin. They were of the same mind where monetary circumstances were concerned, and Martin could easily divine Sean's intentions. Martin wasn't convinced, though, that Sean's hunch about Charli still abusing drugs was accurate. Having only seen her once, when Angela and her daughter had met up with them at the outside seating area of the Coffee Café in downtown Weaverton, Martin could already tell that the girl was far too committed to her long-term sobriety to be a likely candidate for an addiction relapse.

But Sean clung to this idea because it could give him leverage with her mother. After all, stranger things had happened. Many kids with far greater advantages than Charli turned to drugs and sabotaged the rest of their lives for the temporary high and the quick escape from reality—especially these days, what with the global pandemic and all.

Sean's favorite bar was only serving outside these days, but he still could meet up with friends here, and they didn't even have to wear masks. Sean was glad about that because he didn't possess a mask and in fact didn't believe they were either necessary or acceptable. Martin largely shared his friend's views, though he secretly did use a mask when going to stores that required it; he didn't relish the idea of confronting the store manager. Sean had already had an altercation with the bar manager here when he tried to go inside to use the restroom and refused to wear a mask. Calling the manager a "fucking snowflake liberal" didn't exactly smooth things over, but fortunately for them, the bar had seen a major drop in clientele since the more stringent restrictions had been put in place in the state. Right now, their principles had to be sacrificed for the sake of keeping themselves open at all.

When Sean told Martin about seeing Charli burying the glass bottle under a tree, he was pleased to see his friend's eyes light up. "So, maybe it looked like just an old shawl, but there must be more to it than that. Maybe the bottle has a secret bottom or compartment or something, and she's hiding something else valuable in there," Martin suggested.

"You're probably right, buddy."

"You should follow her again, see what she does this time."

Sean smirked. "I'm glad you said that. That is exactly what I plan to do."

The two men ran up quite a tab that day, and Sean became predictably more and more garrulous and filled with boastful self-congratulation. Martin always put up with this behavior, believing that there would come a day when some of Sean's "lucky breaks," as he called them, would rub off on him and he could vicariously bask in his glory.

For the fifth time in a row, Sean slipped out of the bar before the two men had a chance to split the check, and Martin was forced to take care of the whole thing. Martin briefly wondered why he so often found himself in this position, but again he told himself,

Sean is going places, and I'm going places with him. There will be payback one day.

Martin was one of those people who had the ability to believe things that were unbelievable, so long as they seemed expedient to him. And so, he sighed and paid the bill and waited for happier days.

his really is a magnificent piece of work, Charli." The teacher's beaming smile registered, even on Zoom. "I'm not sure you realize just how talented you are."

"Uh," Charli stuttered, not sure how to respond. It felt so unusual to have somebody applauding her like this that she felt more embarrassment than pride, although inwardly she felt a little tingle of excitement. "It didn't take me that long to do," she finally managed to sputter in a weak attempt to minimize her achievement. But Mrs. Marshall was having none of it.

"Well, that's even more remarkable, young lady. That you could just dash off something this unique. But I'm sure you don't want to hear me babbling. What I really wanted to tell you is that we are having an art retreat in Henderson this summer, and I wanted to recommend you for it."

"An art retreat?" It had never occurred to Charli that something she did as a fun pastime could be taken seriously enough to dedicate a whole retreat to it.

"Please don't worry about the cost," the teacher jumped in before Charli could ask any more questions. "It's entirely free. The school was given a COVID grant so that artistically oriented students such as yourself could continue to receive support and encouragement, even in this pandemic. So, for a whole week, we would offer you room and board close to the retreat facility, plus all the classes during the day, which would be appropriately socially distanced. In the evenings, you can spend time in your room, as you unfortunately wouldn't be able to take part in any social activities, but you would have access to a computer and TV, of course."

"Wow, that's amazing." An idea stirred as the teacher spoke, and her spirits lifted at the thought of the opportunity suddenly presented to her. Charli was genuinely grateful and realized that the shock of the offer had caused her to almost forget her manners. "Sure, I'd love to do it. Uh, thank you. I didn't realize you had things like that here." Charli felt secretly guilty that she had described her new home as "hick town" to her mother and complained about the lack of culture compared to Los Angeles.

"Oh yes, of course. We love our artists here in Asheton. Haven't you been to the Riverside Arts District yet?"

Ashamed to admit that she had hardly been into the nearby "big town" of Asheton, Charli said, "Well, we haven't been here very long."

"Of course, you are right. And everything's been closed anyway for the pandemic."

Charli was grateful for that excuse to explain her lack of interest in her local surroundings since moving to this area six months ago.

"That's great news that you can join us!" gushed the teacher. "I will be in touch with your mom soon to go over all the details."

Charli and Mrs. Marshall signed out of the Zoom meeting, and Charli sat back on her bed, feeling more optimistic than she had in a while. She longed to find a way to go back to Q'ehazi, and now a potential means had fallen unexpectedly into her lap. Perhaps it was fate.

But she genuinely regretted that she couldn't both attend the art retreat and revisit Q'ehazi. Charli had never been selected for anything like this before. She hadn't thought of herself as a budding artist or somebody with a gift; she just enjoyed drawing and painting pictures, and she had ever since receiving a set of watercolor paints as a small child—and being reprimanded for attempting to color the walls of her bedroom with pictures of fantasy animals and plants. Charli saw artistic talent as more of a curse than a blessing, since artists were impecunious and seemed to be more invested in their own egos than doing something good for the world.

Charli's idealistic nature was much more inspired by the thought of studying to help to eradicate diseases such as the one currently ravaging the globe and killing people in terrifying numbers. Charli thought of Shashawna, who wanted to be an actress and whose attractive face, buxom figure, and vivacious personality seemed like the perfect fit for that career. Shashawna would have been crowing from the rooftops about being chosen to go on a free art retreat based on the strength of her artistic talent, whereas Charli simply saw this as a pragmatic means to an entirely different end that she very much desired.

The thought of her friend curled her mouth into a smile, and Charli reached for her phone and was just about to text when a sudden noise startled her. The very loud crack made her literally jump in her seat. A gunshot. It sounded impossibly close. Charli had heard gunshots before in the area, but never quite that loud. Her heart thumped in alarm, and she rushed to her bedroom to see where the shot could have come from.

On one side of the house lay a valley of unbroken land leading down to the creek, which was owned by an elderly lady who kept to herself and whom Charli had never seen. On the other side, closest to Charli's bedroom window, lived a young man who owned a motorcycle repair business that he ran out of his dilapidated mobile home on the far edge of his property. That was definitely the side the shot had come from. As trees obscured Charli's view, she ran down the stairs and out the front door, then through the trees dividing the two houses and across the field to the location of the gunshot, which was now accompanied by several more sounding in a continual volley.

Charli spotted two men firing rifles into a thicket of trees at the bottom edge of the property. Most of the shots were hitting a makeshift bullseye and tin cans on wooden stakes just in front of the trees. When the men saw Charli running towards them, they stopped firing and stared at her. As she drew closer to them, she realized that one of the men was their next-door neighbor, the young man called Michael, and the other man was her mother's boyfriend, who stood with a smile on his face as he recognized Charli and noted her alarm.

"What the hell are you doing?" Charli gasped as she came close enough to shout at them.

"Well, if it isn't the little lady," Sean mocked.

Michael had more of a defensive attitude. "We're allowed to shoot out here. Ain't no law against it. We're more'n three hundred feet from your property."

"But what are you shooting at?" questioned Charli breathlessly, feeling quite certain that there must be something wrong in what they were doing.

Michael gestured towards the wooden stakes and tin cans. "Target practice, that's all."

"She's from California," Sean said to his friend by way of explanation.

"Oh, right. Don't got no shooting there, I s'pose." Sean's companion turned away, but Charli didn't let it go so quickly.

"Did you hit any animals or birds?" she blurted.

"Oh yeah. I got a squirrel." Sean seemed proud of himself. "Over there, in the thicket."

Charli said no more to the men but ran over to where Sean was pointing to try and rescue the animal. "He's probably dead already, girl," Sean called after her, but she ignored him.

She quickly found the little body lying on the ground. The eyes of the squirrel were still open, and he was breathing fast, obviously injured badly. Tears stung her eyes, and she brushed them roughly away as she picked up the little, almost-lifeless creature and held it to her chest. She ran as fast as she could back to her house and the relative safety of her backyard. Once there, she stopped to rest for a moment and look at the little creature, but by this time it had stopped breathing, and she could tell it was dead.

Charli couldn't contain herself now. She began sobbing, audibly and with full access to her pain. "I hate humans!" she cried as she fumbled in the dirt beneath an oak tree in their yard, making a small hole for a roughshod burial and envisioning doing the same for her beloved Casper only days before. "Why are they so cruel? Sometimes I hate humans—I really hate them!"

When she finished, her face was stained with tears and soil, but she didn't care. She stumbled back to her bedroom, relieved that her mother was still working her day shift at Ingles. Charli's mood had gone from elated and optimistic to one of despair in a matter of moments. Now she felt utterly drained. She managed to totter into the bathroom and wash her face and hands. Then she flung herself on the bed and picked up her phone, recalling what she had been doing before being so rudely interrupted.

At least there were no more gunshots to be heard from next door. Perhaps they had decided to be kind and stop, at least for the time being. Charli doubted that the decision had been Sean's.

Charli got on Facetime with her best friend, and was glad to see Shashawna's friendly face and hear her warm, throaty laughter as Charli relayed the squirrel incident and the way she'd tackled the two men next door.

"Wow, you go, girl!" Shashawna encouraged. "Nobody gonna be stopping our Charli when she gets riled up about something."

"Yeah, well, I'm not exactly David Attenborough, but I don't like to see people being mean to little animals, that's all."

When Shashawna heard about the art retreat, she was predictably impressed. Still, she couldn't resist competing with her friend by telling her all about the glossy Hollywood parties she'd been invited to, which she couldn't attend with the pandemic was raging. Although Charli loved her friend, she wasn't enamored of the Hollywood lifestyle her friend enjoyed, so she listened more politely than enthusiastically.

"So, how are things in Hicksville?" asked Shashawna. "Other than your fancy retreat, of course."

"Not good," admitted Charli. "I have to visit with my grandparents for Memorial Day."

Shashawna gave a disapproving tut but maybe didn't understand the gravity of Charli's distress.

"If you think this place is bad, you should try over at their house. It's, like, a million times worse. And they are these Bible-bashing Jesus freaks. OMG, no wonder my mom is crazy!"

"You better run away from home, girl."

"Yeah, I wish."

There was a slight lull in the conversation, and this would have been the perfect moment for Charli to introduce the topic of Q'ehazi to her friend, along with her plans for not truly "running away" from home but at least getting away for a few days—to a place that was as far removed from the normal reality of her world as anything she'd ever known.

And yet, Charli said nothing. She had told nobody about her adventures. She almost wondered if they were real. But she wanted to go back, and she would find a way, as soon as she could.

⊙ ⊙ ⊙

Angela had been brought up to believe that there was no problem that couldn't be solved by "spiritual ministry" and faith in the church's teachings. Yet when she'd tried to talk to her pastor about her problems with Charli and Sean, he had been neither sympathetic nor very helpful. She wanted someone to give her advice and not simply throw it back to her to ask God for forgiveness for her sins. She wasn't sure what sins she had committed to make her deserving of such a wayward and perverse child, and she longed for someone to tell her what to do.

Perhaps in an effort to appease its workers, who were considered "essential" and therefore forced to work shifts where they sometimes interacted with non-mask-wearing strangers, her company was offering four sessions of free EAP therapy, which they referred to as "counseling to help with the effects of additional stress caused by the pandemic." Although Angela had been raised to be distrustful of things she didn't understand, she felt desperate enough to give this free service a try.

And so, on this cloudy, sultry morning in mid-May, she found herself sitting in her car outside the house and hoping that the internet was strong enough in this area to handle her first telehealth session with her therapist. Angela's stomach churned as she held the iPad up to her face, turned herself off mute, and increased the volume. The therapist, Elsa, who was an older lady with what seemed to be a European accent, had a friendly and welcoming demeanor, and that put Angela at her ease right away, even if the accent was a little disconcerting at first.

After the initial introductions and explaining that she was new to this in a trembling voice, Angela found herself being more voluble than usual in explaining why she had chosen to come to therapy for the first time in her life.

"I'm usually very private about these . . . personal matters," she faltered, "but I really feel like I need some help right now. I can't do this all alone." This last sentence came out unexpectedly, and with the words came a few tears at the edges of her eyes, which she hastily brushed away with an apology.

"No need to say sorry," the therapist explained. "People often get emotional during session. It's very normal."

This statement emboldened Angela, and she realized how much she had longed to get certain things off her chest, and how much had been stored up inside and for how long. For the next few minutes, it all poured out of her: how hard it had been to continue raising Charli after the unexpected death of her husband; how guilty she still felt about disobeying Mommy and Daddy and their pleas not to marry Chuck Speranza and move to California, and how she felt she was being punished now for those former actions. The therapist listened intently without interjecting or making comments, and this silence propelled Angela to say more than she had anticipated or even wanted. She was surprised at the relief she felt after this small outburst, although she again apologized for having used up so much time with her rambling.

Once more, the therapist brushed aside the apology, and now she asked about Angela's romantic relationships. On this point, Angela was a lot less open. She knew there were some problems in her relationship with Sean, but she had no idea how to articulate them, or even if she was allowed to feel discontented with her situation. She mentioned that she felt he drank a bit too much, maybe, and then felt instantly guilty, as if she had somehow betrayed him with this revelation to an outside person, a stranger. What would Sean think if he knew she was talking about him in this way?

Angela felt unsettled when the therapist took this opportunity to ask if there was any alcoholism in her family, and she wondered aloud if this was relevant. It seemed intrusive to be asked about her family (as if that had anything to do with Sean or her current problems), and she did her best to steer the conversation in a different direction, simply stating, "My childhood was pretty idyllic, really" and that she had no complaints about her parents, who were staunch Christians. Even though a tiny piece of Angela knew she was lying, she didn't allow that piece of her to have a voice, and she fervently hoped that the therapist wouldn't ask those sorts of questions again.

To Angela's relief, soon the fifty-minute session was over, and she realized that it hadn't been too terrible of an experience. It had even been quite nice to have somebody to talk to who didn't seem to be judging her but instead accepted everything she said at face value. Angela surprised herself by thanking the therapist in a way that was heartfelt, and she found herself even looking forward to the next session in a week's time.

⊙ ⊙ ⊙

The day before Memorial Day weekend, Charli received her results back from the DNA test her grandmother had purchased for her birthday. Charli had asked her grandmother to buy her the kit specifically in order to prove to herself and her grandparents that her heritage was Italian on her father's side and Scotch Irish on her mother's side, as she had always believed. This was in response to a snide comment made by her grandmother—"You're not exactly a thoroughbred yourself, darlin'," delivered with a tone of contempt that still rankled—which had badly hurt Charli's feelings.

As Charli input the code she received in the letter to see her results online, she felt confident that she would finally be able to wipe that condescending smile off her grandmother's face when she told her that, yes, she was a pure-bred Sicilian Italian on her father's side—a fact of which she had always been inordinately proud, perhaps because she admired her father so much as an intelligent and successful man from a family of cultured East Coast Italians who had come to the US with nothing and made something of themselves. Charli had always put her father on a pedestal in this way, and perhaps her mother encouraged this, having come from much lower down on the totem pole when it came to intelligence and education.

So, the shock of seeing the actual results was so great that at first Charli wondered if she'd made a mistake—input the code wrong or gotten her results mixed up with someone else. A brief, paranoid thought flashed through her mind that perhaps her grandmother had somehow gotten control of the results and altered them to read like what she had predicted, that Charli's heritage was far from pure and was a mishmash of different ethnicities and races, none of which were in fact Italian.

Charli checked and rechecked the form, the code, the website, her name on the letter, and everything she could before she even considered believing what her own eyes told her. The results that swam before her and quickly became imprinted on her mind:

CHARLOTTE GRACE SPERANZA

30% Scottish

20% Irish

25% Cherokee

10% Polish

8% Dutch

7% German

Charli printed out the results and with trembling fingers took the paper down to her mother, who was in the kitchen, washing up from the night before. Charli thanked God that Sean wasn't there that morning, having disappeared to do a "job" on a construction site that paid well for temporary labor.

"Take a look at this," Charli said in a small voice as she handed her mother the paper.

"Oops, let me just dry my hands first, honey. What is it?"

"You'll see."

"Oh!" Angela took the paper and read it over a couple of times, then looked up at Charli with an expression that Charli couldn't interpret. Angela stood silently for a few moments before she responded. Her tone was embarrassed, almost ashamed. "I've been meaning to talk to you about this."

"What?" This was not the response Charli was expecting at all. She had half expected her mother to provide some explanation for why the DNA results were completely wrong, and explain how they could complain to the company for screwing up the test and mixing her up with another girl. "It's a mistake, isn't it?"

"No, honey," her mother admitted. "Can we talk about this later? I'm in the middle of—"

"No!" Charli blurted. "I want to know now! And I want to know why you didn't say anything before. I think I deserve to know, don't I?" Charli's tone was a mix of plaintive and resentful.

"Yes, yes, of course you do," Angela placated her.

Charli's mood could quickly escalate when she was upset, and Angela was sensitive enough to her daughter's needs to realize that a situation she'd been putting off for years had to be taken care of right away, with everything else put on the back burner, so she called in sick to work and spent a good two hours telling Charli the whole story.

It was quite a story—and not at all the one Charli had believed about herself for her whole life.

Angela explained that she was very young when she first met Charli's biological father, just fifteen, and they started dating in high school. Angela had been afraid to tell her parents when she became pregnant at the age of seventeen—and they were so shocked by their daughter's "disgusting" behavior that they threatened to disown her. Angela begged her boyfriend, Jake, to marry her so that they could keep the baby and bring it up in the right way. But he was just a child himself, with no money and from a very poor family who came from the wrong side of the tracks. As soon as he heard about the pregnancy, he disappeared, and Angela never heard from him again. In later years, she discovered through mutual friends that he had died of a drug overdose. She wasn't very surprised, as she'd known that he had a problem with heroin.

The pregnancy had been an accident; yet once she knew she was pregnant, Angela was happy to have a purpose in life as a mother, and she relished the idea of raising her daughter free from the judgments and fears that had plagued her young life. But this was not to be. Her parents swooped in and took control of Angela and her baby as soon as Charli was born. When Angela met Chuck Speranza, a handsome young man from California who was a sales rep in NC on a temporary work assignment, the attraction was instant, intense, and mutual, and the two married very quickly.

This time, Angela's parents honored their threat to disown her because they couldn't tolerate her marriage to a man of the Catholic faith. And so, Angela became cut off from her parents, who wouldn't even attend her wedding, and she moved to California to be with her new husband. Chuck adopted young Charlotte as his own, and the serendipity of their similar names was not lost on him. The young couple had both anticipated another pregnancy, another child who was their own, but that was not to be. At this point, Chuck started to lose interest in his wife, who was much younger than him and lacked an educational background that would make her appealing to him on an intellectual level. He'd always loved Charli, though, and regarded her as his own.

Charli's eyes filled with tears as she heard all of these facts. She wasn't even sure why she was crying: perhaps it was the shock of discovering that she wasn't who she'd always thought she was; perhaps she understood something of the pain her mother must have gone through as a teenage mom. Charli still mourned the loss of the man she knew as her father, and somehow the knowledge that their connection wasn't biological made her feel even closer to him in a way that mere biology couldn't explain; she also mourned the fact that she would never know her actual father or come to understand her racial and ethnic heritage in a way that could help her identify who she was, or who she might become.

⊙ ⊙ ⊙

Charli was unusually quiet in the car as they drove to her grandparents in Saluda for their Memorial Day visit. This was partly because she was still disoriented by the DNA test's revelations and trying to adjust to this shocking new information and partly because Sean was driving, so she was forced to sit on her own in the back of the car rather than in her customary spot in the front passenger seat. Charli really hated the casual way that Sean drove, and her anger and resentment towards him only grew as she stared at the back of his head and projected her frustration and rage onto his unwitting brain.

Charli nursed a fond hope that perhaps her grandparents would take against Sean, just like they had reputedly taken against her own father—stepfather—Chuck Speranza. But her hopes were dashed when Pastor Richard and his wife, Dorothy, welcomed Sean into their home with genuine warmth. Sean, for his part, knew how to charm his way into their good books, using the sort of religious language and references he knew they would appreciate and which he usually never uttered. Angela was relieved that she wouldn't have this battle to fight, although she was aware of the tension between her daughter and her parents.

Charli sat glumly through their dinner of homemade pork stew with grits, collards, and corn dogs and helped herself to the measly salad, which was the only type of food she craved right now. Since there was nothing in the house to drink but Diet Coke, she contented herself with water and longed for the relative comforts of her own home. Her mother seemed chatty and smiled frequently but allowed Sean to do the bulk of the talking. Grandma Dottie didn't allow her morbid obesity to prevent her from flirting grotesquely with Sean, offering him more of everything and calling him a "big boy." Even Pastor Richard, who was used to dominating every conversation around the dinner table, allowed Sean to take the floor and restrained himself from intoning religious verses in an effort to demonstrate (Charli thought) how much he knew of the Bible.

When there was a slight lull in the table topics, Richard turned to his granddaughter and asked in a demanding tone, "And what about you, little lady? How are you doing at school these days?"

Charli winced inside at being called "little lady," but she managed to respond, "I'm doing fine," not wishing to elaborate further and hating the sudden eyes all on her.

Angela chimed in, wishing to save her daughter from embarrassment and also enjoying the opportunity to gloat a little: "You know, Charli is very smart. She's been getting straight As ever since we moved here from California. Even though there's no in-person school right now, she works hard. I never have to ask her to do her homework."

"There's nothing much else to do at the moment," countered Charli, feeling her cheeks go red and hot. Even though the positive remarks were nice to hear, she hated the condescending looks everyone was giving her. She both craved and hated attention.

Angela continued: "Charli wants to be an epidemiologist."

"A what?" Dottie said in her lilting Southern drawl.

"It's a kind of doctor," Richard explained. "Is that right?" he asked, turning to Charli for confirmation.

"Yeah, I guess so. I'd have to go to med school."

"Oh, my Lord," exclaimed Dottie. "Why go to all that trouble? I think a pretty young lady like you should be focused on finding a nice man and settling down, starting a family."

"I think she's got a few years for that," admonished Richard, shooting a telling look towards his daughter. "But I do think it's a waste of money giving girls a higher education. You may think it sounds like a nice idea to be a fancy doctor with letters after your name, Charlotte, but you'll regret spending your youth with your head in a book—or a computer, I should say—instead of getting out and enjoying yourself with healthy activities."

Charli opened her mouth to speak, but her grandfather didn't give her a chance to respond. Turning to Angela, he asked: "Are you taking her to church regularly, so she can learn righteous ways?"

"Oh, yes." Angela's face turned pink at this lie, so she quickly turned the conversation in another direction. "You know, Sean and I met at church."

"Well, that is wonderful." Dottie glowed, turning another beaming smile in Sean's direction and patting his arm. "I could just tell you were a God-fearing man."

It seemed that everyone at the table was relieved that the subject had turned to something more pleasant than the black sheep of the family, who currently wished the floor would open up and swallow her or that she could be transported suddenly to another location. California, perhaps, at the rehab, where she had felt accepted and never judged; even just back home to Weaverton and the comfort of her bedroom.

Charli thought of Q'ehazi—a world so different from this one that it seemed to be receding into the background. She needed to get back there as soon as she could. It seemed like the only way to preserve her sanity and to feel a little bit like she wasn't an outsider but rather a part of a genuinely loving and caring community of people.

CHAPTER SEVEN

With only the memory of Q'ehazi to sustain her, Charli devoted herself to researching everything she could about the shawl she had found and her subsequent adventures. Interestingly, there was no mention of Q'ehazi anywhere online, nor of any of the unique cultural innovations she had witnessed.

The unusual bottle the shawl had been stuffed inside was made of heavy glass that looked antique. She returned to retrieve the precious object and brought her phone with her to take several photographs of the shawl and the glass bottle that contained it. The bottle itself was too heavy to carry any distance, so Charli buried it more thoroughly and contented herself with adding a few unusual stones to mark the location so she could easily find it again.

She put the photographs on NextDoor and inquired whether any of her neighbors had ideas about the identity of such an object, or if anybody knew of a local historian who could help her discover the date when the shawl or the bottle had been made. Charli was in luck: one of her neighbors did know a local historian she believed could help. And so, she found herself visiting the Museum of Local Folk Art in nearby Swanton.

Since it was about a forty-five-minute drive from Weaverton, Charli chose to go on a day when she knew her mother would be working one of her shifts at Ingles. These days, since so much of her schoolwork was done online from home and her mother was used to working late shifts and leaving Charli to make her own lunch and dinner, it was relatively easy to have a secret life that her mother knew little about.

Charli felt like an explorer or a researcher on an important mission, and she loved that feeling. When she entered the tiny brick building that housed the museum, she enjoyed the musty smell of old books and artifacts and the quiet hush that permeated the old walls and the wooden furniture. Charli asked for the individual she'd been directed to, a Mrs. Helena Eagleby, who looked exactly as Charli expected a lady with that name to look. She was a tiny, wizened woman, possibly in her mid-eighties, with bright-blue eyes that sparkled with interest and intelligence as she viewed the photographs Charli had taken.

"Can you make them a tad bigger, honey?" said Mrs. Eagleby, squinting through her glasses. "I miss the old days when you could just take a photo in your hand and hold it up to the light." The woman had a strong Southern accent that Charli found charming, and she couldn't resist a smile as Mrs. Eagleby studied the photographs for a few minutes.

"Yes, that's a glass battery jar, all right," she declared finally.

"What is that?"

"They used them in the 1920s and '30s to store household items, even car batteries, mostly. They were quite common. Although you don't often see an article of clothing inside, that's for sure. Where did you find it, again?"

For some reason, Charli didn't wish to admit that she had dug up the bottle containing the shawl. It seemed almost like stealing. And she didn't want to have to give it up. So, she told a little white lie. "It was in our house."

"Mabel told me you're in that house by the Vaughan birthplace there, is that right?"

"Yes. My mom rents the place."

The woman scrunched up her already small blue eyes as she

reflected. "Oh yes, I know that old house. The Hopewell family had lived there for generations, but then it got foreclosed on back in 2008, and the bank sold it to one of those fancy investor folks from California. Been a rental ever since." Mrs. Eagleby seemed a little nostalgic. "Back in the day, when I was a little girl, my family lived in Weaverton. That was considered the grandest house in these parts. I always wanted to see inside."

"Doesn't seem very special now," Charli admitted.

"Oh, well, they let it fall into disrepair. And then the new owners 'modernized' it so it was unrecognizable. If you ask me, they should have let well enough alone. But who cares what an old biddy like me thinks." Mrs. Eagleby giggled conspiratorially to her young companion, as if she'd said something quite impolite. "Dr. Brian would be rolling in his grave, I'm sure. It's a good thing he didn't live to see what happened."

"Who's Dr. Brian?"

Mrs. Eagleby appeared delighted to expound upon her story. "Well, he was quite famous in his day, you know. He was a scientist, very smart man. Wrote books, lots of books, about his theories and discoveries and such."

Charli was intrigued. Whenever anybody mentioned the word *scientist*, her ears pricked up. Physics, chemistry, and biology were her favorite subjects, a fact that always bemused her mother, who had just scraped through her lessons at school, particularly the scientific ones.

"Wow, that's cool. But what's he got to do with our house?"

"His family owned that house for generations—before it got auctioned off to the highest bidder. Dr. Brian was dead by then. He'd never have let that happen, I'm sure. But he didn't have any heirs to leave it to, so his nephew David inherited it, but the boy didn't care. David Cosby was from a wealthy family, but he lost all his money and had to refinance the house to pay his gambling debts. Eventually, when he couldn't pay his mortgage, the bank took the house back from him."

"Sounds like quite a soap opera."

Mrs. Eagleby chuckled. "Believe me, my girl, when you've lived in a place for eighty years like I have, you hear more family tragedies than you can shake a stick at."

"Tell me more about Dr. Brian's books."

"Oh, yes. You can probably get hold of a copy at the library. They always used to stock them there, what with him being a bit of a local celebrity and all. His most important book was written in the 1950s, and it's called *Experiences in Time and Space* by Dr. Brian Hopewell. I know I have a copy at home, but I don't think I could lend it to you. It's too precious."

"Oh, no, that's okay. I'll find it on Amazon or whatever."

The woman seemed skeptical about this suggestion. "I know they used to sell it at our local bookstore here. Mabel, do you know if the Goodreads Bookstore is still open?" she called to her colleague in the next room.

"I think so, but they're closing at five with COVID hours."

"That's right. If you hurry, you might still make it."

Charli thanked the old lady profusely as excitement stirred within her as. After checking her phone and realizing it was a few minutes to five, she ran over to the bookstore three streets away, figuring it was easier to go on foot than to spend time parking the car again. To her great relief, Charli made it into the bookstore before they closed, and they even had a copy of the book left on the shelf, so Charli hurriedly purchased it and clutched it in eager fingers as she walked briskly back to the car.

Later that evening, after having dinner with her mother, Charli had the opportunity to open and peruse the book, and certain passages stood out as particularly illuminating. The mystery of the shawl was finally revealed, and Charli was pleased that she had thought to approach her well-informed neighbors with her questions.

When I was a little boy of just five years old, I have a very vivid recollection of meeting my great-grandfather Bradshaw, at his house in Weaverton, the house I would eventually inherit. Old Daddy Brad (as we used to call him), Ernest Bradshaw, had numerous children, grandchildren and great-grandchildren, about 40 in all, I believe. For whatever reason, I was his particular favorite, and so it was to me that he bequeathed the famous Bradshaw shawl, that had been in our family for generations.

It wasn't until I reached my teens that my mother, Henrietta Hopewell, explained to me the significance of the shawl, although even she was surprised that it was myself who had been chosen as its recipient. Ernest Bradshaw died, at the age of 97, when I was still a child, and so I was never able to personally thank him for his generosity, nor could I inquire any more about the provenance of the shawl and its meaning for him. My mother was able to divulge at least the family history surrounding the shawl, and according to her, Ernest had inherited it from his father, who had inherited it from his father before that, and on through the generations, in an unbroken line since the original owner in the late sixteenth century.

Squire Bradshaw was a dignitary from the tiny village of Eyam in Derbyshire, England, who emigrated to the New World on a ship that sailed with Sir Walter Raleigh in 1563 or thereabouts. He traveled with his pregnant wife, and they were part of a cargo of 100 or so English men and women who were of a devout nature and thus being persecuted for their faith in their home country, so seeking a place where they could establish a new colony.

According to the stories passed down by my family members, the squire did not bring the shawl with him from England, but acquired it at some time during his sojourn in the Americas.

My story now diverts into two strands, which you may follow as you wish: the first is the history of the shawl before it made its way into my hands (as the progeny of the original owner); the second is the experiences I myself have had with this almost magical article. I do not wish to digress here, merely to alert you, faithful reader, to the fact that I believe Divine Providence must have sent this shawl to me, as being possibly the only person to fully understand its true worth and meaning. Perhaps Ernest Bradshaw divined something of my nature even as a child—although I was peculiarly quiet and bookish, and not given to demonstrating a keenness for any particular field of study—and that is why he chose me as the inheritor of this most precious article.

In any case, once I realized that, due perhaps to my very reserved nature, combined with a reluctance to marry and carry on the line of succession, I was not going to be blessed with an heir to whom to bequeath the shawl, I decided therefore to dispose of it in a manner that would preclude anybody else from being able to use it to fulfil their potentially nefarious desires. And so, the shawl is now lost to mankind. But I am not altogether unhappy about this outcome, since I do believe that human beings are not yet ready to embark upon the journey that such a shawl could offer.

And now to explain what I believe may be the origins of the shawl. I shall of course stick to the facts of the history as it has been explained to me. And if you feel that my predilection for the bizarre and the paranormal has caused me to read into this history more than is actually there, then I must beg your forgiveness. For I cannot put aside the years of research into quantum physics and the nature of time and space to which I have dedicated my life, nor am I inclined to believe that it was mere coincidence that the shawl ended up in my hands, rather than in the hands of another, who would not have understood its significance.

However, the facts stated plainly are these:

A Brief History of the Bradshaw Family and Its Descendants in the New World from the Sixteenth to the Twentieth Century

My ancestor Matthew Bradshaw was on the ship with Walter Raleigh from England in 1563 and part of the so-called "lost colony." Squire Bradshaw hailed from Eyam, a little village in Derbyshire, England. He was a country squire who intended to settle in the New World, and he brought his young pregnant wife with him.

When Sir Walter Raleigh left for England and the colony was charged with existing on their own, Bradshaw was chosen as the leader of the little band of English men and women. He was given the opportunity to form a connection with the Q'ehazi tribe of Indians (who were descendants of the native Cherokee of North Carolina and the Arawak Indians from the Caribbean). It is believed that one of the tribal members wished to marry one of the English maidens from the colony. These Q'ehazi natives were residing in the flatlands by the coast, known in those days as the Outer Banks. At this time, Bradshaw had to make a choice: should he trust the Indians, who he had been told were "savages" and incapable of moral and ethical thought? Or should he risk the possibility of violent reprisals by taking actions to thwart them that could be interpreted as hostile?

Squire Bradshaw had strong religious principles, and he and the other members of his group were committed to peaceful negotiations. However, they knew very little about the Indians and what they were capable of, nor did they have any experience in this foreign land, and Bradshaw recognized how vulnerable they were. We do not have any written records that could tell us definitively the choice Bradshaw made at this critical juncture in our history.

Here is where the story becomes interesting. According to our historical records, by the time Sir Walter Raleigh was able to return to the mainland of NC almost three years later, he could find no trace of his group of English settlers (beyond the intriguing word "Croat" that had been carved upon the trunk of a tree near where he'd left them), and therefore presumed they had all been killed by hostile Indian tribes. The group was ever afterwards referred to as the "Lost Colony," a group of intrepid English men and women who had lost their lives to cruel and hostile natives. From that point on, relations with all the local Indian tribes became more and more strained; revenge piled upon revenge; many lives were lost in massacres and uprisings, and the Native American culture was almost completely decimated. Now, in the 20th century, the whole of modern American society is built upon this foundation of bloodshed and desecration, which was so far from what the original settlers had intended. And yet, perhaps things didn't need to be this way.

One article remains—a shawl, that the small tribe of Indians known as Q'ehazi had given to Bradshaw as a present for his wife. The really strange and interesting fact is that this gift, according to the stories of my family, was bequeathed to the English man in 1590, i.e., long after the supposed destruction of both the English colony and the Indian tribe itself. While the history of how the shawl came to be passed down through the generations and eventually into my hands is at first murky, we know for sure, due to carbon dating, that this article of clothing was made in the sixteenth century, and my family can attest to the fact that it is not a fake.

Bradshaw's wife, Emily, died tragically in childbirth, but the child, William, survived, and he inherited the shawl, which had been placed in a metal box for safety, with the keeper of the box surprisingly enjoined to "never open it." This child somehow managed to escape the massacre of all of his countrymen and he fled to the western part of the state, where he eventually made a life for himself, worked as a carpenter, married, settled down and had a family.

William, who was born in 1601, gave the shawl to his first-born son, Harold, who was born in 1623, and he passed it to his son Edward in 1650, who gave it to his grandson Robert in 1695. Six generations later, my great-grandfather Ernest Bradshaw inherited the shawl, and as I earlier mentioned, he passed it to me. Although I do not carry on the Bradshaw name, I am a direct descendant of the original Squire Bradshaw who was given the shawl, allegedly by the Indians.

It has long been believed by historians that the English settlers were all killed, probably by Indians, and the Q'ehazi tribe has vanished into obscurity with no records of them extant. Yet how did this shawl manage to survive, and what is its provenance? Could there perhaps be another world in which the destruction we heard about never happened?

My Research into the Phenomena of Parallel Worlds and How These Were Expanded Upon by the Use of the Shawl I Inherited

As far as I understand, nobody before me—apart from the original owner of the shawl, my ancestor Matthew Bradshaw—had ever actually opened the box and looked at the shawl. It was said that the shawl was somehow cursed and that whoever opened it would be cursed also. But as I am a scientist and not a superstitious man, I attempted the deed that none had dared to do before me. I have no regrets about doing this, as the results surprised even myself, and led me on an adventure that has been unsurpassed by any other in my life so far.

I have dedicated my life to conducting research into quantum physics and random particles, and I have been most fascinated by theories posited in the 1920s by other renowned physicists and scientists, including Heisenberg with his uncertainty principle and the aptly named observer effect.

I was privileged to be able to view some scraps of writing that were preserved from my ancestor's journals from the date of September 1563, in which he tells something of his story. He and his wife, Lucy, joined with a group of English men and women who undertook the perilous journey across the sea from the English south coast, probably Dover, to the shores of what is now North Carolina. This group of roughly 100 souls came from all parts of Britain. They were united in their desire to find a New World in which their principles of fairness and tolerance could be appreciated and expanded, and despite a long journey through sometimes rough seas, they successfully made the voyage and landed at Cape Hatteras in the Outer Banks sometime in the late summer of 1563.

They were accompanied and led by Sir Walter Raleigh, who was hoping to make a name and a fortune for himself in the new land; however, he was recalled to England by Queen Elizabeth I, who wished him to help her fight the English wars against Spain. And so, Raleigh had to leave his band of travelers, temporarily, or so he thought, assuring them that he would return and bring more provisions to help them settle into their new home. In the end, the wars, as we now know, kept Raleigh away from the American shores for over three years. When he finally made his return, he was disappointed to discover that all of his colony of English settlers had disappeared, and he presumed that they must have been killed by hostile native tribes. The apocryphal story tells us that Raleigh had asked his compatriots to leave him a sign of their whereabouts, and when he came across the one word "Croat" carved into the trunk of a tree, he made the supposition that they had been taken by the Croatan tribe.

But Squire Bradshaw tells a different tale. According to his admittedly brief and somewhat sporadic journal entries, these settlers did not perish, but in fact joined with a local tribe of natives and were able to successfully make a life for themselves. Bradshaw explains that, shortly after Raleigh's departure, and while his small colony of settlers were attempting to carve out an existence for themselves, they were approached by a small tribe of natives who it was said originally hailed from South America and were part of an extant offshoot of the Aztecs. They called themselves Q'ehazi, and they were tall and lean with dark skin and glossy black hair. The most unusual thing about them, compared to other tribes known of in the area, was their demeanor. They were quiet, peaceful and friendly, and they ate only fish (which were abundant in the waters at that time) and local fruits and plants. They were also well-versed in the use of medicinal herbs, and they had developed a society based on the daily use of the *pukatl* herb, said to induce a feeling of relaxed and focused energy.

The Europeans and the natives formed an alliance in those early days because they both had things to offer each other that were beneficial: the settlers had a knowledge of writing, mathematics, and the production of artifacts from metal, that the natives had never seen before; the natives had a wealth of information about indigenous plants and other resources that could be used both for food and for medicinal purposes. Gradually, over the next few months, they came to learn each other's languages and to appreciate each other's customs.

Bradshaw, as leader of the English settlers, was charged with making decisions for the group. He had been raised in a staunchly religious household and had a strong moral code that normally would preclude intermarriage between different races of people. His experience with these natives, however, had been positive, and he knew the kind of people they were and the values they held, even though other, perhaps more superficial things such as dress and self-expression were very different in the two cultures. There came a time where Bradshaw had to make a decision that was likely to change the course of history. He pondered on it for many days, as he recognized the significance of his choice. One of the natives, a young man who was the son of one of the tribal elders, wished to marry Bradshaw's niece, Ellen, who was 19 and of an age to bear children. Bradshaw was ambivalent about the proposed union.

Would it unite the two cultures, in the same manner as kings and queens of yore would wed princes and princesses from another country in order to cement alliances? Or would it lead to disaster and cause his people to lose sight of their original mission of tolerance and peace, because of their line being watered down and unduly influenced by another culture and race? What was the potential outcome of his choice, either way? Bradshaw delayed his decision for many nights while he wrestled with his soul and prayed to his God to make the right choice, for his people and for all mankind.

I can only surmise what must have happened to my forebear during the ensuing few days, as corroborating records from that time are scarce. Squire Bradshaw wrote (in barely decipherable script and using a form of Old English that required some translation on my part) in his journal about the unique experience he had, right after he carved the word "Croat" into the trunk of a tree. Bradshaw described a "dream" where he met the people of the Q'ehazi tribe and became friends with them, and he saw the unique and beautiful hand-woven shawls that the women made, and they gave him one. According to Bradshaw's writings, he "woke up from this dream" and came back to "reality" in which his little band of pilgrims were all killed by the Indians. Indeed, his journal appears to have been abandoned, as it ends almost in mid-sentence. This journal was passed down to me, along with the shawl, which has remained remarkably intact and well-preserved through the centuries. The shawl, when I inherited it, had been placed inside of a metal box, and I am assuming had not seen the light of day since the time when it was first acquired by my ancestor.

Upon reflection, and the scientific research into quantum physics for which I have gained some little notoriety amongst my peers in the past two decades, I arrived at the conclusion that Bradshaw had somehow managed to exist momentarily in two parallel worlds or realities: one in which he made the choice to join with the natives, and one in which he did not. The latter choice led to the world in which I and all my predecessors are existing. The former choice led to an alternate universe which has been running parallel to our world ever since.

It is my firm belief that this parallel world, which was originated by my ancestor, Matthew Bradshaw, in the sixteenth century, still exists today, and in a sense runs along the same timeframe, as two parallel but never intersecting lines can stretch into infinity yet never meet. This article, which was present at the split between worlds and therefore has a "foot in both worlds," as it were, can be utilized as a kind of a portal or door, that will enable passage between the worlds.

Dear Readers, those of you of whom it can be said are possessed of a more "rational" mind, i.e., not given to belief in anything which has not been proven by your own direct experience, may be inclined to disapprove of the subsequent elements of my story, and this is why I have chosen to bury them in this tome's appendix. Thus you are able to ignore these aspects and focus on the parts of my story that are more logical and therefore more believable. However, those readers who are more drawn to the mystical and who are possessed of a more credulous nature, not needing proof of direct experience and able to suspend your disbelief for the entertainment of a good story (whether it be true or not), will enjoy reading about my experiences with the shawl, which were done partly in an attempt at scientific exploration, and partly (I must admit) in a spirit of fascination with the seemingly impossible.

Following the results of my own personal experiences, and recognizing that this ease of passage between worlds might result in negative consequences, both for the traveler and the worlds themselves, and not wishing to potentially subject others to these unintended consequences with their unknown and unpredictable outcomes, I elected to dispose of the shawl, after using it myself to test my theories. Thus, I sacrificed my desire for scientific validation of my theory, that parallel worlds are not only in existence but may be reached from our own world, on the altar of practicality and reason, judging that it was best not to risk the health and safety of others for what might be a fleeting and inconsequential gain.

There are moments of regret at my decision. But for the most part, I am glad to have literally and figuratively closed the door on any further investigation of this fascinating journey.

⊙ ⊙ ⊙

Charli felt a certain sense of shock, and also recognition, as she read these words, particularly the ones describing Dr. Brian's ideas about parallel worlds. She wondered why Dr. Brian had decided to lie when he claimed in his book that he had destroyed the shawl, rather than telling the world he had in fact buried it in a glass bottle. Perhaps he was worried that the land of Q'ehazi would be invaded and destroyed by people who couldn't understand its worth. Perhaps, at the last moment, he did after all rethink his decision to destroy the shawl and decided instead to bury it inside a glass bottle, where it might one day be found. Perhaps Abbe was right, and Charli who was "meant to" find the shawl. Charli recognized that, somehow or another, she had been chosen for a special mission, and she needed to act wisely. The coincidence— and perhaps significance—of Charli having discovered her part-Cherokee heritage relatively recently was also not lost on her, and she felt validated to know that something other than her feelings connected her to the world of Q'ehazi.

To Charli's great and intense disappointment, she searched in vain for the "appendix" where Dr. Hopewell had supposedly written about his own experiences with the shawl, but this section of the book was nowhere to be found, and perhaps had been eliminated in subsequent publications of the book, as her copy was a fourth edition, printed in 1999.

⊙ ⊙ ⊙

Charli obsessed over this other world and everything she'd learned and experienced during her brief visit there. It was often on the tip of her tongue to spill the beans. She imagined the glow in her eyes as she told the tale of finding another world adjacent to this one, where people and things were just the same and yet fundamentally different.

But something always stopped her from speaking about it. She imagined too the looks on people's faces if she spoke about this "other world" that remained unseen. Surely, they would think she was completely nuts, or had been doing drugs, or was making it all up to get attention. Who would believe such a fantastical tale? It had been such a magical experience that she wondered now if she'd dreamed it. Perhaps she was indeed going crazy.

The only way to confirm that she hadn't dreamed the whole thing was to revisit the place where she'd buried the shawl and attempt to repeat her actions. But first there were the end-of-semester exams to get through.

Charli was not usually cunning or deceitful, so it was uncharacteristic of her to lie to her mother about something as important as where she was going to be for a week. She was surprised at how easy it was to make her mother believe she was going to the art retreat in Henderson that her teacher had invited her to and that she would "probably be too busy with class" to call or text on a daily basis. Now that she had a car, Charli could drive to a place close to her home and leave the vehicle and make it seem as though she had gone somewhere in it, although her intentions were entirely different.

◉ ◉ ◉

Angela felt a lot more comfortable today as she spoke to her therapist—again on Zoom, but this time in the relative privacy of her sunroom rather than in her car, now that both Sean and Charli were out of the house. Angela wasn't sure why she felt such shame and guilt about talking to a therapist, but these feelings inhibited her from admitting to anybody else what she was doing and caused her to feel secretive. The therapist's now familiar and kind face immediately made Angela feel at ease, and she exhaled her tension in a sigh at the beginning of the session, not realizing she'd been holding so much in.

The therapist noticed this sigh and remarked on it, wondering aloud what could be causing this level of tension for her client. Was the stress she was feeling work related or more to do with relationship difficulties? Angela paused before replying, somewhat conflicted over how much she wished to reveal, but once again, when she had started talking about her troubles, the words spilled out faster than she'd anticipated, and the therapist's nods and gentle vocal prods incited her to carry on with her story.

Angela had so wanted somebody to share these things with before, but there was nobody she could trust to support her without judgment or even to understand why it was so difficult. She explained how worried she was about her daughter, and how that occupied much of her time and energy (although a small part of her recognized that this "worry" was mostly to do with herself and how to cope with her daughter's emerging independence, and what it would mean for her future as a young woman).

"Charli was always such a good girl when she was little," Angela opined, wanting to let her therapist know that she loved and was proud of her daughter. "She was smart, too, much smarter than me, and more like her dad." Now Angela explained how Charli had worshipped her father—too much, perhaps—and how hard it had been when her father was taken away from her so young and in such a shocking manner.

"And I feel guilty because there are even things about that I haven't told Charli." When the therapist pressed her, Angela wasn't quite ready to reveal how she'd discovered that her husband had been cheating on her the night of the fatal accident that claimed both his life and the life of his mistress. Her feelings were so conflicted even now—such a mix of regret, disappointment, anger, grief, guilt—that she couldn't begin to explain or address them, so she swept the whole incident under the carpet and focused on other things and other people.

Angela preferred to speak about how Chuck's death had impacted Charli, and how the girl had gone from being a popular and vibrant member of her school with excellent grades to withdrawn, rebellious, and oppositional, a teenager who didn't seem to care about her academic prowess or social skills, and who started to hang out with a "bad crowd of kids" who used drugs as a way to cope with their unwanted feelings. It was the therapist who put her finger on something that Angela hadn't realized: "I guess Charli must have felt abandoned by her father, and maybe even by you."

"By me? How did I abandon her?"

"If you weren't able to grieve openly for him, you also were not letting her grieve, and so all that emotion got shut inside and had to find an outlet somewhere."

Angela didn't say the words "I see," but a lightbulb moment pricked at the edges of her consciousness.

The words continued to tumble out, and Angela felt tears coming as she spoke about the years since Chuck's death and how difficult they had been for both of them. Charli's increasing drug use had led Angela to send her to a rehab facility in California for a three-month stay, and even though the treatment helped Charli to overturn this habit before it ruined more of her young life, her resentment had solidified the rift between them into something unspoken but deeply felt.

Angela had felt so lost during this time that she reached out for help to her parents, the same parents who had disowned her for marrying outside of their religious faith fifteen years before. Now that she was a young widow, her parents gladly took her back into the fold and offered her a place to stay with them while she got back on her feet. Even though Chuck came from a wealthy family and had therefore provided adequately for his daughter, the money he'd left would not keep Angela and Charli forever without her working to support them both, and the rents in California were prohibitively expensive, so returning to North Carolina seemed the only viable option.

Angela wished she could have explained her reasons for the move more successfully to Charli, who was bitter and unhappy about leaving behind the world she knew, and all her friends, to make a new life in a state that she regarded as "backward" and "uneducated." But Angela couldn't handle Charli alone and fervently hoped a fresh start could bring back the vibrant, intelligent, and popular girl she had been before.

However, eight months staying with her parents did not have a good effect, either on her or her daughter, and the tension in the household was palpable. Her parents did not appreciate this oppositional teenager, who seemed to represent everything they disliked in the world—and the feelings were mutual. As for Angela, her naturally unconfrontational nature was constantly triggered by the fighting and negative atmosphere.

So, when Angela was offered the opportunity to work as an elementary school teaching assistant in Weaverton, she jumped at the chance, both to do a job she loved with little children and to move far enough away from her parents to avoid their pervasive influence while still being able to stay in the same state and enjoy the cheap rents. It seemed a cruel blow that after only six months in this job, the pandemic began, all the local schools were forced to close, and the children had to homeschool. At least Charli was doing relatively well now. She hadn't exactly had the opportunity to make new friends but was at least doing well academically and regaining her interests and ambitions.

The session ended, and it seemed so sudden that Angela felt

disappointment at not having been able to broach the aspect of Sean and her concerns about his drinking. Still, she felt a huge wave of relief wash over her that she'd been able to share this much, and from the knowledge that at last her troubles were being taken seriously and she had some hope for the future.

⊙ ⊙ ⊙

"I've got to go to work now, honey. Are you sure you'll be okay, and you have everything you need for the art retreat?" Angela popped her head into Charli's bedroom at 8 a.m. one morning in early June. Charli was still lying in bed.

"Yeah, I'll be fine, Mom." Charli smiled and was unusually affectionate towards her mother, who she normally would have spurned for being overprotective, because she felt guilty about the lies she'd had to tell to preserve the secret of her visit to Q'ehazi.

Angela normally could intuit when her daughter was being less than truthful, but she was already late for her shift, and she was also distracted by her guilt about the ways she sometimes ignored her daughter's needs if they conflicted with Sean's. She'd made an internal commitment to do everything she could to encourage her daughter to stand on her own two feet, embrace her talents, and strive for the achievements that Angela herself had been denied, so the art retreat seemed like a gift sent from heaven to help her daughter, and she wasn't going to do anything to sabotage that.

Charli's expression seemed benign and happy, if a little sleepy, as her mother gave her a kiss on the cheek before heading out the door. Inside, though, Charli's mind was racing, and as soon as she heard her mother turn the key in the lock, she literally sprang out of bed with excitement.

About half an hour later, with her backpack carefully stuffed with items as if going away for a week, Charli drove her car to a nearby side street and set off across the fields to the creek and the place where she'd left the shawl two months earlier. She took in the sights and sounds all around her as usual, but she remembered how heightened her senses had been in the other world and wondered if she would experience the same intensity of emotion and sensation in that place, or if it was like the first high from a drug she would always be chasing.

Arriving at the familiar redbud tree, she experienced a twinge of excitement bordering on anxiety. She hoped that there were not other, less pleasant adventures in store for her this time. Charli wasn't normally an anxious person, but she wasn't sure what to expect and whether she was prepared for it. *How do you prepare for a trip to a foreign land, where nobody else has been before you, and there are no goalposts or rules to follow?* "Just bring your sunscreen," Charli joked out loud as she set about digging into the earth with her hands to recover the bottle.

Fortunately, as she'd forgotten to bring a spade and had to do the whole thing with her hands this time, she hadn't dug the hole very deep. She eventually managed to loosen enough earth to pry the glass bottle from its hiding place. Then, with slightly trembling fingers, she opened the bottle and gazed at the multicolored shawl with its vivid hues. Yes, it was still there, and it looked exactly the same.

Charli stood and carefully draped the shawl around her shoulders. Suddenly, she heard a crackle behind her and swiftly turned, expecting to see an animal or a bird. But there was nothing, just a gently swinging branch, as if a bird had just flown off.

When Charli faced the mountains again, which was where she had gone with Abbe when she'd first entered the Q'ehazi land, she closed her eyes briefly and then opened them again, hoping to see the tear in the fabric indicating the portal to the other world. At first, it was pretty indistinct, but if she squinted her eyes almost shut, she could see a vague line hovering in the air about a foot or so away from her. It was much closer this time, and she easily reached out and touched it, feeling again the raspy texture beneath her fingers.

She didn't hesitate and pulled apart the tear to step through. Determined to waste no time, Charli set off across the grass to the spot where she had met her friend weeks before.

⊙　⊙　⊙

Sean adjusted his position and bent down lower to watch Charli from his vantage point shrouded by the trees. He held his breath as she whipped around at the sound of the leaves beneath his feet. She soon turned away again.

Sean had been keeping a careful eye on Charli, especially when her mother was at work and thereby leaving Charli free to shoot herself in the foot. As soon as she dumped her car, he knew he was in for a treat, so he followed her at a safe distance and ensconced himself in the thick shrubbery to watch.

What Sean saw as Charli stepped through the tear made him wonder whether he had lost his mind or perhaps drunk too much whisky the night before. *She vanished into thin air!* One minute, she'd been standing there with that stupid shawl on, and the next minute she was reaching into the air and making some weird gestures for a couple of seconds—then, whoosh, she was gone. What a trip!

Sean waited a few moments after Charli disappeared, then jumped out of his hiding place and ran over to the spot where she'd pulled her vanishing act. He'd taken out his cell phone, intending to snap a picture of Charli as proof that she was doing something clandestine, and he momentarily forgot it was in his hands and dropped it on the ground in his confusion. Now he had no idea how to proceed. He'd seen the girl make some strange movements with her hands, so he did the same, but that didn't work. He paced the whole area, wondering if she had somehow jumped behind a bush or something he didn't initially spot, but Charli was nowhere to be found.

Then, he spotted it. At first, he thought the brown line must be a twig suspended in the air by the wind or a spiderweb—and yet there was no wind today, it being a very still, hot day in June, and no glimmer of spider silk. Was it an alien object that had fallen from the sky?

His unimaginative mind was unable to comprehend something as unimaginable as a whole other world. So, he gave up trying to figure out what was going on here and focused on crashing his way through whatever it was. Sean was convinced that Charli was either up to no good or had secret access to something valuable—and for both reasons, he wanted to make sure she didn't get away from him this time. He walked directly into the line.

Once past the weird distortion, Sean recognized only that the scenery around him was pretty much the same as what lay behind him. Not being given to reflection, he didn't ponder on or notice what it meant to step into another dimension. Nor did he observe a metamorphosis in the hues and sounds around him, as he was not particularly sensitive to these things ordinarily. If he had noticed a change, maybe his actions would have been different. But he was bent on a mission.

Sean strode quickly and purposefully ahead for a good ten minutes but failed to find Charli, though his attention was captured by something up ahead and to his left: a red glimmer. Sean was struck by how unusual it was to see something sparkling out in the open, as if pronouncing its beauty unabashed to the world. He was even more intrigued when he moved closer and realized that beside the shiny red object was a large waterfall he had never seen before, cascading over rocks to a lotus-filled pond full of clear water. Some hieroglyphics were carved on the rocks, but Sean didn't recognize any of them as English words.

Beside the pond, a man sat with his head bowed over a book.

The man was quite old, thin, and frail looking, with very dark skin. *Like a jungle native,* Sean thought scathingly.

If he'd been of an aesthetic nature, Sean might have recognized the scene as being quite beautiful, but he tended to focus on the utility of things rather than their intrinsic value. For this reason, once Sean realized that the sparkling red light he had seen from afar belonged to a huge, rose-colored rock atop a plinth, his mind raced with possibilities.

That's got to be a ruby, he thought, a rush of greedy anticipation making his mouth water. *Bigger than any ruby I've ever seen. Jesus, that would be worth millions back home!*

Sean found it difficult to take his eyes off the beautiful red rock once he realized what it was—which was probably why it took him a few moments to recognize that the man had stopped reading and was actively trying to engage his attention. The man stood and waved at Sean in an agitated manner but did not speak aloud.

He's a jungle bunny. Probably doesn't even speak English, thought Sean. Still, he decided to give the man the benefit of the doubt.

"Hey, buddy, that's quite a rock you've got there."

The man suddenly approached Sean and smilingly held out his arms as if prepared to hug him. Although this seemed like a friendly gesture, Sean was bemused at the guy's apparent inability to talk. He was also suspicious of this sudden onset of friendliness from a stranger and backed away, putting up his hands in a defensive manner.

"Woah, hold on there. Do I know you?"

The old Black man was gazing at him intently, as if trying to communicate, but he still didn't say anything. Sean suddenly had the idea that maybe this guy was a deaf mute, although why he would have been chosen to guard this precious object was beyond him. Quite a stroke of luck, though, because this dumb guy would never be able to spill the beans about who took the rock.

Sean knew of a great way to persuade people to do what he wanted without the need for words, and now was the time to implement it. He always carried a gun on him, especially if he was venturing into an unpredictable situation, so he drew the pistol from his pocket and pointed it at the man.

"Just back away from the rock, boy, and let me take it; then you won't get hurt."

The expression on the man's face was more confused than afraid, and he didn't put his hands up. Sean wondered if the man was stupid as well as mute.

"So, I get it. You're here to watch over this ruby rock or whatever it is. But it's not doing much good here, is it? I mean, nobody can see it out here in the wilderness. How about if I just borrowed it for a bit?" As Sean spoke, he approached the red rock, which now looked even more shiny and precious. Sean was so entranced that he took his eyes off the man, who was probably not much of a threat anyway, and stuck the gun back in his pocket.

The stone was probably almost a foot in diameter and had been cut into facets, each of which caught the sun's rays so that it sparkled and shone in a way he had never before seen.

"Oh my God, this is incredible. Martin is going to freak when he sees this," Sean murmured, mostly to himself. The man was waving at him again, but he hadn't approached Sean and remained at a distance, so Sean wasn't too concerned. After all, Sean was the one with a deadly weapon.

Sean was amazed at how easily he lifted the red rock off its plinth. No secret booby traps or hidden guards sprang at him. Although the rock was extremely heavy and the weight of it almost brought him to the ground, Sean regularly lifted at the gym and was very motivated, giving him all the energy and drive he needed to carry it with him. Fortunately, the distance back to the house was relatively short, and Sean judged that he could make it if he gave the job all his effort. So, with some straining of his back and arms, he prepared to haul the gem off.

The man had snuck up behind him and now frantically tapped him on the shoulder. Sean had intended to use the gun as a deterrent only and not to actually shoot the guy, but partly by reflex and partly to teach the man a lesson he wouldn't forget, Sean swung around and shot him in the leg. The old man collapsed on the ground, where he writhed in agony, clutching his injured leg.

"I told you, you fucking idiot!" Sean yelled. It wasn't that he had any ill will towards the man, but he didn't like impediments. "You fucking asshole, get out of my way! Fucking loser. I told you already, stay away from me!"

Once the man was no longer being a nuisance, Sean hurried off with the red rock in his arms and retraced his steps. He still hadn't acknowledged to himself that he was not in the world he'd known his entire life, but he couldn't deny that there was no way the place he'd just found had been there and accessible all this time without him knowing it. He simply ignored the mystery.

Sean staggered along the path under the weight of the ruby, using visions of the money he'd earn by selling the rock to motivate him to continue despite his discomfort. He could be very determined once there was a strong motivating force to drive him on, and this was potentially the best thing that had ever happened to him—an incredible stroke of luck that he should act upon fast.

Sean had enough memory to get back to the redbud tree, where he momentarily rested against the trunk and gazed down at the rock. When he looked up again, he thought there must be something wrong with his eyesight because everything was suddenly blurry, but fortunately it cleared up as soon as he stumbled a few steps forward and found himself back beside the creek. In fact, he fell on the ground and lay there for a few moments, panting with the exertion. His cell phone was still lying at the base of the tree where he'd left it. When he picked it up, he realized that he'd been gone for just over an hour.

After checking to see if there were any messages—there weren't—Sean called Martin and spoke breathlessly: "Hey, pal, get your ass over here quick as you can. I'm by the creek at the back of Angie's place. I need you to bring the wheelbarrow with you. It's in Angie's shed. She always leaves the door open, so you can just grab it. I've got something pretty fucking amazing to show you."

Sean couldn't resist crowing to his friend about his new find, but he didn't want to waste time on the phone, so he didn't tell Martin what they would be carrying back to the house. Martin said he'd be right over, and Sean decided to wait there for him rather than spending any more of his energy lugging the rock on his own.

He figured he could always go back to that same place, now he knew how to get there, and find more of these rocks if he needed to, although he was so sure of the monetary value of the one he already had that he didn't think he'd need to go back for quite a while. *But you can never have too much of a good thing!* he reflected.

CHAPTER EIGHT

Charli walked for a long distance before she encountered any other people. As before, she was entranced by the vivid colors around her and the sharp detail of the sounds. The sky was that cerulean blue associated with the Carolinas, and a few pale, wispy clouds floated by as if they had nothing much to do. The temperature was warm but not sultry. The air felt refreshing, like a glass of sun-warmed spring water.

As Charli walked, she became aware of a sound piercing the normal soft hum of animals and nature. At first, she thought it was a strange animal making the eerie noise—a coyote, perhaps, calling to its mate? Then she recognized the voice as human. It sounded a little like a yodel, with its rising and falling cadence. There was a response from the nearby hills, and this unusual dialogue continued for a few minutes as Charli learned to recognize the sound. Now she realized what it must be.

Abbe had told her of the Q'ehazi tradition of "hollerin'," or calling to each other across the hills and meadows. She'd said it was a traditional form of communication first used in the 1600s by the original settlers of these lands. This type of call-and-response in order to alert or warn about some noteworthy event had not been superseded by more modern forms of contact such as cell phones and computers, even though those were also available. Charli was entranced by the idea that communication could take a variety of forms—both human and technological, using both auditory/oral and extrasensory methods.

Taking in all of these sensations, Charli's step and mood

was buoyant, full of positive expectancy such as she had never felt before. It reminded her of being a small child who trusted in everything and believe that absolutely anything was possible. Charli's natural cynicism had begun early in life, so this optimism was unfamiliar to her, but it felt like a distant echo from a time long gone. The crunch of twigs and dry grasses beneath her feet and the birdsongs and the sound of the water flowing in the creek once again seemed to join together in pleasing harmony.

Charli kept to the path that spread out ahead of her with trees flanking it on either side. After a while, the path opened up, and Charli beheld fields and meadows stretching in front of her. Some of the fields had crops planted in them. The time being early morning, there were as yet no people working in the fields, but the land had obviously been cultivated by humans.

After walking for perhaps a mile, Charli saw a gray line stretching horizontally from right to left, where the road would have been in her world. She spotted movement on this line. Shapes would appear on one side and move across her field of vision slowly to the other side. It was a little like a river with leaves floating along it, except these shapes were much larger than leaves.

As Charli approached, she discerned that the shapes were human beings. The ground gave way to a gray surface the width of a small country road—in fact, about the same as the one on which her own house was placed. But this road was almost entirely taken up by a wide conveyor belt, which was transporting all of the people she had seen. It moved at a fairly slow speed, with access ramps every few yards or so. Some people were seated and reading as if they were on a train. Others, who were maybe in more of a hurry, were walking or running down the middle of the conveyor belt.

And now Charli realized that there were actually two conveyor belts moving in opposite directions, exactly like trains on two separate tracks. Both were occupied by people. Charli wondered how long this conveyor belt was, so for a time she walked alongside

THE WORLD BEYOND THE REDBUD TREE

it, though it didn't appear to have an end to it. Sometimes she smiled at the people on the belt, and they nodded to her in acknowledgement and smiled back a friendly greeting. She passed people making their way onto the belt using the ramps.

It seemed to Charli as though it would be relatively simple to enter the belt and travel in either direction. Charli considered that she was here to experience all there was to experience in this strange new world, so she ascended a ramp to the conveyer belt heading to the left, which she imagined was east, and found herself riding along with the others. Since she enjoyed walking anyway, she sauntered down the center aisle, slowly passing the few seated people and catching sight of the folks traveling in the other direction. To Charli's surprise, there was nothing covering the conveyor, and she wondered briefly what would happen if it started to rain—would people just get wet, or perhaps nobody traveled in bad weather?

A breeze whispered past her, and the warm, moist air felt pleasant on her skin and caressed the loose strands of hair that fell over her face as she walked. She was glad she had decided to wear her sensible shoes for the trip and that she hadn't brought anything with her other than a light jacket in case the temperature turned cool. The backpack her mother had insisted she take to the art retreat had been left in her car. Charli didn't like the idea of being encumbered by anything here.

Alongside the road, Charli saw occasional small knots of people engaged in various activities. Some were now harvesting or planting crops in fields; some were seated at outdoor desks where they worked on computers; a small group of children sat on the ground in a semicircle around an older lady speaking aloud and pointing to words written on a board. It was so strange to hear somebody speaking out loud that Charli's attention was instantly drawn to this phenomenon. The woman was speaking in English, but it had a strange accent or lilt to it, like Old English, which had not been spoken for many generations in Charli's world. The pleasant sound reminded her of the Shakespeare plays she had seen and Chaucer poems she had read for her English literature classes. The children were mostly quiet and listening intently.

Up ahead, Charli could just make out another group of individuals, but this was a larger group of adults, and they were clustered around an individual wearing an official-looking cape. It was an older Black woman with a commanding voice and presence, who was also speaking aloud in the strange, old-fashioned English dialect. As the belt brought Charli closer to the crowd of about fifty or so people, she realized the speaker was Sovereign Aurora. Charli felt a rush of excitement. *Surely Abbe must also be there, somewhere in the crowd*, she thought. Sure enough, she soon made out the distinctive features and overflowing hairstyle of her friend, seated among the others.

Charli hastily departed the conveyor belt using one of the ramps and made her way over to her friend, trying to be as unobtrusive as possible so as not to disturb the progress of events. The event seemed to be an official and formal occasion, judging by the quietness and the serious expressions of the audience. The sovereign was dressed in dark and somber colors, not like the clothes she had worn at the concert at all.

Charli found her friend and took up a seat beside her on the grass. As soon as Abbe noticed Charli, she gave one of her customary huge smiles and hugged Charli tightly as she spoke without words: "I'm so glad to see you, my dear friend." Charli responded in kind, and felt instantly relieved and full of that warm contentment she remembered feeling in Abbe's presence.

"What is happening?" Charli asked with a thought question.

"It's a fairness test," replied Abbe in similar fashion. "We always have these types of sessions in the open air so that many people can participate."

"Oh, I see. Was that what they were hollerin' about earlier?"

"Yes. Calling everybody to the court. The sovereign is making a decision on what to do. We can also give our opinions if we wish."

The sovereign spoke aloud once more and indicated two people who were seated at the front of the crowd and who were obviously the subjects of the fairness test.

"Barylos, my daughter, from the Village of Teachers West and Metlin from the Village of Scholars and Historians South are in dispute over who should teach the children from the Village of Farmers South when they are learning about the myths and stories of the Old Age. Barylos believes that all lessons should be taught by those from the Village of Teachers, and Metlin believes that lessons concerning historical facts should be taught by the Village of Scholars and Historians. We have heard from both Barylos and Metlin with their arguments about why they believe as they believe. Now I would like to hear from anybody in the crowd who has an opinion to give, or a fact to input."

Various people in the group of onlookers spoke, and all raised their hands to signal their desire to contribute before speaking. To hear voices in that normally quiet place felt a little strange to Charli, but she was glad to witness how respectful everybody was and their willingness to listen to each other, even if they had a dissenting point of view.

At one point, Charli spotted another familiar face in the crowd. She felt a little thrill run through her as she recognized Joslyn, Abbe's brother, whom she had met on her last visit. She was again surprised at this visceral reaction of excitement, nervousness, anticipation, and anxiety all mingled together, both pleasant and unpleasant at the same time.

When she smiled in his direction, he noticed her as well, and his face lit up in a similar smile. Charli wondered if she was reading his expression truly or if she was so affected by her own emotions that she imagined his happiness on seeing her, but at any rate, her heart beat even faster as their eyes met in a moment of mutual recognition. He nodded as if to say, "I see you," and then she felt or heard the unspoken words: "I'm glad to see you, Charli." She couldn't help her smile from broadening as she sent back the message without sound: "I'm glad to see you too, Joslyn."

The fairness test continued for a half hour or so, with the people giving their softly worded feedback. Charli was surprised that nobody so far had come up with a suggestion that she thought was glaringly obvious. She kept waiting for somebody else to speak it aloud, but nobody did. On a whim, perhaps because of the little thrill inside still lifting her spirits at the sight of Joslyn, Charli did something she never ordinarily did—she put her hand up to contribute to the conversation.

"I have a suggestion."

Charli expected censure and braced herself for a negative response. She had often been deemed "too opinionated" by her teachers at school and "too idealistic" by her peers. Charli had always had a strong sense of right and wrong, and the importance to her of doing the right action far outweighed any material benefit a person might receive, in Charli's opinion. She had come to realize that not everybody shared her views, though, so she often kept her feelings to herself.

But here in this place, she felt safer than usual, and from everything she had learned about Q'ehazi so far, she had the impression that to these people, values were more important than power or money or fame for its own sake (which were the things her culture and friends in her own world espoused).

Sovereign Aurora turned and seemed to see Charli for the first time: "Ah, young Charli, I remember you. You are Abbe's friend, are you not?"

"Yes."

"Tell us your suggestion, please."

Charli's nervousness disappeared as she spoke aloud with a clarity and conviction that surprised even her. "I can see both people's points of view and that they both wish to contribute something. What if you divide the class time in two, and Barylos teaches half and Metlin teaches half? That way, the kids get to learn even more because they get both sets of information, and everybody wins."

Although nobody spoke in response to Charli's suggestion, there was a general aura of receptivity from the crowd. Abbe smiled at her friend and spoke without words: "Good job. I think my mother likes your idea."

"We are glad to hear your suggestion, Charli. I believe that would provide a fair allocation of labor for our two people. What do you think of this, Barylos and Metlin? Can I get your impression? Is that something you would be prepared to try, at least?"

There were nods from the two individuals in question. However, when Charli happened to glance in Barylos's direction, she noticed the young girl glaring back at her and realized that not everybody had been entirely happy with her intervention. Abbe pulled at Charli's sleeve, having noticed this small interaction, and used silent words to speak to her privately: "Barylos is my sister."

"But she's White," Charli was going to respond, then held her tongue, recognizing that things were different in this place, and much was possible that was highly unusual in her own world. "She seems angry," Charli observed.

"Don't worry. She's always angry about something."

"But why should she be angry with me? I just made a suggestion."

"Perhaps she is jealous that our mother is paying you so much attention. She's been trying to attain a state of grace for a while now, and Sovereign Aurora always says she's not ready yet."

"Oh, I see." Charli recognized that look of resentment on Barylos's face. She'd seen it before, in class, from other students when she'd gotten an answer right and a teacher had praised her.

Charli didn't understand why; she never courted extra praise or attention, but she often had these reactions from her peers.

Sovereign Aurora continued speaking aloud to the crowd: "Very well, then. That is what we shall do. For the time being, we will divide the lessons up among these two individuals. We will then get feedback from the children as to how much they are learning from both, and we will also take that into consideration before we decide to take this matter further. Thank you all so much for participating. You are free to leave."

The crowd began to disperse, and Abbe and Charli rose from the ground and mingled among the others. Charli secretly hoped that she would be able to spend some time with Joslyn, but he departed quite quickly from the group once the meeting was over, although not before giving a friendly goodbye wave to her and Abbe. It was apparent that most people had some other activity to occupy themselves with, and Charli wondered how she should spend her time.

This wasn't something she had considered before deciding to come back to this world, and with no way of contributing or being useful, she suddenly felt like an outsider. Abbe explained that she had music practice after the midday meal and that Charli was welcome to join them if she wished. Suddenly, Sovereign Aurora was by Charli's side and had taken both of her hands in hers.

"Thank you so much for your comment, young Charli" were her unspoken words. "Although you are only sixteen, it seems you have an old head on your shoulders."

"Yes, people are always saying that sort of thing," Charli acknowledged.

"Here in Q'ehazi, we value wisdom very much, no matter where it originates. The attainment of a state of grace is our greatest prize."

"What's a state of grace?" Charli knew the literal meaning of the words but not what they represented to the Q'ehazi people, or why this was so important.

"I believe it is something you will discover for yourself, in its fullest capacity. But quite simply, it is the ability to feel empathy for all human beings—"

"And animals," Abbe chimed in.

"Absolutely, and all of God's creatures on this earth; an ability to spread harmony, joy and positivity; to make a contribution; to be of service; and to overcome the pleasures and needs of the ego."

"Wow, that's interesting. I was just feeling bad that I'm not very useful here."

"Even the fact that you care to be useful and to make a contribution demonstrates that in your soul, you are headed on the right path. I am so glad Abbe found you—or you found her; I'm not sure which way it was. In any case, you are very welcome here in our world."

"Thank you," Charli said without words and with sincere gratitude. These people were amazingly accommodating. She wondered with a sudden chill what would happen if someone with evil intent tried to infiltrate their world—would they be so friendly and welcoming then?

Abbe picked up on her thought question and responded: "We do not welcome everybody here. A person who wishes to join us permanently has to be invited by one of our members, and they must demonstrate that they are able to achieve a state of grace in order to be accepted fully into the Q'ehazi world."

"I see."

"But, Charli, I see that the sun is high in the sky. It is time for us to take our midday meal. Are you hungry? Will you join us?"

Charli was in fact starving and very grateful for the offer. The girls walked away from the road, into an area of dense trees where a few tables had been set with plates and silverware. Charli was amazed at the delicious and wholesome nature of the food served to them. She was especially surprised to learn that everything was grown and produced locally. Charli also learned that the Q'ehazi people ate no red meat, but they did eat chicken and fish harvested from their farms. The people who served them did so willingly and with smiling faces. Apparently, they were the servers, and that was their chosen occupation. Some of them were also farmers and cooks.

When Charli asked how much people were paid for their various jobs, she was astounded to discover that there was no such thing as money in the Q'ehazi society. Everything was handled by bartering and mutual exchange. Once a week, all the members of each village would get together for a so-called trading day, in which they offered and accepted goods and services for exchange and barter. Once she got over the initial shock, Charli realized how this could make life a lot simpler. Without money being hoarded in vast quantities by a few rich people and desperately needed for survival by the majority of individuals, life could be a lot fairer for everybody. This world's customs made sense to her in a way that her world never had.

After lunch, Sovereign Aurora asked Charli if there was anything she particularly wished to see or experience during her visit. Charli's main passions in life, as far as she was concerned, were medicine and research and becoming an epidemiologist, and she shared this information with Aurora. When the sovereign told Charli that her son, Joslyn, was training to become a healer and that he lived in the Village of the Healers, Charli had difficulty getting Joslyn's face out of her mind and thought it would be great serendipity if she could bump into the young man again. However, having been a spontaneous part of the fairness test earlier that day, she was also fascinated at the idea of seeing how the schools worked and how the history of the Q'ehazi was taught to the children. There were so many things she wished to see and discover, yet she only had a week for all of this exploration.

Charli's experience was made easier by the people she met because they accepted her so readily. Their generosity overwhelmed her and made her feel a little guilty. She hoped she could repay them somehow, but their lives seemed so perfect already that she doubted she could contribute in any meaningful way. It didn't occur to her at first that she would, or could, stay in this new world forever.

While Charli was talking to Sovereign Aurora, another woman came up to her and introduced herself as Maudina. This woman spoke aloud in the first instance and gave Charli the customary hug given to all strangers. Her hug was as warm and affectionate as Abbe's had been, and the woman's smile made her seem instantly approachable, like the sort of person to whom she could tell all of her troubles without fear of judgment or censure. Charli was surprised to learn that this lady was the sovereign's older sister.

The woman was White and in her late fifties, and had a face that had once been beautiful, large green eyes, and a mass of curly white hair that stuck out from her head in all directions. Her clothes were ample and colorful, and her smile was broad.

"It is true we look nothing alike," explained Maudina, "and that is because we have the same mother yet different fathers."

"Oh, you mean like cats," Charli blurted out before she could stop herself. She hid her mouth behind her hand in awkward embarrassment at a comment that could be construed as rude.

Fortunately, Maudina reacted with a peal of girlish laughter. "Yes, you are right. Except we are not from the same litter but born a few years apart."

"I see. And you are also a sovereign, or a . . . princess?" asked Charli, hoping to redeem herself by appearing respectful.

"Oh, no, I'm not royalty at all," responded Maudina with a gleeful expression. "I have far more fun than Aurora."

Charli was beginning to like this woman. Here was an individual who seemed to genuinely like being who she was, without any need for external validation or power. She wasn't a weak person, like Charli's mother, and her strength didn't come from feeling superior to others. "What do you do, then?"

"I'm lucky. I get to play all day," Maudina replied with a twinkle in her eye. "You see, I've always loved the arts, and so I run the Arts Academy, where we do things like acting, singing, dancing, writing and painting."

"You work with children, then?"

"No, all ages. Adults need to play too, sometimes. Actually, a lot of the time."

Now Charli realized what it was she liked most about Maudina: her playful spirit.

"That sounds nice," Charli said, somewhat enviously.

"I suppose the most serious thing I do is to run the Dreams Academy."

"You mean, where you decide what your dreams are and how to pursue them?"

"No, I'm not talking about dreams of the future, but dreams you've had while asleep."

"That's serious?" Charli was mystified. She'd always thought dreams were an aberration that served no purpose whatsoever. Most of the time she either didn't remember her dreams or was trying to forget them—the unpleasant ones, at least.

"Yes. We believe that dreams are important messages from the subconscious, and that we need to listen to the messages they contain."

Charli couldn't keep the skeptical expression from her face, although she was trying to remain open to everything she learned in this world, especially the customs and characteristics that were the most odd or unfamiliar to her.

"It is an ancient custom inherited from the Greeks who lived thousands of years ago," Maudina continued. "We practice dream incubation and train people how to analyze their dreams."

"Wow! Well, I'd like to learn more, for sure."

"You are welcome to visit us anytime." Maudina gave Charli a farewell hug and a kiss on the cheek as she departed, her long, brightly colored dress flowing behind her.

Later that afternoon, Charli was invited to join a class of schoolchildren. The class was very similar to one in her world; the children had not yet learned the art of thought connection and were all speaking aloud and listening to the teacher, who was doing the same. The only difference was that the classes were held outside in the open air, yet with quite sophisticated desks and computers, which indicated that their technology was every bit as advanced as in Charli's world—maybe even more so.

To Charli's great surprise, a little before three, the teacher rang a bell, and class was dismissed for ten minutes. But the children didn't go home, or to recess. They gathered up their computers and papers, put plastic sheets over their desks, and retired with the teacher and Charli herself to a long, narrow building that Charli later discovered was called a longhouse. Once inside the building, and after a brief break, they got out their computers again and started to work. At three o'clock precisely, Charli realized why they had done this when the heavens opened and it rained heavily for about thirty minutes. She remembered being caught in a heavy rainstorm like this on her way back to her world a couple of weeks earlier. When she remarked to one of the children how strange it was that the rainstorm occurred at the exact same time, the child seemed surprised.

"Well, of course. It's the daily rainstorm."

"But doesn't it happen at different times, or sometimes rain for longer?"

"No. Why would we do it that way?"

The teacher explained that the Q'ehazi scientists had long ago learned how to control the weather, and that they had concluded it would be beneficial to have a small amount of rain every day and always at the same time so that people could take the proper precautions. Charli remembered Abbe briefly mentioning their technology and was amazed again at this very sensible idea. *That must be why the Q'ehazi people don't bother living in buildings,* she thought. They could manage with just treehouses and longhouses if the temperature was always the same and the rain was completely predictable.

"That's correct," said the teacher. "We only have a few brick houses on the ground, and they are historical artifacts from before we controlled the weather, when we felt it was necessary. There are some lovely old buildings from the time of the first settlers hundreds of years ago, and we keep them for posterity."

"So you sleep in the treehouses at night?" Charli queried.

One of the children laughed at this question. "No, we sleep in our beds, of course."

"He means in our hammock. We each get a hammock to sleep in—"

"Or sometimes several people in one big hammock," added one of the children with a grin.

Charli wondered where she would sleep that night, and if there were any spare hammocks for visitors such as she. But she determined that everything would work out, as it invariably did in this place, so she didn't feel the need to worry.

Charli was a little surprised at her own equanimity about this unfamiliar situation. Perhaps it was because she was in a new world where everything was strange anyway, so she couldn't predict anything and therefore there was no point worrying about it. Usually, in her world, Charli was the sort of person who didn't do things spontaneously, who liked to plan and plot out her future in predictable ways. Her mother often castigated her for this because Angela was a far more spontaneous person than her daughter.

In fact, Charli often judged her mother for this character trait, feeling that Angela was far too passive about life and apt to just let herself land wherever the wind blew her. And yet, that was what Charli was doing now. Perhaps because nobody knew her here, and so she could be anybody she chose and didn't have to live up to anybody's expectations—even her own.

Charli stayed in the Village of the Teachers for dinner, and then she traveled to Abbe's village, as she had arranged to meet her that evening. There was another concert of the musicians, as there seemed to be on most days, and to Charli's great delight, Joslyn was also in attendance. She was even able to sit next to him. Blankets had been spread out on the grass for the onlookers, and Charli and Joslyn sat on a blanket close to the front of the audience. Charli had the same feeling she'd had before, of excitement and anxiety bubbling up inside her chest. The feeling intensified when she realized that she and Joslyn were both sitting cross-legged, and every now and then their knees would gently brush against each other as they swayed in rhythm with the music. Charli tried not to think too hard about how she felt, though, because she didn't want her thoughts to be read too clearly. That was one aspect of regular mind-reading that Charli found a little difficult to accept.

Later that evening, when it came time to retire to bed, Abbe and Charli made their way to Abbe's family longhouse, which was in a densely wooded area behind where the concert had taken place. In front of the longhouse, Charli found many hammocks strung up among the trees. Some were already occupied. The place was silent apart from a few snores and the hum of night creatures like cicadas, crickets, and frogs. Every hammock had a piece of netting over it for the insects, and each was a different color and design. Abbe took up residence in a hammock that she said was her own, and she gestured towards a spare hammock Charli could sleep in, beside Abbe's.

As Charli lay next to Abbe, enjoying the gentle motion of the hammock swaying in the wind, the two girls had a long, silent thought conversation where they each learned more about the different worlds they inhabited. Charli told Abbe of everything she had learned about the history behind the shawl, and Abbe was as amazed as Charli had been but also not disbelieving of the idea that the two worlds existed in parallel dimensions. They both felt lucky and grateful to have the opportunity to have a "foot in both worlds," as Charli described it.

The more Charli discovered about Q'ehazi, the more she loved it and longed to stay forever and make this her home. Abbe explained that people lived not in nuclear families but in large, extended families of many aunts, uncles, cousins, and grandparents who all congregated together in one longhouse for things such as meals and social events. Charli was also delighted to learn that when children were born, they were given songs written by their mothers and/or fathers, which were taught to the children as soon as they were old enough to sing. Children chose their names themselves, at an age when they were considered old enough to be able to make a decision about such things, usually around fifteen years old. Charli couldn't imagine being nameless for most of her life up to this point.

The Q'ehazi people were very connected to nature, in ways Charli had never dreamed possible. For example, they were able to communicate with trees and plants and retrieve messages from them, since they understood that trees and plants had their own unique methods of talking to one another and had learned how to tap into this. This was the reason for their highly evolved medicinal expertise based upon plant and herb extractions Trees were regarded with the same affection as pets and sometimes given names, such as "Evergreen, the standing tall tree" or "Hunchback, the bent tree" or "Docile, the slender pine tree." Trees and plants were thus regarded as living beings, as worthy of respect and value as animals or human beings.

Each creature possessed value in nature that contributed to the harmony of the whole. For this reason, perhaps, the Q'ehazi people of this particular district had constructed a library for birds where many different species congregated and lived among the books so that the humans could communicate with them as they read.

All the new knowledge, along with the gentle rocking of her hammock, made Charli sleepy. It was perhaps midnight or later, and Charli felt tired and worn out from all of the excitement and wonderment of the day. The blanket of stars above her and the chorus of night animals provided a gentle lullaby, and she drifted off to sleep.

hen Martin first saw the huge red stone his eyes grew wider than Sean had ever seen them before. "Man, where did you get that?" he gasped.

"That's for me to know and you to wonder." Sean guffawed, both at his own joke and at his friend's astonishment. When Martin said, "Asshole" under his breath, Sean pretended not to hear. Right now, he needed his friend's help more than he needed to have his ego massaged.

"Whatever. It weighs a ton, and I've got to get it back to the house before Angie gets home."

Martin was used to Sean keeping things from the girlfriend he lived with, and he never expressed an opinion about his friend's actions, anyway. If he was compliant with Sean's requests, he might benefit in some way. The stone was much bigger than the blue diamond in the movie *Titanic* and could be worth millions of dollars.

Martin's lifetime of living paycheck to paycheck had given him a craving for money that was never quite satisfied. He often imagined a different sort of life for himself, where he was admired rather than despised by the people around him. What drew him wasn't so much the things money could buy for him as the status of being one of "those people" with their aura of confidence and power that only money could generate.

So, Martin helped Sean lift the stone and put it in the wheelbarrow. Even using this to carry the rock, it took a great deal of effort to get it back to the house, and both men were sweating by the time they arrived on the back porch. It was now time to unload the rock somewhere, and Sean decided on the shed in the backyard, which was windowless and currently full of garden equipment. Sean moved aside a tiller, weed eater, garden rake, hose, and shears and stacked them in one corner of the room while complaining about what a messy woman Angela was. Then he cleared off the top of a large wooden work bench in the middle of the room. When the two men hauled the rock onto the table from the wheelbarrow, neither of them noticed that the rock was a little smaller, possibly because they were so tired that they simply wanted to get the job over and done with.

They went back to the house, and Martin joined Sean in the sunroom for a beer or two (which turned into six by the time Angela arrived home from work at around 5 p.m.). Sean was already feeling the warm glow of alcohol in his bloodstream, and he greeted Angela with a hearty slap on the backside. "Hey, babe, what's for dinner?"

As usual, Angela bit back her first reaction to both this comment and the sight of Sean's friend, who she disliked and hoped wasn't intending to join them. "I don't know. What do you want?"

"Whatever you want, kid. You know me, easily pleased." Sean flung open his arms in a gesture of tolerance.

Angela was about to leave the room, planning to ignore the fact that Sean's friend didn't look in a mood to leave before dinner and hoping that this passive-aggressive action might get her the result she wanted.

"Oh yeah, and make enough for three," Sean called out after her as she exited to the kitchen.

"You know Charli's away for the week, right?" was Angela's deliberately clueless response.

"Sorry, she can be thick sometimes," Sean explained to Martin. "She makes up for it by being a great cook."

"It's okay. I'll go home." Martin was not one to court

confrontation, and he recognized Angela's feelings about him as less than welcoming.

"Oh no you won't. After what you did for me?"

Martin was secretly pleased. It wasn't often that he got a good home-cooked meal; plus, he was happy that Sean appreciated his efforts to help carry the stone.

Sean followed Angela into the kitchen. "You're going to be pleased when I show you what Martin and I brought back today," he boasted as she busied herself collecting ingredients for dinner. "You'll see how we both deserve the best meal ever. How about a steak?"

"We've got steaks in the freezer, but they'll take a while to thaw," Angela said in a tired tone.

"Okay, whatever you like, babe, as I said, but just cook three. You've got hungry guys to feed."

"Sure." Angela pursed her lips in a habitual gesture and took some pork belly out of the refrigerator. "I've got these. Will that do?"

"Fine."

Once Sean had left the room, Angela's breathing became more regular, and she put on music from her iPad while she busied herself in the kitchen. Sean never spent much time in here, so it was her safe space at home and a haven of tranquility, no matter how tired or stressed she was feeling. It had been a long day at work, and she'd had to confront a shopper about not wearing a mask. Nevertheless, Angela usually felt more comfortable outside the house, although she missed Charli considerably and was looking forward to her daughter's return.

Angela's sense of discomfort around Sean was always heightened when he had one of his friends with him because she had an odd sense that they were ganging up against her, even though Martin never said anything overtly hostile or negative and in fact hardly said anything to her at all. For all Angela enjoyed the feeling of coming home to a man, as soon as she stepped inside that house where Sean resided, it was as if a spell had been cast over her. She felt powerless to overcome the spell, and so she just carried on with her life, making herself as small and unthreatening as possible so that she wouldn't incite any reprisals.

She couldn't control Charli's behavior, though, and Charli wasn't at all afraid of Sean and even seemed to deliberately confront him and push back, which often sent Angela into a panic. She wished her daughter could be more passive, and yet she knew that wasn't Charli's nature, as the girl was much more like her stepfather, with his assertive and dominant nature. Angela was sometimes as intimidated by Charli as she had been by Chuck Speranza when he was alive—which was supremely ironic, given that the girl was hers and not his—and she often wondered if Charli had inherited anything from her at all.

Angela acceded to Sean's demands regarding dinner and dutifully laid the table for three people. As usual, she did her best to cook as delicious and substantial a meal as she could, and the men were both pleased with the results. After the meal, Martin surprised her by offering to wash the dishes, and she was going to accept his help, but Sean wanted her to see the object in the shed that he'd been crowing about for the past two hours. Angela had no real expectations, but she followed the two men over to the shed and waited while Sean opened the door and shined a flashlight onto the workbench in the center of the room.

"There you go," he stated proudly. "What do you think of that?"

In the weak light of the shed, all Angela could see in the center of the table was what looked like a rock about the size of a football and a dull shade of maroon. She tried to act as pleased and surprised as Sean was expecting, but she couldn't tell what was so special about this rock.

"I'm sure it was bigger than that when we brought it in," Martin couldn't help saying.

But Sean was in denial about any change to the rock.

"It's a fucking ruby, or something like that. I don't know, but worth a ton of money. And me and Martin busted a gut to get it over here."

He seemed displeased that Angela's reaction to the rock was so lukewarm.

"Yes, I'm sure," she reassured him. "It's hard to see it here in this dim light."

"Yeah, you're right. We'll take it out in the morning, and you'll see. This thing shines like the North Star." Sean was happy with this explanation, and his mood brightened again, but he was moving from jovial to hostile drunkenness, and Angela knew what would happen next.

To her relief, Sean and Martin decided to go out to the local bar, so Angela was free to clean up and get an early night. She'd be asleep by the time Sean got back, and in the morning, he'd probably have forgotten most of what transpired anyway.

To her surprise, though, despite his hangover the next morning (which was instantly cured by a "hair of the dog" beer first thing), Sean was still enthusiastic about taking out the stone in the daylight, where he could finally demonstrate its inherent value.

Angela and Sean went down to the shed at around nine, and Sean flung open the door to the shed with a grand gesture, as if he were Svengali revealing a great trick. However, by this time, even Sean had to recognize that the stone had shrunk considerably in size overnight and was now about the size of a grapefruit.

"Shit!" Sean picked up the rock and brought it outside into the light. There, Angela could see that it was the same dull, dark maroon as the night before but a lot smaller.

"I don't get it. I just don't get it." Sean was so genuinely amazed by the changes in the stone that Angela felt a little sorry for him.

"Why is it smaller?"

"I don't know. It wasn't like this at all when I picked it up. It was huge, and bright red, like the biggest ruby you ever saw." Sean saw the pity on Angela's face and was infuriated by it. He wished fervently that Martin were there to back up his story. "Martin saw it, too. I'm not crazy, babe."

"No, I know. Perhaps it just seemed bigger—"

"No, no, no! It *was* bigger. It weighed a ton. Jesus! Piece of shit! I can't believe I wasted my time on this!" Sean flung the stone on the ground in his anger and frustration, and some of the rock broke off, leaving a huge crack in the side.

"Oh, Sean," Angela began, stooping to pick up the partially shattered rock.

"Don't you 'Oh, Sean' me!" he warned in an aggressive tone while wrenching Angela's arm away from the pieces of broken rock.

"Ow!" Despite his roughness, Angela continued trying to clean up the mess Sean had just created.

"I said leave it alone, woman!" Sean bellowed.

"I'm just trying to help," whimpered Angela.

"I don't need your help, you stupid bitch!" This time, Sean grabbed her arm and used it to fling her across the room, where she banged her shoulder against the hard walls of the shed. Now Angela started to cry, with soft tears falling down her cheeks.

Fortunately, Sean was in no mood to continue the argument. He stormed out of the shed, cursing under his breath and not bothering to give a backwards look at Angela, who was now cowering against the wall, having dropped to her knees.

CHAPTER TEN

A wave of peace and tranquility washed over Charli, which was unlike anything she'd ever experienced. She'd felt happiness before, of course, in response to something going right or some unexpected joy, such as receiving a wonderful birthday present or a visit from a dear friend or passing a difficult exam. She had felt the excitement of anticipation, such as for the taste of chocolate ice cream after the main course, or hankering after a long-awaited vacation in a beloved place. She had also felt the pangs of disappointment, the pain of rejection, the sting of anger when plans were thwarted, and the frustration of an unfair accusation or a wrong decision. But she had never felt this kind of inner stillness and contentment that she could only describe to herself as peace.

Charli wasn't sure if these feelings were due to the unusual-tasting mixture Abbe had given to her that morning. Charli had tried a few drugs in her world with negative consequences, and so was a bit nervous about taking a substance she knew nothing about, but Abbe told her that this mixture was from an herb used by all the Q'ehazi people—a wonderful herb that was responsible not only for curing ailments but also for enhancing mental clarity and inducing a calm state of mind akin to the meditative state. Abbe had this drink every morning, rather than coffee or tea, as a way of both energizing and relaxing her to have the best day possible. Since Charli admired just about everything she had seen of Abbe and her family so far, she was persuaded to follow her friend's example. Even though the drink tasted a little strange and left a bitter aftertaste, the effects of it were immediate and quite pleasant.

Charli had read about people experiencing inner peace, usually when they engaged in regular meditation or were much more spiritually enlightened than her, a teenage girl on the cusp of adulthood. But if she hadn't experienced it now, she wouldn't have believed it was possible for somebody like her, whose brain never seemed to turn off and was constantly active and alert. Yet here she was, among this group of people who all seemed to be experiencing it too. It was as if all the cells of her body—which ordinarily were vibrating and rushing around, bumping into each other—had decided to calm down and remain still, breathing and oxygenating at the same steady pace as she was. Perhaps this was the higher plane of existence she had read about online, or perhaps she was in a hypnotic trance or some other altered state. All she knew was that it was pleasant and supremely relaxing.

A mellow chorus of animal and insect hums surrounded her: the chattering of tree frogs; the chirping of cicadas; the tinkling of water from the nearby waterfall into the pond; a slight rustle of wind through the trees; a distant, lone bird calling to its mate. And then the inner voice, which was more like an attunement, yet the words and thoughts were clear in her head. As she looked up at the minister—a White man in his thirties dressed in a pale-golden robe, whose curly hair hung to his shoulders—Charli was aware that the words were coming from him, even though his lips were not moving, because his gaze was fixed on the congregation before him, and the others were gazing back at him.

The thoughts were conveyed not in a didactic or autocratic way but gently, as a passing stream. It was possible to either hold on to them and process them each individually or to argue them in your mind, or even to let them go with no further ado. Charli was in the process of letting the thoughts wash over her and taking them in to digest later, when she had more time to think about it. She enjoyed the opportunity to let go of everything else and just be, for a few moments.

Sometimes she held her eyes closed because then there were fewer distractions. And sometimes she opened her eyes because everything was still so new to her in the Q'ehazi world that she didn't want to miss anything. With her eyes open, she saw that she was seated on the ground in a large circle of about fifty people quietly gathered around the minister, who stood with his arms outstretched and his head lifted towards the sky.

They were outdoors, yet there were several manmade structures obviously used to celebrate some form of religious ritual. The pond to the right of Charli was about fifteen feet across and had a beautiful waterfall constructed of stones, many of which glowed in various colors as if they were precious or semiprecious gems. The water in the pond was clear as glass, and lilies and cattails floated on its surface while koi fish swam beneath. Around the pond, colorful flowers and plants gave a beautiful, rainbow-like aspect of reds, blues, and yellows.

Around the circle in which the onlookers sat was a larger circle of huge, blue stones topped by intricate carvings. And in the center of the circle with the minister was a marble plinth, also elaborately carved and covered in hieroglyphs. The sky above them was blue as a baby's eyes, and the mosaic of trees held many different shades of green, from dark, forest green to almost yellow. Charli wondered if, in addition to the herbal drink, this lovely and peaceful place was why the sermon had such a calming effect on her. She had always hated church services when her parents had taken her, but this was entirely different.

"We are all one," came the unspoken words from the minister, "and we are put here on this earth to love one another as equals, and to respect and value all life, whether human, plant, or animal."

Some of the attendees began to sway slightly from side to side. Most of them wore smiles or serene expressions.

"We know that God is our father, in the truest sense of the word. That is, not like a human father. But he is the father of the universe, the creator of everything. His seed impregnates and conceives and creates life, in all its many forms. And our mother is the earth, this beautiful planet that we are charged with honoring and caretaking."

Charli realized that Abbe was holding her right hand, and every now and again her friend would give her hand a slight squeeze, as if to say, "I'm still here; you're still okay." Then she felt Abbe's body shifting from right to left with the others. Charli followed along, and she soon sensed the person on her left doing the same thing, until the whole crowd was swaying, as if they were one person with fifty souls, all feeling the same thing at the same time.

Which was when Charli realized that everybody had started singing. She heard the tune and the words aloud and gradually began to hum along, even though the words were unfamiliar. It seemed that everybody else knew the song and had probably sung it many times before—apart from Charli and a few young children who sat in the front of the circle and who had picked up the swaying and the tune to join in with a hum as Charli had. Charli felt bonded to the people in this group through her participation in this ceremony.

Charli's tranquility persisted even when the service was over. People rose and congregated in small groups prior to leaving. Abbe gave Charli a long hug, and this close bodily contact comforted Charli, who had been feeling a little overwhelmed by everything she had recently experienced.

Although Abbe now had personal business to attend to, she introduced Charli to friends of hers, who were shortly going to be playing the Q'ehazi game, which was a regular Tuesday-afternoon activity, usually carried out in the open air before the daily rainstorm at 3 p.m. Charli liked the sound of a game and relished the opportunity to play along. She was quite competitive and often won at games such as Monopoly and Scrabble, being, as she believed, of a high intelligence and a good strategic thinker. She wondered if this might be her opportunity to demonstrate that she knew a thing or two. She had been feeling a little intimidated by how happy and confident most of the Q'ehazi people were, seemingly all of the time.

Abbe's friends guided Charli to a location where the game was about to be played. This time, people were seated in chairs rather than on the ground, and around a large circular table. It was evidently some kind of board game, as there was a large wooden board in the center and several wooden and metal "pieces" that would be used by the players. Charli sat next to an older gentleman who agreed to act as her mentor and coach.

As it turned out, he was the perfect instructor for her, as he was a history professor and could explain the history behind the game, and indeed the aspects of Q'ehazi culture that led to its creation. The professor's name was Avendo. He was a small, wizened man with fine gray hair that seemed to float around his head and a kindly face. His manner was mild, and yet a fierce intelligence shone out from his dark-blue eyes. Charli had an immediate respect for him.

The game was called "the game where everybody wins." Charli learned many things about it by watching and talking with Avendo. Charli was amazed by the existence of a game that had no winners and losers and was played with a sense of collaboration instead of competition. Avendo could tell how impressed she was with these concepts, and he pressed a book into her hand, saying, "This is a gift for you."

"Wow, for me? Thank you very much." Charli turned the book over in her hands. It was small with just a few parchment pages and a cover that was quite ornate, like one of those books in fantasy films set in the Middle Ages.

"It's so beautiful," Charli couldn't help noticing.

"Not only that," replied Avendo, "but it is very precious because it will tell you all about the Q'ehazi history and culture, much more than I can reveal to you now. There are only a very few books like this in existence, since we are mostly an oral culture and tell our history through storytelling. But I happened to have a copy of the book, and I want you to have it, since you seem so interested."

Charli was honored to have such a valuable book bestowed on her without her even asking. She didn't know how to thank the professor, but Avendo seemed to understand, and he smiled and wished her happy reading. Charli put the little book inside her jacket pocket, where it would be safe until she could read and digest the contents.

After about an hour, Charli noticed the girl sitting across from her was clutching her stomach in an alarming way. The concerned people on either side of the girl asked her what the matter was. Charli gathered that the girl had some stomach pains, possibly from eating something that disagreed with her. The other players called for a healer to come and administer some herbs.

Although Charli was well aware that Joslyn was training to become a healer, she was surprised and secretly overjoyed when the healer who came to call on the girl was Joslyn himself. When he spotted Charli among the game players, he smiled in recognition, although he didn't have much time to be friendly. Joslyn led the sick girl off to the side and guided her to a secluded spot where he could help her further. Charli asked her companion if she could follow them and find out more about how people in the Q'ehazi world were healed, and Avendo agreed to accompany her. She was genuinely interested to find out about the Q'ehazi's medical practices but of course also intent on seeing Joslyn as much as she could.

So, together, she and Avendo went to one of the few enclosed areas in Q'ehazi, where they found Joslyn administering herbal medicines to the girl. Charli's companion asked Joslyn if it would be acceptable for them to visit, and Joslyn asked the girl if she minded having another person observe. The girl said she didn't mind at all. She didn't seem capable of minding anything other than feeling better. Charli felt like a first-year medical student observing a resident doctor. The idea brought a smile to her face, and she sat on a chair and watched how Joslyn handled the situation. Avendo, meanwhile, bid farewell to Charli, reminded her to read the book he had given her, as it contained much interesting information about Q'ehazi, and returned to his daily work activities.

The setup was a little how she imagined a medic's tent would be in the field. The enclosure was made of some clear, heavy, plastic material, and inside, all the equipment and instruments were clean, white, and very sterile. While there was certainly high-tech machinery inside the tent, there were also shelves and shelves of bottles likely containing herbal potions and elixirs, so the tent looked like something between an old apothecary shop and a modern hospital unit. Joslyn was in his element here, and he deftly gathered ingredients, made them into a potion for her to drink, and also gave her a small bag of dried leaves and herbs, instructing her to make it into a tea when she got home.

The girl looked so pale and wan that Joslyn asked her if anything else was wrong. In Charli's experience, doctors were rarely interested in a patient's feelings or in talking to them beyond getting a brief description of their symptoms and giving them a diagnosis before administering medications. His manner resembled a therapist more than a medical doctor.

The girl proceeded to spend a good fifteen minutes talking about her current emotional situation, which was quite complicated. She had been under a lot of pressure, she said, because she was preparing to move to another village, away from all of her friends and family and people she knew. While she had herself made the decision to leave because she wanted to follow a certain profession and that was the best way of doing it, she was also conflicted about having to adjust to new people and a new location.

Joslyn explained to the girl that her stomach problems were probably partly a result of the stress she was under and her attempts to navigate these underlying feelings of anxiety and adjust to the unfamiliar environment she was about to experience. The girl was reassured by Joslyn's words, and when she thanked him and prepared to leave, Charli noticed that her step was much lighter, and her skin had regained its normal color.

Joslyn had clearly been trained in both the physical body and the brain's complicated psychology. She had never witnessed anything like that before, and she wished others in her world could see the benefits of this kind of treatment. Since she herself wanted to join the medical profession, Charli was excited to learn that there were ways of approaching physical maladies other than just prescribing drugs.

Charli was also delighted that Joslyn had time to sit and chat with her for a time after his appointment had ended. She had no desire to leave and go back to Abbe's family longhouse, even though it was getting rather late and the chorus of frogs signaled the approach of nightfall.

Joslyn was happy to show Charli his arsenal of potions to help with various ailments and "predicaments," as he called them. All of his diagnoses linked the mind and the body. "This can help with anxiety and stomach indigestion," he would say, or "This ointment will ease shoulder pain and stress from being overburdened by responsibilities," or "These herbs are good for headaches and irritability."

One herb seemed to occupy a special place in the room, as it was kept in a very large bottle, much larger than all the others, and was labeled with both its name and the note FOR GENERAL CONCERNS. Joslyn was glad to tell Charli about the history and importance of the herb.

She discovered that this was the pukatl herb renowned among the Q'ehazi people for generations, and the same herb in the concoction Abbe had given her before that morning's sermon; and now she recalled that Dr. Brian Hopewell had mentioned it in his book. Joslyn told her that the Q'ehazi people might never have become what they were if they hadn't discovered this wonderful medicinal herb and started using it many generations ago, when they were still living in tribes. It was partly due to this herb that the people remained gentle and nonaggressive; it had qualities that "soothed the nerves" and helped dissipate strong emotions of fear and anger, thereby allowing them to better access the inherent sense of harmony and spirituality that connected them to nature and every living being around them. It was also useful in many of the more common maladies that affected humans and could be used as a general panacea to help people feel better, both physically and emotionally.

The original Q'ehazi native tribe had been using the herb for centuries when they introduced it to the European settlers of the Roanoke Colony. (Charli was reminded of Dr. Hopewell's hypothesis. In this world, rather than killing most of the native "Indians" and regarding them with hostility and suspicion, the settlers had joined with them to form a new world where the best parts of both cultures were combined.)

The herb was grown from the seeds of the pukatl tree, which was indigenous to this region and to no other. The seedling took at least ten years to grow into a mature tree of about five feet tall, at which point it would start producing the flowers where the seeds could be found. Even though it would continue to grow, eventually reaching a height of twenty feet or even higher, the tree bloomed and blossomed just once a year to produce the flowers and seeds which could be used for medicinal purposes. And many pukatl trees lasted longer than humans, some even reaching hundreds of years old. The oldest pukatl tree in existence was no more than a mile from where they were, and it was revered for its longevity and its beauty. The huge tree with spreading branches was believed to be almost 500 years old.

Joslyn handed Charli a small cloth bag that housed a few of the pukatl seeds and suggested that she plant them in her own world to see if they could grow there. Charli thrilled at the thought. She placed the pouch next to the book Avendo had given her, in her inside jacket pocket.

While Charli chatted with her newfound friend, an older man entered, limping on his left leg, which had a large bandage around the thigh. He greeted Joslyn warmly, and Joslyn asked him how he'd been since the injury. Joslyn gently removed the bandage from the wound, which was still gaping and quite bloody so that Charli squirmed internally at the sight (although she tried to maintain her composure, for the sake of not appearing to be a wimp in Joslyn's eyes). Charli was impressed at how well Joslyn kept his cool, simply offering the man a seat so that he could be tended to in relative comfort.

Joslyn tenderly washed and dressed the man's wounds and administered some ointment, as well as giving him a hot tea made partially from pukatl. Joslyn spoke to him in quiet tones. Probably recognizing that Charli was unaware of the story behind his injuries, the man spoke aloud: "I was by the Honor Stone at the Sacred Circle a few days ago, as I had some questions to ask the oracle. You know, I spoke with Sovereign Aurora about the problems I've been having with my wife recently, and she told me to look within my own heart and find my guiding wisdom, which is always best done when I can be in a quiet, peaceful place like that."

Joslyn nodded at this reflection.

"It was a beautiful morning, and I was starting to feel some peace and contentment for the first time in a long while, knowing that things were going to improve so long as I took Sovereign Aurora's advice to keep a loving heart towards my wife and always listen to what she has to say, even if I don't at first understand it. The birds were singing, and I was gazing at the waters of the fountain, and sometimes reading from my book of meditation verses. Then I heard a noise behind me, so I turned around and I saw this man—"

"Who was it?" Charli couldn't resist asking.

"Well, I don't know. I've never seen him before. He did look unusual because he had colored patterns on his arms and his neck."

"What do you mean 'patterns'?" asked Joslyn, intrigued.

"Pictures on his skin, like the ones our ancestors used to wear when they dressed as warriors."

"Oh, you mean a long, long time ago?"

"That's right, before the Q'ehazi people, even—when they were warriors and fighting amongst themselves."

"What were the pictures?" asked Charli, dreading the answer.

"I'm not sure. I think one was a snake—that's right, a snake that was crawling around his neck."

Charli's heart sank further. "Did he have dark hair and a little beard?"

"I think so, maybe, yes," the man replied, looking at Charli now as Joslyn continued to minister to his wounds.

"What happened next?" inquired Joslyn.

"I saw the man walk right up to the Honor Stone and rip it from its perch! I was so shocked and amazed that I just stood there for a few seconds and watched him do it. He was smiling!"

"Oh my God!" exclaimed Charli with horrible prescience, although she didn't at first want to believe it.

"When I realized that he was planning to run off with the stone, I asked him to please put it back. I was sending him thought messages, but he didn't seem to understand me at all. I asked him why he would do such a thing. I put out my hand to try and stop him. I didn't want to fight him. I just wanted to stop him taking the stone."

"Did he yell at you?" asked Charli.

"Well, yes, he was shouting all sorts of words, curse words and insults. I don't even remember what he said now. He wasn't exactly complying with my wishes," the man said with a wry grin.

"That's terrible," exclaimed Joslyn.

"But you haven't heard the worst part. When I put out my hand to try and stop him, he pointed some sort of a weapon at me. I suppose it must have been a weapon because he kept threatening me, and his face was very aggressive."

"What kind of a weapon?" asked Charli. The use of the word *weapon* rather than something more specific made her think of a Star Wars movie.

"I don't know really. It looked like a short, black . . . stick. But it was no stick. It made a very loud bang, and then all of a sudden there was a terrible pain in my leg right here"—he pointed to the wound—"and the force of the blow made me fall down to the ground."

Charli put her hand over her mouth in shock. "You mean he shot you?"

The old man seemed confused by her question. "Shot? I don't know what that means. All I know is when I looked at my leg, there was blood coming from it, and a lot of pain. I had heard stories of devices like this exploding black stick from visitors, but I had not comprehended their meaning; to be in its presence was horrifying."

"Oh my God!" she said again. What was most horrifying to Charli was that Sean had used a gun on this defenseless, harmless man. "Then he ran off with the stone?"

"Yes. I suppose he was angry and wanted to hurt me. I was crying out, asking him for help, but he wouldn't listen. Then he ran away."

"I'm so sorry," Joslyn said as he stroked the man's arm gently. "Your wound has healed well so far. And I'll do my best to help you feel more comfortable."

"Thank you," the man said gratefully.

Joslyn noticed that Charli had gone very pale and silent. "Are you okay?" he asked her, this time with the unspoken words.

"I'm okay," replied Charli, unable to smile in response. "But there is something I have to do right away." She said aloud to the old man, "I'm so sorry this happened to you. I will do my best to put things right."

And with that, she left, and started running towards the place where she had last seen Abbe.

have to go! I have to go right now!"

"But I thought you were going to stay for a week?"

"I know, but that was before Sean—" Charli inhaled a big gulp of air. She was panicking, and the words slithered out of her mouth before she could stop them. She gave up all ideas of speaking with her thoughts now; the situation was too urgent. "You remember I told you about Sean?"

"Your mother's boyfriend?" In order to accommodate her friend's urgency, Abbe spoke aloud now in a soft, melodious voice. "Yes, you told me about him. Not a nice person, you said."

Charli snorted. "I probably said it harsher than that, but yes, a pretty evil guy. And I just learned that he was here!"

"In the Q'ehazi world?" Abbe seemed stunned. Perhaps it had never occurred to her that somebody other than Charli would be able to enter their world.

"Yeah, I know. It's messed up, isn't it?" Charli didn't wait for an answer. "He took something—a big gemstone or something that's valuable—"

"The Honor Stone at the place of the waterfall," Abbe mused.

"I guess so, yes. It was taken from that place where we had the religious ceremony earlier. But not only that, he shot somebody and knocked them down. He hurt them." Charli was so distraught that she failed to notice the confusion in Abbe's eyes at the word *shot*. Charli's eyes welled with tears as she thought of the terrible nature of this crime, which was hers, too: she had brought evil to the Q'ehazi from the violent world she thought and hoped she had left behind. She felt guilty and ashamed.

"Why take it away? Couldn't he just appreciate its beauty by leaving it there?" queried Abbe.

"He probably didn't even think about its beauty. He just wants to sell it, for money."

"Money?" Abbe considered this word—not as if she'd never heard it before but as if it were a laughable concept.

"I know that the Q'ehazi people don't have money. But you don't understand how important it is in our world. Money is . . . literally everything; it's everything!"

Charli didn't want to appear dramatic, but the combination of her shock and horror over what had just happened with Sean and her impatience to get back to her world and address the wrongs that had been done, coupled with her inability to articulate this huge difference in worldview between her culture and that of Q'ehazi, made her words come out more forcefully than she intended.

"Oh no, I'm so sorry." Abbe's sympathy was not what Charli had wanted or anticipated. She expected some kind of hostile reaction, or an expression of outrage, a desire to punish and condemn. But that was not in Abbe's nature. "Is the Honor Stone keeper okay now?"

"Yes, he's okay. I think he'll recover, with Joslyn's help."

"Thank goodness."

Charli was on the point of explaining that the old man had been shot by a gun and that his wound would take some time to heal. But then she realized that the concept of guns was almost as foreign to these people as the concept of money, and she didn't have time to embark on that subject. She made a mental note to come back to it later.

"I have to go and find him—Sean, I mean—and stop him."

"What is he planning to do?"

"I don't know. That's the whole thing. He's capable of anything if he thinks it will get him what he wants."

"How can you stop him?"

"I don't know!" Charli wailed. She was irritated by Abbe's questions, which suggested that she did not grasp the horror of the situation; she seemed focused not on righting the wrong but rather on obstacles and motives Charli hadn't anticipated or wished to consider. "I just know I've got to go back and do something," she exclaimed with conviction. Action was what was called for now, any action, to demonstrate that Sean couldn't get away with his devilish plan, whatever it was.

Abbe put a sympathetic hand on her friend's shoulder. "Let's go, then."

"Are you coming with me?"

"Would you like me to?"

"Absolutely! Yes!" Charli enthused, and the two girls set off across the fields. Charli wasn't sure if the spot by the redbud was the only portal into another world, but it was the one she knew of, and she felt it was familiar and safe as an entry point.

Charli's thoughts raced even faster than her feet, calculating all of the ways in which Sean might have found an entrance to the Q'ehazi world. Perhaps there was another portal she knew nothing about. Perhaps he had followed her. What were his reasons for coming? The unanswered questions crowded her head and forced her onwards. If only she could fold back time and stop it all happening. She felt devastated that this pristine world had been tarnished, and that it was all her fault.

Finally, the girls arrived back at the creek. Charli was in such a hurry that she didn't hesitate but plunged straight ahead, momentarily forgetting about her friend just a short distance behind her.

Although the tear between the worlds was only visible in Charli's world, she had discovered the last time she came through that if she placed one hand on the trunk of the redbud tree and bowed her head to look down at the ground as she passed this particular spot, that action was enough to pass through the portal. She had only discovered this by accident in ducking her head to avoid the heavy raindrops of that scheduled Q'ehazi rainstorm.

When she looked up again, she saw the familiar vista of her own world in front of her. The difference between the two worlds was subtle, and yet very real. Charli was going to point out the differences in the two worlds when the sight of her friend stopped her. Abbe was breathing very shallowly, gasping for breath and hunched over, holding her sides.

"What's the matter?" Charli felt a twinge of fear.

"It must be the air," Abbe gasped. "Oh. I . . . can't . . . breathe."

"Oh my God, oh my God, what can I do to help?" Charli was distraught. She helped her friend straighten up but felt helpless. "I'm sorry. I didn't know—"

"I know. Of course you didn't. But I have to go . . . back now." Abbe's words came in short little sentences. And now she gave up speaking altogether and just telegraphed her distress in the thoughts that Charli knew so well.

Charli realized what she must do. She helped her friend back through the tear, which was still fortunately visible to the two girls. She had a hunch that the tear would not last forever in her world, and all she cared about right now was that Abbe was safe and well.

The last thing Charli saw of Abbe was her friend's face—pale and ashen, yet smiling bravely at her through the tear—before Charli fell back into her own world. Anger and grief welled up in her heart. If it was the last thing she did, she would fight Sean and win. Her determination to defeat him at that moment knew no bounds. Charli quickly reburied the shawl in its glass bottle before speeding home as fast as she could.

When Charli arrived back at her house, she was breathless, and her legs ached from running. It was about nine o'clock at night, so the light had already faded, and Charli had to make her way across the fields using only the moon and starlight to guide her. By the back porch, the motion sensor lights noticed Charli's presence and led her the rest of the way up the back steps to the glass door to the sunroom. Charli saw from outside that her mother was sitting in the sunroom with her feet up, reading one of the novels she enjoyed so much and sipping on a glass of wine.

As soon as she flung open the glass door to the sunroom and saw her mother's shocked face, Charli regretted coming home first, but there was nothing she could do about it now. In her impulsive decision to leave Q'ehazi and rush back to her own world, Charli had forgotten many things for which her mother now demanded an explanation. Why was she on foot and not in her car? (Charli had left the car in Ox Creek and walked to her portal location by the redbud tree.) Where was her backpack? (Charli had left the backpack in her car before going into the Q'ehazi world, as she'd only taken it for her supposed trip.) Why was she returning so late in the day? Charli fended off the questions as best she could and was noncommittal about the story she'd planned to tell her mother about her visit to the art retreat. Her best defense was to change the subject.

"Where is Sean tonight?"

Her mother stopped in mid-sentence and looked at Charli in utter bafflement. "Why are you interested in him all of a sudden? What's gotten into you, Charlotte?"

"It's just . . . he has something of mine—something I need," Charli responded lamely, trying to keep the tremor out of her voice.

"For heaven's sake, you haven't even told me anything about how you've been the past few days. You never called or texted while you were away. And now you want to know—"

"I know, I know. I'll tell you later; I will, Mom, honestly! I just need to go now. It's urgent. I'm sorry." Charli gave up on trying to fend off her mother and took off through the house to the other side, where she exited again through the front door, with her mother's voice still ringing in her ears: "You're going out again?! What are you doing, Charli?!"

Charli knew exactly where Sean would be at this time of night. Her mother had complained to her often enough about Sean spending virtually every night at the local bar with his friends, and he would be there again, Charli was sure of it. All she had to do was retrieve her car and drive over. There, she would confront him and find out what he had done in the Q'ehazi world. Charli didn't have a very firm sense of what she would actually do, but she knew what she wanted to say: that he was a bastard to follow her and steal a precious gem, and to shoot and hurt a man who meant him no harm. She wanted him to know that she knew what he'd been up to, and that he couldn't get away with it because she would tell others and they would discover what a lowlife criminal he was.

Charli had visions of Sean being hauled off to prison or otherwise being taken away from society so that he could no longer influence her mother and she'd never have to put up with him again. Charli was convinced that once her mother saw what a bad man he was underneath that charming exterior, Angela would recognize that Charli had been right all along, and she'd return to being the fun-loving mother of Charli's childhood. Sean had taken her mother from her, and she couldn't forgive him for that. He was going to have to answer for his crimes, and now was payback time.

To her great relief, the car was exactly where she'd left it. She patted the hood affectionately as she caught her breath: "Thanks for being here for me." She felt like her car was the only loyal friend she had right now. It would get her to where she needed to go.

Hopping inside, Charli felt the usual rush of excitement at having her own transportation. It was something she had longed for, for years, as a symbol of independence and freedom, and even though it was an old car without a lot of horsepower or gleaming status, the fact that she'd passed her test and been awarded a car for her sixteenth birthday was not only a mark of pride and accomplishment but also her entry into the adult world, where she could go wherever she wanted whenever she wanted.

Charli's hands trembled as she turned the key in the ignition. When she pulled out into the road, she failed to look behind her and narrowly missed another car, which sped past her, sounding its horn in annoyance. Charli felt a rush of adrenaline and breathed deeply, trying to calm herself as she traveled along the narrow country road to downtown Weaverton.

She glanced down at the GPS screen of her car and tried to input the address of the local bar. Partly because her concentration was distracted and she was tired and emotional, and partly because the street lighting in this part of town was barely adequate, Charli didn't see the car headed straight towards her on the opposite side of the road, and she didn't realize that she had drifted across the central barrier. By the time she heard the loud blare of the other vehicle's horn, it was too late to avoid the head-on collision. Everything went blank.

◉ ◉ ◉

When Charli regained consciousness, she looked up and saw the face she least wanted to see.

"So, you're back with us, kid," said Sean, not unkindly. Given Charli's current condition, he felt a modicum of regret at the disparaging remarks he'd recently made about her to her mother, but he was secretly rather pleased to see Charli in this weakened and vulnerable position; it gave him the upper hand for once. When Angela had called him half an hour earlier to say that Charli was asking about him and was probably on her way to see him at the bar, he hadn't brushed off her urgent request that he "go and find Charli" and in fact set out in his car on the road back to

Angela's house. Though he doubted Charli could convince Angela of any wrongdoing on his part, he worried about what Charli knew.

"What are you doing here?" Charli managed to gasp out, raising herself on her elbows as much as she could and brushing the hair off her forehead. She shielded her eyes from the lights of police vehicles surrounding them.

"Your mom called me. She was worried about you. What the hell were you doing?"

Charli couldn't respond because at that moment a young policewoman came up and knelt beside her. "How are you, honey? That was quite a wreck back there."

"I'm fine." Charli struggled to her feet in an effort to prove the validity of her words. She blinked in the fierce light and could just make out a few figures hovering around the two crashed vehicles. "What about the other—"

"They're fine. The car isn't, though. Is your mom on her way?"

"Yep." This was Sean's response, before Charli could interject. Charli felt suddenly helpless and small.

A young man in a yellow jacket appeared on Charli's right, and the policewoman turned away to answer a call on her personal intercom. "How are you, young lady? No broken bones, anyway. You're really lucky."

"Yeah, I . . . think I'm okay," Charli ventured.

"You'll have to come back with me to the hospital."

"But I feel fine."

"It's protocol, I'm afraid. We'll have to do a drug and alcohol test too."

"I wasn't drinking or anything, just tired."

"Well, we need to make sure of that. Is this your dad?" he added, indicating Sean, who was still hovering, with something resembling a smirk on his face.

"No," Charli blurted, not wanting there to be any confusion as to his role in the proceedings. "He's just . . . my mom's friend."

"Well, your mother will need to come get you."

"I can let her know where Charli is," said Sean, attempting to take charge of the situation.

"That's fine. We're taking her to Cedar Springs General. We've got a stretcher here for you."

"No, no, I don't need that," Charli responded, feeling more and more embarrassed and ashamed.

"Well, get in the ambulance as soon as you can, miss." The EMT headed towards his vehicle, which was where most of the lights were coming from.

"I want to call my mom," Charli whimpered. She wished so much that Sean were not there to see her like this. She'd imagined herself accosting him, accusing him for what he did in Q'ehazi and having the pleasure of seeing him with his back against the wall, not strong and confident as he seemed now.

"Sure," said Sean. "Where's your phone?"

"Uh . . ." Charli searched her mind desperately through the fog of shock befuddling her brain. She couldn't remember the last time she'd had the cell phone. Was it back in Q'ehazi? Was it in the backpack she'd left in the car? Or had she forgotten it at the house when she'd left so suddenly on her way to find Sean at the bar?

"Not a problem. We can find it later."

Charli saw that smirk appearing on Sean's face again, and she knew that this situation was just what he'd been waiting for. She was determined to say something before the inevitable distractions of hospital staff and tests and her mother fussing over her distracted her from her mission. So, she burst out: "I know what you did!"

"What are you talking about?" Sean was still smirking, but there was an edge of fear in his voice.

"You stole the Honor Stone from Q'ehazi. You just took what wasn't yours!"

Sean snickered. "Was that what you call it? Well, it was just sitting there. Why shouldn't I take it?"

"You're a thief and a bastard!" Charli was yelling at him now. "And you hurt somebody. You shot that guy! How could you? He was defenseless. They don't even *have* guns in Q'ehazi! They don't even know what a gun is!" Charli suddenly realized she was shrieking and must have sounded hysterical.

"What the hell are you talking about? Jesus, that was an accident. He came up behind me. It was just reflex. It was his fault for coming after me like that."

"That stone wasn't yours to take!"

"Well, you'll be glad to know it was worthless anyway. I don't know why I bothered lugging the thing back to the shed. Just a fucking rock, and I'd thought it was ruby or something worth a lot of money—"

"It's worth something to *them*, much more than money. I know money is all you care about." Charli almost spat out the word *money*, for which she had a new disdain after being among the Q'ehazi.

"You'll find out, kid. Money is what makes the world go around." Sean looked proud of himself and not contrite at all. "Anyway, now I know how to get them, there's probably plenty more rocks where that came from. It was so easy. If they don't want people to take their rocks, why put them on display like that? How stupid!"

Charli felt aggrieved at his disparagement of the Q'ehazi people, who were her friends and people she aspired to be like. But she needed information more than she needed to express her disgust at Sean's behavior. "How did you even get into Q'ehazi?"

"I just followed you, kid. You went there first, didn't you?" Sean said. "What do you call it? Kuhazee? What are they, Indians or something? Sure have a lot of colored people—"

Charli opened her mouth to yell at him some more, but now the

EMT came back with a jacket that he draped over her to keep her warm, and he ushered her into the waiting ambulance to take her to the hospital. Charli suddenly realized who the EMT reminded her of, with his warm, soft voice and gentle manner. With a pang, the vision of Joslyn's face came to her, and she longed so much to see him at this moment that it made her breathless. They didn't look at all the same, as the EMT was a White guy with red hair and blue eyes, but something about them both was unusual.

Sean sauntered back to his car, and Charli saw that he was making a phone call on his cell now, probably to her mother. "He could have let me borrow his phone," she muttered bitterly. "I just wanted to talk to my mom."

"It's okay, sweetie. You can call your mom from the hospital. We have phones there, you know." The young man had a round, boyish face and large, blue-green eyes, and his voice soothed Charli. She realized that she'd actually gotten off pretty lightly; she was physically unhurt as far as she could tell and hadn't hurt anybody else. As for the car, she knew the insurance would cover the cost of the damage, and although her mother would be angry with her, Charli intended to defend herself by telling her mother the truth about her boyfriend.

It occurred to Charli, even in her currently befuddled state, that she was sitting right in front of a medical person who was there to help, someone sympathetic who could maybe assist her. Charli often wanted to contact the police, or some kind of authorities, about the way Sean was treating her mother. But she didn't know where to begin. It was never the right situation to call 911. Yelling and insults didn't seem like bad enough behavior to be taken seriously, and Charli feared being laughed at or ignored; those few times when Sean actually hit her mother, Angela seemed determined to pretend nothing had happened.

Now here Charli was with a seemingly sympathetic person standing. Perhaps she could unburden herself at last.

"I want to talk to someone . . . at the police station. It's about . . ." Charli spotted Sean ambling back in their direction from his car, and her voice suddenly lowered. "I just want to talk to someone."

"Sure, sweetie, you can do that. As soon as you finish at the hospital."

To Charli's relief, Sean was not allowed to travel in the ambulance with her, and she imagined he would not be inclined to follow her to the hospital. She sat in the back with the EMT (who was called Taylor, she learned) while she listened to the ambulance drone and they rushed through the streets. She was almost amused to think that she had caused all of this drama.

"I've never been in an ambulance before," Charli admitted in an attempt to strike up a conversation with this attractive and sympathetic stranger.

He smiled back at her and seemed to welcome the chance for a connection. "Well, I hope you never will again, young lady. Do you mind telling me where you were going in such a hurry, in the middle of the night, when you should have been home with your mama?"

His tone was more teasing than accusatory, and Charli felt heartened to tell him the truth. "I was actually going after Sean—that guy you met."

"At the accident? Who I thought was your dad?"

"Yeah, crazy, huh?"

Taylor shrugged. "I've heard crazier. So, what's your beef with him?"

"He's not my dad. He's my mom's boyfriend. And I can't stand him."

"Oh, I get it. What happened to your real dad?"

Charli looked away for a second and compressed her lips. "He died. Five years ago."

"Oh, I'm sorry." Taylor put out a comforting arm and patted her on the shoulder.

"Thank you."

Charli turned her head to him and noticed that his hands were small, with manicured nails and smooth skin. His arms were slender, freckled, and pale, and his mop of thick, curly red hair hung around his shoulders in an unruly mass that, together with his smooth, round face, gave him the appearance of a little boy.

"How old are you?" she asked impulsively.

"Oh, I know. I look like a kid," he replied with a grin. "I'm twenty-six." At Charli's surprised expression, he said, "Right? I still get carded if I try to buy a beer."

"You should grow a beard or something," Charli suggested.

"Well, I tried, but it didn't come out right."

Taylor had a pleasant voice with a slight Southern accent that made the words come out slower than normal. The tone was a little high-pitched for a man and low-pitched for a woman—in fact, almost completely a blend of male and female. Charli felt comfortable with him in the same way she had with Abbe and her brother. Charli formed strong impressions about people as soon as she met them, and her impression of this young man was of someone safe, warm, and approachable.

"I've been wanting to talk to someone about Sean. But I didn't know how, or who to talk to. You see, he's not just a mean guy. Sometimes he hits my mom."

Taylor looked serious now, and his brow furrowed in concern: "You've seen him do this?"

"Yeah. I saw them have a fight once, and he pushed her to the ground. My mom's started seeing a therapist. I don't know why she doesn't just say something to her."

"Maybe she has."

"I don't know. My mom's such an idiot." Tears pricked at her eyes. She felt ashamed and guilty, as if she were giving away family secrets. And yet she didn't want to carry this burden all by herself anymore.

Taylor reached out a comforting arm once more. "Has he ever tried to hit you or threaten you in any way?" His voice was warm and reassuring.

"No, he's never done anything to me. Apart from following me. But no, it's just my mom. I wish she could stand up for herself. But she just takes it. If it were me, I'd fight back."

"Atta girl!" Taylor handed her a pamphlet about domestic violence with a phone number on it. "Now, I want you to call these people if you need to, okay? If you ever feel in danger, or your mom. Just call them, twenty-four seven."

Charli thanked him, realizing she'd been secretly hoping Taylor would give her his personal phone number like in the movies when people met through a crisis and then found themselves in a romantic relationship. Charli had been pursued by boys her own age at school, but she never found them attractive. An older man, though, someone with a kind heart and a sympathetic nature, as well as a maturity and experience about the world—that was appealing to Charli in a way that she had only so far fantasized about.

As they arrived at the hospital, both Taylor and Charli were distracted by the sequence of events: people opening the ambulance doors and escorting Charli to a hospital room while she was checked out by a nurse with a brusque manner and a much less sympathetic attitude. The nurse seemed to believe that Charli had been involved in an accident while driving drunk. Charli clutched the pamphlet Taylor had given her as a kind of memento, hoping that maybe one day she could get some actual help for her situation.

About an hour later, when her mother arrived at the hospital, Charli noticed her having a conversation with Taylor in another room, and she worried whether the EMT would mention anything about what Charli had revealed to him.

Charli felt drowsy after taking the painkillers the nurse insisted she take, so by the time her mother came over to her, Charli felt too drained to tell her anything, and Angela was too relieved to see her daughter safe and well to question her. Charli barely remembered the drive home in her mother's car, although she did have a memory of her mother tucking her into bed like she had when Charli was a little girl. This was something she hadn't done in years. For once, Charli allowed her mother to be protective and reassuring and to treat her like the little girl Angela still wished her to be.

◉ ◉ ◉

Charli was woken the next morning around 9 a.m. by the sound of a bird she heard most mornings around this time. It always sounded to her like the plaintive mewing of a cat. The bird had woken her from a blissful dream about Joslyn. She still had a smile on her face and a warm, glowing feeling at the memory of the dream, but the feeling quickly faded as she recalled the events of the evening before and the reasons for her very deep and long sleep. With a pang in her stomach of mingled dread and sadness, she recalled that Sean had admitted he had been to Q'ehazi and taken the stone, and even to shooting and injuring the old man. The most concerning thing was that he planned to go again, to try to collect more stones that he believed would be valuable enough to sell here in their world.

With that thought, Charli leaped out of bed. Her muscles were stiff and achy from the accident, but being young, she shook off her lethargy and moved straight into action. She saw her backpack on the floor, and now she remembered leaving her cell phone in it before going through the portal days before. She was relieved someone had retrieved it from the wreck. After scrolling through her messages and texts and not seeing anything concerning, she left it on the charger by her bed. Next, she went to the kitchen to make coffee and saw that her mother had already left the house for her shift at Ingles. Recalling now what Sean had said about lugging the stone back to the shed, Charli decided to visit the shed and see if the stone was still there. She threw on her jacket and headed out back.

When she walked into the shed, Charli saw a rock about the size of an apple lying among some tools and garden implements in the center of the wooden bench that took up most of the room inside. Charli wondered if this was the rock Sean had thought was so valuable and had found so heavy. The rock looked like granite or stone, the sort of thing Charli saw every day, but small veins of red crystal glowing in the center could represent something more valuable.

The shed door opened behind her, and she whirled around.

"Shouldn't you still be in bed, young lady?" Sean said with a sneer.

"I'm not staying there when you're wandering about," retorted Charli. "Was this what you worked so hard to bring back from Q'ehazi?"

Sean appeared aggrieved. "Yeah, but the rock was a lot bigger before. I don't know what happened."

"I do. It couldn't take the air." Charli was proud of her knowledge, and for being able to catch Sean off guard.

"What are you talking about?"

"Nothing from Q'ehazi can withstand the air in our world. It's toxic to them." Charli knew her face was getting redder by the minute, and she couldn't keep the tremble out of her voice. "You're not welcome there! You're not welcome here with my mom, either! Why don't you just disappear?" She couldn't help herself; the words vomited out of her before she could stop them or consider the wisdom of her words.

"So *that's* why. You just explained it to me, girl. Now I know how to keep my rubies safe until I can sell them for lots of money. I'll just cover them up so they don't get air on them. And if they disintegrate after I've sold them to some loser, that's their problem, not mine. Don't worry, I'm going to be very welcome with your mom when I tell her how I've made millions of dollars. And you. Wouldn't you like a nice new car to replace the one you crashed? I can get you that."

"Except you won't. Because you only care about yourself. And anyway, I don't care about cars. I don't want to live here anymore. I hate this place and everybody in it."

"Oh boy, I wonder what your mom would say if she could hear that."

"Not her. But I hate you. I hate you!" Charli wanted to fling something at him, so she picked up one of the tools on the bench and cocked it back threateningly.

Sean laughed at her efforts. "Oh boy, you're a little tiger, aren't you? I better not let you get out of here."

"What the—"

Before she could stop him, Sean had stepped back out and shut the door behind him. To Charli's horror, she heard the key turning in the lock. "You better stay there till you calm down," Sean shouted through the door.

Charli rushed over to the door and tried vainly to open it, but it was locked shut. The shed had no windows in it, and there was no other way out. She rattled the door desperately, calling as loudly as she could for help. But she knew that this was useless. Her mother was out at Ingles for a good few hours, and the nearest neighbors were too far away. Unless somebody happened to pass by and hear her yells, she was out of luck.

After a while, Charli gave up and reasoned with herself. There was no point getting all in a state about things. Eventually her mom would come home and would wonder where she was, and even she would think to look for her in the shed after she'd exhausted all other possibilities—especially when she saw her daughter's phone was still in her room and her bedroom door had been left open.

All Charli could do now was wait. She turned on the pale light in the shed from the single bulb dangling from the ceiling so that she could see a little. Then she remembered the book about Q'ehazi history the professor had given her. Since she had nothing else to do at this moment, she pulled the book from her jacket pocket and started to read.

CHAPTER TWELVE

Around seven that night, Charli finally heard the key turn in the lock to the shed, and her mother's astonished face appeared in the doorway. "Good heavens, Charli. What are you doing here?"

Charli was hugely relieved to see her mother at last but didn't want to admit to her about the altercation she'd had with Sean. How could she explain what they had been arguing about? "Reading," she responded, waving the book briefly.

"In this light? You'll damage your eyes!"

"It was okay." In truth, it had not been very easy to read under the small bulb; plus, the shed was rather muggy. But Charli stubbornly refused to show weakness.

"Well, come inside now. I've got dinner ready. I looked all over for you. This was the last place I imagined you'd be. And why is the door locked?" Angela asked with a sudden realization that Charli could not have locked herself inside the shed, and there would have been no reason for her to do so.

"That was Sean," Charli admitted.

"What are you talking about?" Angela's voice registered concern and suspicion, as if she suspected Charli of lying.

A light drizzle began to fall on their way back to the house, but the air was warm on this summer evening, and Charli was glad to be outside at least.

"I know you think Sean is the greatest thing since sliced bread and all, but he is in fact an asshole."

"I've told you before, Charlotte—"

"Yeah, yeah, okay. He's not a nice person," Charli said with deliberation and a hint of familiar sarcasm in her voice. "He locked me in the shed."

"Why on earth would he do that?"

"I guess he didn't want me to get out."

"So, when did this happen?"

"This morning."

"You've been in there all day?!"

Charli enjoyed seeing the horror on her mother's face, also recognizing that for once her mother believed her about her boyfriend's bad behavior. Now perhaps her mother would change her attitude towards Sean.

"Yes, I was there all day," pronounced Charli, almost proudly, relishing her mother's discomfiture.

"Why did you go to the shed in the first place?"

That was an unexpected question and not one that Charli cared to be honest about. "I dunno. I was just . . . wandering about in the garden, and I saw Sean in there—"

"What was *he* doing in the shed?"

"He was looking at that stupid rock of his."

"Oh, I see. The rock," Angela responded with a small tut of disapproval. They had now arrived in the dining room, and Charli started dutifully setting the table while her mother brought food in from the kitchen.

"You know about his rock?" Charli was surprised that Sean would have even mentioned his prize to her mother.

"Yes, he showed it to me. Made a big fuss about how valuable it was. It looked fairly ordinary to me."

Charli had an idea now. "When did he show it to you?"

"Oh, I don't know. It was while you were away. Tuesday morning, I think."

Charli calculated. *So, three days ago.* "How big was it then?"

Angela frowned in both concentration and confusion. "I don't remember—"

"You know, just roughly how big?"

"Well, I guess about the size of a football or something. Why does that matter? Why do you want to know?"

"Oh, no reason. Just curious." But clearly the rock had gotten significantly smaller in the past few days, even though in the shed it had been somewhat shielded from the air. If Sean was planning to go back to Q'ehazi, did he realize he could use the shawl to find the portal? Did he know where she had buried it? That hadn't occurred to her before, and it now felt even more urgent that she get back to the creek and into Q'ehazi.

However, Charli didn't want to alert her mother about where she'd really been. She felt territorial about this secret place she'd discovered, and she worried that the wonderful Q'ehazi universe could be infected and destroyed if people from her world knew about it and were able to visit at will. It was also likely that her mother wouldn't believe her or even indulge the possibility long enough for Charli to prove the other world's existence. Not to mention, the revelation tended to disrupt one's entire worldview— unless one was Sean, who just folded the discovery into his general view that everything could be exploited for profit. In any case, Sean's visit had been destructive, and she had to take action to stem the damage before it got any worse.

"I wonder where Sean is now. He usually comes for dinner. I didn't even get a text from him," Angela murmured, looking distractedly at her phone.

Charli suddenly felt sorry for her mother. She wondered what the attraction was and why Angela couldn't see what a toxic person Sean was and how he used and abused her. Perhaps it was because Angela's own father had been such a strict disciplinarian. Angela had no idea how to fight back or even that she should.

Charli frequently determined to be a person completely unlike her mother—to be a woman with strength and power but also with kindness and empathy, a person that the Q'ehazi would say displayed a state of grace. Charli felt a fleeting desire to tell her mother all about the wonderful land she'd discovered that lay just beyond the creek and yet so far from everything she knew.

But then, her distrust returned, and she held her tongue. She'd confided in her mother before, and it had not ended well. She never felt that her mother understood her or had real empathy for what she was going through. While well intentioned, Angela didn't have the capacity to see beyond her own narrow view of things, even though she loved Charli in her own way.

So, Charli didn't answer her mother's question and didn't reveal what she knew about her mother's boyfriend. She believed that Sean's true nature would eventually be revealed, and whatever she said wouldn't make much difference.

Charli did have one burning question: "Did Taylor say anything to you about Sean last night?"

"Who's that, dear?"

"You know, the EMT who brought me to the hospital in the ambulance. I saw you talking to him."

"Oh, so it was a him. I thought it was a her."

Charli was stunned and irritated by her mother's reaction to her question. "What are you talking about?"

"The redhead, right? I thought I was talking to a woman, although she did have kind of a low voice, now I come to think about it. Is she—he—one of those non-gender . . . type people, then?"

"If you mean a trans person, maybe." Then she thought about Taylor's similarity to Joslyn, and "non-binary" came to mind, which might have been what her mother meant. "Well, I don't know, but what does it matter, anyway? The point is, did he say anything about Sean?"

"No, I don't remember her—him, mentioning anything about Sean. Why would he?"

But by this time, Charli had stormed out of the room. She felt too angry to respond to Angela's futile question—angry at her mother's insensitivity; angry that nothing had been done about Sean; angry at being distracted by her own inner confusion at being attracted to somebody who was halfway between man and woman because Charli hadn't yet clarified for herself what her sexuality was or would be. She'd felt attracted to girls before but wasn't sure if it was a sexual thing or a desire to connect with someone she could aspire to be like. She was attracted to men, too, although just men—like Joslyn—and not "little boys" (as she disparagingly referred to the boys who approached her at school). The confusion of emotions whirled around in her head, and she couldn't get it straight.

She went upstairs to her bedroom. She had to get back to Q'ehazi and stop Sean doing whatever he intended to do before it was too late. As soon as her mom was out of the house, Charli would make her way there.

⊙ ⊙ ⊙

As soon as Sean turned the key in the lock of the shed, ignoring Charli's pleas, he felt vindicated. Finally, he'd managed to get one up on this teenager he'd secretly hated from the first moment he saw her. Ironically, the things Sean hated most about Charli were the aspects of her that were most like him: her stubbornness and refusal to show weakness; her independence of spirit; her opinionated nature and her direct expression of her feelings even when it was uncomfortable for others.

To Sean, these were distinctly unfeminine traits, although he had little idea of what feminine really was, beyond vague ideas gleaned from magazines and TV shows. In Sean's personal experience, women were never like that in real life, but he clung to an idealized notion of what they should be.

Charli had inadvertently helped him understand why the stone had gotten smaller and what he could do to prevent that happening again. Inwardly gloating, he sped across the grass to the creek, with the intention of furthering his plan. Sean gave the impression of being lazy because he didn't follow prescribed rules and was petulant when crossed, but the truth was that he could be spectacularly determined and resourceful when necessary, and his laziness was simply a mask for his dormant cunning.

Sean valued money more than anything else in the world because in his experience, it was the only thing that could bring security and power and therefore protect him from pain or suffering. The power that money inevitably brought was much more valuable to him than love or even happiness. He figured, *What good is happiness if you don't have any control over it?* The vulnerability that love required was alien to Sean's nature and experience. Vulnerability meant weakness, and weakness meant danger.

The idea that a source of money existed just beyond his reach and yet tantalizingly easy to procure was too much for him to resist. There was also a sense of entitlement, as Sean was both surprised and disgusted by the fact that people could just leave precious gems lying around like that, as if begging to have them stolen. It was as bad as leaving hundred-dollar bills on the ground. Valuable assets like that should be in a safe deposit box or kept in the bank or at least behind glass with alarms to protect them, and not just visible for all to see, with some idiot standing next to them who didn't even carry a firearm or any means of protecting himself. In Sean's estimation, if people were foolish enough to engage in that kind of behavior, they deserved to get robbed.

Sean had used this same logic when stealing before, and

his lack of conscience demonstrated a missing link in his moral development that psychologists would probably say stemmed partly from his early lack of ethical education or role models growing up. As Sean sped through the fields towards his goal, his mind wandered to the first time he'd ever taken something that wasn't his.

Sean's third foster mother, Harriet—who, ironically was one of the kinder mothers he'd known—was married to a wealthy banker, and they lived in an affluent neighborhood in Chicago. Harriet had lived a fairly sheltered existence and was of a trusting nature, so when Sean admired the large ruby-and-diamond ring she wore on her right little finger, she allowed him to borrow it, "just for fun, just for the day." She also believed Sean when he told her that he'd "lost" the ring because the boy seemed genuinely contrite.

When her husband came home and beat the boy for his carelessness, Harriet pleaded with her husband to stop, especially when the boy cried and sobbed and insisted that it had been an accident and he was sorry and would do anything to make it up to them. Eventually Harriet's husband relented, and Sean retired, whimpering, to his room, where Harriet imagined him metaphorically licking his wounds. She couldn't bear the thought of the little boy's upset and tear-stained face, so she visited him later and tenderly told him that she didn't mind, that it was only a ring, and that one day he would be able to buy all the rings he wanted.

Harriet didn't realize that Sean had hidden the ring in a secret compartment of his small suitcase and intended to sell it, attracted more to its monetary value than its inherent beauty. He'd expected a beating for his trouble, and he knew how to endure such things through long experience; in fact, he prided himself on being able to take any amount of physical pain when a prize was at stake. Sean's assessment of the situation and his behavior wasn't at all altered by the fact that Harriet was kind to him and believed in him. When he sold the ring for quite a large sum a few months later, it was the proudest moment of his life; he saw it as a demonstration of his tenacity and resourcefulness.

Sean arrived at the redbud tree beside the creek and easily retrieved the glass bottle from its hiding place. He didn't bother to re-bury the bottle after taking out the shawl. It contained nothing else of value. Charli had been wearing the shawl when he saw her disappear, so he had an inkling this was a key strategy to finding the waterfall again. His hopes were fulfilled when he held up the material and his eyes immediately focused on the brown line he'd spotted before. He had not seen it a second ago.

Once the shawl had fulfilled its purpose, Sean flung it on the ground and clumsily pushed through the distortion.

He made his way back to the waterfall. His plan was to find more of the stones and bring them back to his world. Only, this time, he'd be more sensible and wrap them up carefully, away from the polluted air of his own world—for as long as it took to sell them to somebody else, who'd have no idea that they had such a short shelf life. Sean also had enough presence of mind to bring with him a small shovel in case he needed to do any digging.

As he approached the waterfall, he saw from a distance that several people were standing around this time. They didn't seem to be speaking, but they gazed at each other in meaningful ways. Sean wondered if they were all deaf and dumb in this country. He decided to hang back until he could find out more about who they were and what they intended to do, keeping out of sight behind a patch of trees.

When the little group of people moved aside for a few minutes, to Sean's great delight and surprise, he saw that the huge ruby rock had now been replaced by three somewhat smaller but even more gorgeous ruby gems. They stood on a small plinth overhanging the waterfall. Sean's mouth watered as he thought about how easy it would be to take one or all of those rocks—and this time, he'd know how to keep them secure. They must be worth millions of dollars!

His body trembled with excitement. He felt certain that the people would eventually go, and then he could run up there and take the rocks. His small knapsack was probably big enough for all three. And he didn't even need the shovel. *This is going to be so easy—I can't believe my luck!*

CHAPTER THIRTEEN

Charli woke from a profound sleep the next morning to an ache in the pit of her stomach. She couldn't remember when she'd been more miserable. Now that she had the energy to comprehend the full extent of events, the force of what had transpired hit her: Sean had taken a precious rock from Q'ehazi and displayed no remorse about it; plus, she could not stop him if he intended to go back for more rocks or hurt more people in Q'ehazi, and she dreaded to think what Sean could accomplish with no holds barred.

Charli thought miserably of the friends she'd made back in Q'ehazi and how much that world meant to her: Abbe, with her wit and vivacity; Sovereign Aurora, the wisest person she'd ever met; and of course Joslyn, who stirred in Charli emotions she'd never felt before. These people understood her better than anybody in her own family or her own world, where she'd always felt like a misfit and an imposter. She fervently wished that she'd been born into Q'ehazi and been able to take advantage of the wonderful parenting and society they enjoyed. Charli cursed her fortune at having been born into this world, with all of its hate and division and greed and envy.

Unable to bear her frustration any longer, Charli leaped out of bed and flung herself into the bathroom, where she started running the water for a hot shower. Her emotions were so intense that she didn't realize she'd started singing to herself, and quite loudly, one of her favorite songs: "It's time to try defying gravity. I think I'll try defying gravity. And you can't pull me down." Feeling the water running down her skin and breathing in the steamy air always seemed to liberate Charli's thoughts in a particular way, and in the shower, her mood suddenly shifted from despondency to determination.

She threw herself out of the shower as quickly as she'd entered it, toweled herself dry, and practically danced into the bedroom adjoining her bathroom, then changed into something sensible for traveling. Charli couldn't wait any longer for her mother to be gone, but, fortunately for her, Angela was still sleeping in before a night shift at Ingles, and the girl demolished breakfast unimpeded before starting her journey.

◎ ◎ ◎

About six hours later, Angela woke to her alarm warning her to get up in time for her night shift. Her first thought was to wonder about Charli's whereabouts, as the girl had been acting so strangely recently. When Angela searched all around the house, including the shed this time, her worry intensified. This was becoming a theme: Charli nowhere to be found and with no reasonable excuse. Her daughter had always been a bit defiant but never to this extent.

Angela wondered if she should start believing what Sean often suggested—that Charli was running with a "bad crowd" and may have already relapsed. Angela had been terrified of something like that happening to her daughter. She had heard so many stories of what parents went through when their teenagers used illegal substances. Angela's religious upbringing made her naive about things like drugs and alcohol, even though her own father drank more than he should—and secretly—while at the same time admonishing his children for indulging in such pernicious and "evil" habits. Thus, Angela and her siblings were never allowed the freedom to roam that she allocated to her own daughter. Angela had hoped that Charli was sensible enough to enjoy her independence without allowing herself to be led astray.

The door to Charli's bedroom had been left wide open, with clothes strewn all over the floor, the computer unopened, the phone on the bedside table, and the bed unmade. It was unlike Charli to leave her bedroom in a state of disarray. She'd always been an overachiever and a little OCD, even. This was so uncharacteristic of her, even if the secrecy and the rebellious streak were not so unfamiliar.

But then, teenagers were changeable, weren't they? Many of the young parents that Angela saw on television in dramas and reality shows, complained bitterly about how they felt they didn't know their kids anymore, that their personalities had changed beyond recognition, and they never intended or expected to raise such little monsters. Angela herself had always been rather proud and grateful that her little girl hadn't disappointed her but instead did her best to excel at whatever she chose to take on.

Angela did recognize that her relationship with Sean had thrown a big wrench into the works, damaging her relationship with her daughter, but she hoped this was just a temporary situation and that eventually a détente would arise. Angela's own feelings towards Sean were ambivalent at times, but she was afraid to be on her own, and he provided her with a sense of security that only a man could.

Angela noticed something on Charli's bed that she hadn't seen before: an old book with very worn covers. As she turned the pages, she was surprised to find it in such terrible condition, some of the pages literally turning to dust in her hand. She wondered where Charli could have gotten such an old book and why she would be reading something like this, which didn't look like part of her summer reading. Surely, whatever the book was, Charli could get hold of a better copy than this. Angela dropped it in the trash can, intending to dispose of it as soon as she took the trash out later that day.

Angela also felt a little disgruntled that Sean had failed to show up for dinner the previous evening, or even to let her know where he was or when he intended to visit again. Since he'd been living in the house with Angela and Charli, Angela expected his presence during the daytime as well as the evenings. She always felt a little lift in her heart when she arrived home and saw his black Toyota in the carport outside her house, knowing that he would be there when she got inside. She'd given him a key so that he could come and go as he pleased.

But this time he hadn't even called or texted. She figured it would be appropriate to call Martin and find out if he knew where Sean was. That was not something she'd ever attempted before, but then, Sean had never disappeared for an extended period.

When she told Martin who was calling, she was gratified that he didn't sound annoyed but instead had a reasonably friendly tone. "Hey, Angie. How are you?"

"I'm doing fine, thanks. I just wondered if you've seen Sean recently?"

Angela wasn't sure how to interpret the slight pause that followed.

"Uh, no, I haven't seen him since . . . when was it? That night you called him about Charli, and he found her on the road—"

"Wednesday?"

"Yeah, that's right. He didn't come to the bar last night. Thought he was with you, actually."

"No. I thought he was with you." Angela chuckled briefly at the humor of the situation.

"Everything okay?" Martin's voice held a note of genuine concern, even kindness.

"Oh sure. I just wondered. But I'm sure he's fine—just busy, I guess."

"Yeah, he must be busy at work or something."

"Right, right."

"Well, you take care then."

"Okay, thanks."

When Angela put the phone down, she felt a sense of abandonment she hadn't felt in a long, long time. Since before Charli was born, maybe. And she hated that feeling. It was an old wound triggered by a new trauma to ache again. The house seemed unnaturally quiet and still. She wished she'd been a bit more sympathetic to Charli the last time she'd seen her. She wished fervently that she understood her daughter better, but the truth was that her own flesh and blood was as much of a mystery to her as any stranger. Still, Angela was aware that Charli had a good heart. She'd witnessed the love and care Charli always gave to animals.

Somewhere in the back of Angela's mind was a glimmer of a new thought, a thought that perhaps Sean was not the right guy for her after all, or that maybe his treatment of her wasn't always deserved. In arguments between her daughter and her boyfriend, she'd always taken Sean's side because on the whole she believed in supporting her partner above all else. But she was starting to rethink her priorities as she realized that Charli, although young and not always communicative, genuinely cared about her mother and wished to defend her.

As Angela rubbed the bruise on her shoulder from Sean's violence towards her a few days earlier, she wondered if she could leave him. The thought first felt like a rebellious notion that left her feeling ashamed and guilty by default, but the more it took hold in her brain, the more it seemed like not such an outlandish idea. And when she imagined what life would be like without Sean, a wave of relief washed over her, not unlike the relief one feels when they have been in a very dangerous situation for a long time and are finally safe and well.

The memory sneaking back into her consciousness after years of trying to push it down and bury it where it would never be found was the knowledge that her own father was similar to Sean, in more ways than either he or she cared to admit. By investigating her relationship with Sean during therapy, Angela had been provoked into admitting that some aspects of it were familiar to her from her childhood: not only the drinking and the denial that it was a problem, but also the "abuse" (as her therapist called it, though Angela herself had never dared to admit such a thing).

Angela had never thought of it as abuse when her father had demeaned her, called her a "stupid bitch," or come home drunk and rageful, but now she realized that it was, and that it had affected her in more ways than she knew. And the time when he had come into her bedroom in the middle of the night—she had believed up until now that it was just a bad dream for which she was inadvertently responsible by even having the idea that her father could do such a thing; now she wondered if that really had happened, and happened more than once.

Of one thing Angela was absolutely certain: she never wanted Charli to have to endure abuse from any man. If Angela couldn't protect herself, she could at least protect her daughter. Her own mother had been a passive recipient of everything her husband told her and prescribed for her, and Angela vowed that she would not make that mistake—if it wasn't too late. Maybe there was still time to reverse some of the effects of her upbringing and not hamper her own child by carrying on those hurtful traditions.

For the first time, the possibility of leaving Sean brought a sense of freedom that she'd never anticipated.

harli eyed the ground beneath the redbud tree where the shawl had been originally buried. A gleam caught her eye, and she spied the glass bottle lying on the ground beside the tree—empty. "Damn!" she hissed through her teeth. "The bastard took it with him!" Then she spotted the shawl on the ground by the tree and realized that he must have simply flung it aside when he passed through the tear.

She gently picked up the woolen piece, horrified to see that not only had it markedly faded but also many of the threads had disintegrated, and half the shawl had essentially disappeared—so different from when she had originally found it in the glass bottle, vibrant with color as if it had only just been made. Charli's eyes filled with tears again.

Charli remembered what Abbe had told her the last time she was in Q'ehazi: "I have heard that nothing from Q'ehazi can survive the atmosphere in your world." Charli reflected, *No wonder whoever took this shawl in the first place placed it inside a glass bottle and then buried it in the ground. That was the only way to ensure its survival.*

Luckily, Charli was able to pass through the tear with the fragments of shawl. She hurried along the path towards the longhouse where she knew Abbe and her large extended family lived. When she got there, Charli encountered just one older lady, who was busy sewing in the pleasant, early-morning sunshine, and told her that most of the people from her village were present at the fairness test for the stranger, which was being held in the "usual place." Fortunately, Charli knew where this place was and how to get there because she had been present when Metlin and Barylos were trying to find a solution to their disagreement over the classes.

When Charli arrived at the large outdoor arena, about a hundred people were gathered as spectators and commentators, which was a larger crowd than before. Sovereign Aurora stood in the center of the circle of onlookers, presently speaking aloud in her sonorous and resonant voice. Charli guessed this audible speech was for expediency.

The crowd was too large to pinpoint someone she knew, so she took a spare chair between two people she'd never met before, who nevertheless smiled a brief welcome.

Charli was aghast to see that the very person she had come to Q'ehazi to confront appeared to be the defendant in this "trial" and was standing next to the sovereign, his hands defiantly in his pockets and his head cocked, with a disdainful smirk on his face. During a pause in the sovereign's speech, Charli turned briefly to the woman beside her and indicated with her face and her thoughts, "What's going on?"

The woman was White, and she had a large, round, ruddy face with a friendly expression. She inclined her head towards Charli and spoke without words: "That man there is not from our world. He was discovered trying to steal some of our stones from the Sacred Circle yesterday. I heard that he visited before and he hurt one of our people—Jason, from the Village of Teachers, who happens to be an uncle of mine. This man wounded Jason with his weapon and knocked him down, then removed our sacred Honor Stone from its plinth and took the stone back to his world."

"Is he going to be punished?" Charli was secretly gratified that Sean would finally get his just desserts, and that she didn't have to administer them. Charli had always believed in the idea of karma and that people who did wicked things would eventually have to pay for it, either in this life or the next. Of her mother's rather strict Catholic religious beliefs, "Vengeance is mine saith the Lord" had always resonated particularly for Charli. She hated the thought that injustices could be ignored or go unresolved; so the woman's response was both surprising and disheartening.

"We don't believe in punishment here. It is not part of our ways. You must be a stranger too, and we welcome you." Here, the woman gave Charli a hug, in the usual Q'ehazi manner of greeting strangers. "You will discover that we do things somewhat differently here, and we hope you will learn our ways and maybe even wish to join us." This tracked with what Charli did know about the Q'ehazi, but she found it difficult to adjust her ideas about reward and punishment.

Now the sovereign was speaking again, and Charli paid attention to her words.

"I wish to ask you again, Sean, why was it that you chose to steal the stone?"

"It was just sitting there."

"So, that means to you that you should take it?"

"Well, finders keepers."

Charli really hated Sean in that moment. She wished he would wipe that stupid smirk off his face. How dare he desecrate the Q'ehazi people in this way, bringing his vile ideas into this beautiful, pristine world? How could he harm one of these wonderful people with impunity? She felt her face grow hot, and her hands balled into tight fists. She wanted to punch him.

"I mean, why didn't you have someone guarding it if it was so valuable? I'd say it's your own stupid fault—with all due respect, uh, Sovereign."

Sovereign Aurora did not fall for Sean's insult bait but carried on in her calm and measured tone: "The Honor Stone was placed there so it could be enjoyed by all our people. We share the stone. It doesn't belong to anyone. We all love and appreciate the stone. So, what would be the need to guard it?"

"Okay, so if it doesn't belong to anyone, then it doesn't matter if I take it, right?" Sean said this with finality, as if he'd won the argument.

"By taking the stone, you are saying that the stone now belongs to you alone. Because you have removed it from a place where it can be enjoyed by everyone."

Sean nodded as if he could see her point.

"In your world, would it be right to take a stone such as that?"

"Well, I don't know about right. I probably wouldn't do it, because I'd get caught and then there'd be trouble." Sean gave a brief laugh, indicating that he still believed he had the upper hand in this debate.

"So, in your world, you do things based only on consequences to you personally, rather than an intrinsic knowledge of what is ethical behavior or that which would benefit the whole community?"

"Huh?" Sean seemed genuinely perplexed by this question and uncertain as he continued: "I don't know why nobody took it before now. It was just sitting there, glowing, like 'Take me.' It must be worth millions of dollars—or whatever you use for money here."

What the sovereign said next prompted such an expression of genuine shock from Sean that Charli wanted to laugh: "We don't have money in Q'ehazi. We believe in the noble truths we have gleaned from an old book, telling us that the love of money is the root of all evil. We stopped using money over five hundred years ago. Money is a human idea that promotes inequality, greed, disharmony, and hatred. The only currency here is love, and our world is better because of that."

Charli had heard of this idea before (and read about it) but never put so eloquently and simply. The concept obviously made so little sense to Sean that it was as if the sovereign were speaking a whole different language. He was literally speechless and stood for a few moments with his mouth hanging open.

"We also don't believe in punishment for wrongdoing. Because punishment doesn't achieve anything in the long run; it just creates needless suffering."

"What *do* you believe in then?" This was said in a much smaller voice. Sean actually sounded like he was digesting the import of the sovereign's words, and his state of confusion made him appear a lot less confident.

"We believe in learning. We believe that negative actions stem from misguided learning. In your case, you learned that money was the only thing of value or of worth, and so you coveted it. You learned that in order to be safe from suffering or pain, you needed to make yourself powerful and invincible. Whereas, in fact, power and money don't in the end bring happiness, and they certainly don't bring an end to pain."

"Right" was Sean's flummoxed response.

"When you have genuinely learned this, there will be no need for punishment, because you will automatically be released from the pain you are trying so hard to avoid."

Some onlookers in the crowd murmured their agreement and nodded. Charli, however, reserved judgment.

"There will be no punishment, but you will be escorted back to your world, and you will not be allowed to reenter Q'ehazi. While it is our policy to welcome and embrace strangers, those who do not act in accordance with our principles shall not remain. And those who wish to become more than just temporary visitors must demonstrate that they can attain a state of grace in order to do so."

The sovereign seemed to look directly at Charli as she said this. But the sovereign hadn't shown she'd noticed when Charli first arrived, and Charli couldn't be sure if it was a trick of the light. Nevertheless, she loved Q'ehazi so much that she did wish to stay forever—if there was a way to fulfill her obligations at home first.

"Okay, but how are you going to keep me out? I wasn't exactly invited in the first place." Sean spoke defiantly, undeterred by the disapproval of the crowd.

"It is true that the tear in the fabric of our world was created without our knowledge. But now we know that it exists, we will take steps to have it repaired so that it can no longer reappear. The talisman you used to open the portal—the shawl—will by now have disintegrated, and you will not be allowed to carry anything else back with you to your world. And now my sister is going to escort you to get something to eat." The sovereign pointed to Maudina, who was sitting close by in the crowd. "And then someone else will escort you home."

To Charli's amazement, the sovereign now pointed directly at her and called her over. So, she *had* been recognized.

Charli felt disappointed at being lumped in with Sean. Even though she was from the same world as him and had been brought up with many of the same beliefs, she wished to shed those like a snake sheds its skin. But she dutifully left her seat and approached the sovereign. Sean, at least, was surprised to see her there, although he said nothing to her directly.

"What do you need me to do?" asked Charli, hoping to both ingratiate herself with the sovereign and also demonstrate that her loyalty was to the leader of the Q'ehazi and not to her own countryman.

"You will also escort Sean back to his world."

"Me? But why?" Charli was astonished, and her immediate reaction was one of hurt that she'd been pushed away and out of Q'ehazi alongside this man.

"We will talk about this in a little while. In the meantime"—the sovereign gestured to her sister—"please take Sean to get something to eat and prepare him for his journey back." She turned to the crowd. "Thank you all for taking part in this important expression of Q'ehazi community. You may go about your day. I wish you all a pleasant afternoon." The people in the crowd rose and began to disperse. As had been the case at the last fairness test and the concerts Charli had attended, the usual murmuring of people who have been silently watching an event that has ended was not happening here, as people were communicating with each other by thoughts not spoken aloud.

Someone else had overheard the interaction between Aurora and Charli. Barylos had been sitting close to her sister, Abbe, and she now rose from her seat and addressed Charli aloud, as if she didn't believe this stranger was capable of conversing in the normal Q'ehazi fashion. She sneered at Charli. "You will need to learn how to forgive if you wish to attain a state of grace. And perhaps you don't realize that you can't stay in Q'ehazi without doing that."

Charli had no idea how to respond. The girl was passing judgment on her that she couldn't refute. It was true that she was a stranger here in this world, much as she longed to be included. The thought crossed her mind that maybe she could never be completely a part of Q'ehazi, because she had already been tainted by her own world, with its greed and violence. A wave of sadness washed over her at the thought as Barylos walked away with a smirk indicating she'd had the effect she wished.

A few seconds later, Abbe came up to her friend and gave her one of her characteristic warm hugs. "I wish I could stay," she said without words, "but I have a rehearsal now. Take care, Charli. I hope to see you again one day."

"You too," Charli replied, her heart temporarily warmed by this expression of affection from her friend.

The sovereign now gestured for Charli to accompany her, and

they both set off across the grass. Sovereign Aurora walked ahead of Charli with confident, quick steps. Even though she was quite possibly twenty or thirty years older than Charli, she was so fit and strong that Charli struggled to keep up with her. Charli suddenly felt like a foolish little girl. She could understand the value of the Q'ehazi principles, but they seemed so hard to live by, forcing her to set aside her own ego and all of the things she'd been taught to esteem. Yet she was eager to learn and improve, and she sensed that the sovereign valued her enthusiasm and passion, even if she was not yet able to live up to Q'ehazi ideals.

Eventually, they came to the edge of a lake where the waters were so still that Charli could see all the way to the bottom, to the stones and pebbles that lay there and the little silver fish darting among them. Sovereign Aurora took up a position on a large, flat rock overlooking the lake, and Charli sat next to her. The sovereign's gaze stayed fixated on the lake while she gently stroked Charli's right hand with her left fingers in a friendly and affectionate gesture.

Charli was frustrated that Sean had been allowed to escape scot-free, despite all of his transgressions. Her sense of justice and fairness was offended by the thought that a person who so manifestly demonstrated evil intentions could continue on his path of destruction.

Now the conversation between them was conducted in the silent speech that Charli was becoming familiar with.

"I don't like to think that a person like Sean can just do whatever he wants and get away with it, without any repercussions. You only saw what he did in Q'ehazi, and you don't even know about the times he's been mean to my mom, and even hit her." Charli's eyes filled with tears as she realized how inarticulate she was at expressing her rage against this man who seemed hellbent on destroying her peace forever.

The sovereign maintained her equanimity. "We in Q'ehazi believe there is no sense in raising specters from the past. During an argument or debate, we like to focus on what is before us and make our decisions based on that. People can change, you know." The sovereign smiled reassuringly at her young companion. "There are so many things you don't know about this world, but you will come to know them in time."

"I guess so." Charli looked down at the ground.

"I can tell how much you love Q'ehazi. Even though you are not from our world, I feel that you could become part of it because you are open to learning and changing for the better."

Charli had a powerful urge to tell the sovereign that she was part Cherokee, as if this connected her to the Q'ehazi people in a visceral way. But before she had the chance, Aurora continued, turning to look at Charli with her kind eyes. "We are all born with flaws, to be sure. And it is our job to learn and grow stronger and healthier every day. Here in Q'ehazi, it is maybe easier to do that than in your world, where there is little support for grace or valuing of it. Do you understand what I mean by grace?"

Charli didn't really, and she shook her head. "I heard the word at church when Mom took me, but I didn't really know what they meant by it, and I'm not sure they did either; it was just a word that sounded good."

"Here in Q'ehazi, a state of grace is the most important thing to attain. It's not necessarily easy, but we are all striving for it in our different ways. We occasionally have visitors who wish to stay here, and only those who show they are able to attain a state of grace are asked to remain. Of our people, it is necessary to attain a state of grace over time if you wish to have a leadership position within the community. We believe that the job of bringing the next generation into the world is an onerous task and not one to be undertaken lightly or without a full understanding of its complexity and responsibility. Therefore, only the wisest and healthiest people in our community are given that task. It has served us well for many hundreds of years and generations of people."

Aurora's ensuing smile was surprisingly girlish in its authenticity and unpretentious charm. "But I am boring you with this long-winded explanation."

Charli giggled. She had been feeling a little sleepy.

"The fact is, I feel that you would be capable of attaining a state of grace. And I would be happy to have you join our community. But first, I wish you to accompany Sean back to his world so you can demonstrate to him the true nature of the Q'ehazi teachings, and he can experience what it feels like to have his hate and fear met with only love and forgiveness."

"Can I really forgive him?"

"I think you can—if you realize that underneath his bravado lurks a little man who is full of fear and insecurity, who believes that only money and power can be his friend. Perhaps you can feel compassion for him."

Charli meditated on this idea for a moment. "Perhaps."

"Perhaps I have more faith in you than you have in yourself," said the sovereign, smiling again.

Charli smiled back. "I'm glad you have faith in me, anyway. You're good at seeing the best in people."

"Seeing the best in people is my job. I brought you to this beautiful lake because sometimes only nature can help us to heal our anger and fear and bring us perspective on the things that really matter in this world."

Sovereign Aurora's presence was so warm and reassuring that Charli felt she could ask the older woman anything and confide in her, even about subjects she would never broach with her own mother. "I don't think Barylos likes me very much. I don't know why." She hung her head as she said this.

Aurora touched her shoulder gently: "Everybody has an opinion, and not everybody will like you, no matter how much you try to win their approval. But regarding Barylos, she has her own concerns. There are things she needs to change within her heart, and only she can do so. She is already twenty-seven years old and has not yet completed the hardship mission. Perhaps she is afraid to do it; I don't know." Aurora's face became contemplative.

"What is the hardship mission?"

"Everybody must complete this before being able to attain a state of grace. We believe it is very important to develop and enhance empathy, and that you cannot do that unless you have struggled to overcome obstacles yourself. Spending a month in isolation with nobody else to help you is designed to test you and eventually bring you closer to the state of grace."

"Did you complete the hardship mission also?"

"Oh, yes, of course."

Charli smiled and asked the question that had been on her lips since she had first met the sovereign: "I hope you don't think I'm nosy, but . . . do you have a husband?"

Aurora smiled in response: "I do. I was married first to Maydon, who is the father of Barylos. After his death, I married Joslyn and Abbe's father, Serano, who is thankfully still alive."

"So, is he a sovereign too? Or a king or something?"

"He is not automatically a sovereign, no. However, a very special person. And certainly a king, but just of my heart." Sovereign Aurora rose to leave and held out a hand for Charli to rise also. "And now it is time for us to part, just for a time, and you will take Sean back to the creek so he can rejoin his world."

"What about me? Can I stay here?"

The sovereign didn't respond to this question but took Charli's hand and guided her back to the meeting area where the fairness test had taken place so that Charli could meet Sean there.

Aurora reassured Charli that they didn't need fond farewells, as she would probably be seeing her again very soon, and that helped Charli to feel more certain that she was welcome to stay in Q'ehazi once she had fulfilled her mission to accompany Sean.

Their reverie was abruptly terminated when Charli noticed a young White man running across the fields towards them. He was shouting something that was at first indistinct and became clearer as he came within a few yards: "Come quickly, come quickly. The man from the other world has been taken ill!" At this point, they heard a sound like a yodel from far away. The sovereign raised her head, listening intently to the sound, then took Charli urgently by the arm as she said silently, "It's the warning holler. We must get back as soon as we can."

All three moved swiftly towards the dining place. Charli spotted a small crowd of people gathered around Sean, who appeared to be lying on a stretcher. His whole body was racked by coughs. He was moaning, his face had turned a horrible shade of blue, and he kept repeating, "I can't breathe. I can't breathe. Get me out of here!"

Charli went up to him right away. Initially, she suspected him of malingering for attention, and all thoughts of forgiveness vanished: "What's the matter with you, Sean?" she demanded.

When he saw Charli, his expression turned to a pleading one she'd never witnessed before. "Oh, thank God you're here," he moaned. "I need to get home as soon as I can. I'm having an asthma attack," he attempted, between gasps. "I need my inhaler, fast."

He looked so genuinely distressed that Charli couldn't help feeling a pang of pity for him. "Okay, I'll take you," she agreed.

"You'll need some help," Sovereign Aurora announced. "He won't be able to walk, and he's too heavy for you to carry alone. I have asked my sister Maudina to accompany you." The older lady was dressed today in more practical garb than previously, and appeared ready to take on the arduous task of transporting the man on a stretcher across fields and through trees.

The sovereign turned to Charli and gave her a brief hug and a kiss on the cheek. "You will need to hurry now. Be well, my dear."

Charli felt so overwhelmed with all the activity and the flurry of emotions inside her that she couldn't respond but simply took one end of the stretcher while her companion took the other and made her way across the grass to the now-familiar path back to the tear.

CHAPTER FIFTEEN

Charli heard Maudina's laborious breathing behind her as both women heaved their heavy cargo
across the fields. She turned her head briefly and found that the
woman's face was red with exertion. "Do you want to rest a bit?"
she asked silently.

"Yes," Maudina agreed with relief. "I know you're in a hurry,
but I'm not as young as you, and this load is heavy." The two women
carefully set down the stretcher so as not to awaken its occupant,
who was now unconscious. They sat under the shade of an apple
tree for a few moments, listening to the birds and the babbling of
the nearby creek.

Maudina mopped her face with her colorful scarf. "This kind
of exercise is not something I'm used to," she admitted with a wry
grin. "It's normally dancing and yoga that keeps me fit. Which is
probably why Aurora thought it would be good for me."

"I'm sorry to put you through all this." Charli felt guilty that she
had caused so much pain to the Q'ehazi people by inadvertently
introducing this rogue element into their world. She wished she'd
created a different ending to her visit.

"I don't mind, really," said Maudina, putting her hand on the
girl's shoulder. "I wanted to have the chance to get to know you
better, anyway."

Charli smiled back. "I wanted to get to know you too. Actually,
it's really cool what you do. Analyze dreams? I don't know anybody
in my world who does anything like that. And I always wondered if

dreams weren't just random, you know? Like, they have a message or something, right?"

"I believe so, yes." Maudina sat in quiet reflection for a few moments before continuing. "I had a dream the other night that really did intrigue me. For the first time in my life, probably, I wasn't sure how to analyze it."

"So, what happened?" Charli had never met anyone willing to talk about such an esoteric topic, and she was thrilled to have this opportunity now.

"Well, I had the dream just before waking up in the morning, which is when we normally have what we call venting dreams—that is, dreams where the subconscious mind is letting go of unwanted emotions like fear and anger. By the way, if you ever have a nightmare just before you wake up in the morning, don't worry. It's not destined to come true; it's just your subconscious venting out unwanted or old fears and insecurities."

"Wow, that's amazing."

"Yes, our subconscious minds certainly are amazing fonts of knowledge, for sure. But this dream, while it was perhaps linked to some fear I have been harboring, the specific nature of it was something I've never before encountered."

"Go on," the girl encouraged.

"As you know, there is not much sickness here in Q'ehazi, because we have managed to almost completely eradicate most diseases due to our substantial knowledge and use of medicinal herbs and plants. So, the idea of a disease infecting a lot of our people is not even in my mind, or not in my conscious mind, anyway. And yet my dreaming mind conjured the idea that our world, the world of Q'ehazi, had been invaded by a terrible virus that was infecting people, and killing many of them, making them terribly ill, so that they died within days of being infected. I'm not sure if that is a symbol of something I am fearful of, or . . ." Here,

Maudina stopped, clearly taken aback by the look of shock and bewilderment on Charli's face. "What's wrong?"

"You dreamed about a virus killing people? That's nuts. That's exactly what really is happening. But in my world, not yours."

"Really? You mean, literally killing them?"

"Yes," Charli stated with urgency and passion. "And it's all over our world. It's what they call a pandemic. That means everybody in the whole entire world is in danger of being infected. It's literally killed . . . I don't know how many—certainly hundreds of thousands of people, and infected millions of people."

Maudina seemed overcome with a mix of emotions—grief, shock, fear—and took Charli into her arms. "You poor girl. No wonder you wanted to stay here. That's so terrible. I can't even imagine."

For a few minutes, the two women sat like that, comforting and reassuring each other. Maudina wanted to know if Charli herself had been infected by the virus, and she reassured her companion that she had not, but she knew of people who had, including her grandfather, and she herself was extremely careful in taking all precautions.

Charli was glad to make a new and close friend of this woman, who although she was a lot older than Charli, and probably the same age as her mother, had such a youthful spirit about her that Charli felt she was in the company of someone who could understand and empathize with her on a deep level.

After a few more minutes, they climbed to their feet and lifted their load, realizing that they only had a limited time before the rainstorm was due to appear.

About a half hour later, Charli felt the first drops of rain landing on her arms and began to walk faster and faster, urging Maudina along. The older woman was much stronger than she looked, though less concerned about the forthcoming rain. When the raindrops turned heavy and constant and a flood of water was unleashed upon them, the two women tried to shelter in various trees, but it was no good. The only recourse was to continue on.

Charli felt in her pocket that the packet Joslyn had given her had become loose, and some of the seeds were escaping. Desperate to reseal the packet and save as many seeds as possible, Charli pulled it out, attempting a delicate balancing act with the stretcher in her right hand as she fumbled with the packet in her left.

Because she was looking at her hands and not at the ground beneath her, she tripped on a loose branch and tumbled headfirst onto the grass. The packet flew out of her hands, and all of the seeds were dispersed on the ground. She and Maudina both dropped the stretcher now, and Sean groaned.

"Oh no, oh no, my seeds, my seeds!" Charli wailed, distraught. She couldn't bear to lose her precious seeds, which were the only tangible things she possessed of the Q'ehazi world. Despite the rain pelting her, she scrabbled around in the dirt, trying desperately to retrieve some. But because the sky had darkened during the rainstorm, and because the raindrops were large and heavy and impeded her vision, it was near impossible to see anything, let alone a small seed among leaves and branches.

"My dear, we must continue if we are to get to your world in time to save this young man," exhorted Maudina. Sean's whole body was contorted by racking coughs in confirmation.

"But my seeds," Charli moaned helplessly, the rain mingling with hot tears she couldn't staunch.

"We can give you more seeds another time. For now, we must go. There is only a short distance now."

Maudina was right. When Charli looked at Sean, she felt sorry for him. He looked small and beaten, and his face was red and puffy. Right now, the urgent needs of this man were more paramount than her own longings. Charli grabbed the stretcher again, and the two women hobbled the remaining steps to the creek.

By resting one hand on the trunk of the redbud tree and looking down and then up, she could induce the haze in front of her that told her she was entering the other dimension. Maudina was a little bemused to see how Charli accomplished this feat. She helped Charli gently remove Sean from his stretcher and prop him up against a tree trunk. At least here in Charli's world, the rain wasn't pelting them with heavy drops. The sun was shining, and it was a pleasant day, if a little warm.

But Charli couldn't ignore Maudina's breathless gasps, and she swiftly helped her friend carry the stretcher back through the tear into the Q'ehazi world. Charli thought again of the seeds scattered on the ground a few yards behind them. *Could I just go back?* she wondered, but then her eyes fell on Sean slumped unconscious by the tree, and she knew she didn't even have a few moments to spare.

She and Maudina hugged briefly, and Charli turned back, retreated through the tear, and left the world of Q'ehazi behind her. It all happened so fast that Charli couldn't even take in Maudina's sad and sympathetic expression as the woman said goodbye to her young friend.

Charli refused to think about what she'd sacrificed; the crisis at hand needed her full focus. She found Sean's cell phone in his pocket and used it to dial 911, then described their location in a voice shaky with fear and tiredness. Charli waited for the paramedics to arrive and told them as much as she could about Sean's symptoms, as he had again lost consciousness. They told her where they were taking him, and Charli walked across the fields back to her house. Behind her, the final fragments of the shawl drifted away on the wind.

It was only then that she realized the full extent of her circumstances now. With the seeds gone, she had lost all hope of ever going back to Q'ehazi. The tear would be sealed off, leaving nothing to connect her to the people in the other world. The pain in her heart was so overwhelming that she almost sank to the ground. Tears streamed down her cheeks. She would never see Abbe again, or the wonderful Sovereign Aurora, or Joslyn, who had stirred in her feelings she never expected to feel again for any living soul.

CHAPTER SIXTEEN

When Sean woke up, he had no idea where he was. As he slowly regained consciousness and looked around, he accurately guessed from the plain white walls, solitary airless window, and smell of disinfectant that he must be in a hospital. He tried to piece together the events leading up to this unfamiliar setting, as if they were fragments of a dream he was trying to remember. He did recall having a pretty bad asthma attack; being carried back home on a stretcher; huge raindrops falling on him; falling to the ground with a heavy thud that was painful to his back. Perhaps after that was when he'd lost consciousness.

But he was too tired now to give it much thought and just wanted to rest. He noticed tubes protruding from his arm, and a machine on his left beeped slowly. The tubes were hooked up to a bottle of liquid suspended on a metal tripod.

As Sean pondered these things, a young woman entered the room and came up to his bed with an air of efficiency. "How are you doing, Sean?" she asked as she adjusted the tubes and bottle of liquid. She was in her early twenties or thereabouts, African American, with large, dark eyes above her N95 mask and a tousle of curly black hair tied back from her face. Her voice was gentle and sympathetic.

Sean, however, was irritated by her presence. "What am I doing here?" he demanded. "And what the hell are you pumping into me here?"

The nurse was not fazed by his questions but answered him calmly.

"You had an asthma attack," she began.

"I know that, but it shouldn't have landed me in the hospital. All I need is my inhaler."

She looked at him intently now, as if she had significant information to impart. "You are very sick, Sean," she said solemnly. "It's not just asthma. That's a symptom, yes, but you need a lot more than an inhaler."

"What are you talking about?"

"You tested positive for COVID-19. We have you in for observation and monitoring, and we hope you don't get any worse because we only have four ICU beds in this hospital, and three of them are full already."

"Oh, come on, that hoax? What bullshit. I just have bad asthma, and sometimes it makes me cough." As if on cue, Sean started coughing. "I don't believe that virus crap on the fake news. It's no worse than the flu."

"Don't get upset; it'll make it worse," the nurse warned, gently persuading him back down on the bed as he tried to raise himself.

"I'll get upset if I want to. Don't tell me how to feel." At least, that was what Sean was trying to say, but now he was so racked by coughs that he could hardly get out the words, and he sank back. He was so overwhelmed by tiredness that it was easier just to lie down, although he longed to tell this girl what he thought about her advice.

The nurse sighed, wrote something in her ledger, exchanged the bottle for another new bottle of liquid, and left the room, realizing that she was in for another long day.

⊙ ⊙ ⊙

Charli breathed a sigh of relief when she arrived home after her mother had already left for her shift at Ingles. Now she'd have some time to herself to collect her thoughts before the inevitable interrogation she felt certain her mother had planned for her—not to mention her mother's reaction to learning Sean's whereabouts.

When Charli went up to her bedroom and saw that the history book the professor had given her had been dumped in the trash, being now almost entirely destroyed because of sitting open to the air for most of the day since she'd left it there, she felt so despondent that she openly wept. Charli's desolation was only heightened by her sense of responsibility for doing everything wrong. Not only had she lost the seeds, but she also hadn't been able to stop the disintegration of the stone Sean had taken; she had been unable to care for the shawl since Sean had left it outside of the glass bottle for too long; and now even the history book was lost to her because of her carelessness.

Thank God Charli had at least read the whole thing and remembered most of the information contained there. She knew she would never forget anything the Q'ehazi had ever told her, as it was burned in her memory as securely as any computer chip.

The girl slumped on her bed and allowed the tears to fall freely. She didn't have to put on an act for anyone. She was grieving the loss of so much—of the wonderful Q'ehazi world that she loved and to which she could never return; of her beautiful and wise friends, Aurora and Abbe and Joslyn; of the opportunity she had to live a better life and "attain a state of grace," as the sovereign had put it.

As Charli sniffed away the remaining tears and held her aching head in her hands, swinging her feet back and forth on the high bed, she mulled over this final thought. She had hoped to attain the state of grace necessary to remain in Q'ehazi, but perhaps she could try to attain it even in her own world. Surely it was still something to strive for, even if nobody understood the reasons why.

Suddenly, Charli felt dirty and sweaty. Getting clean always felt like beginning anew, so she pulled off her extremely muddy shoes and flung them into her closet without attending to them further; then she pulled off all her clothes and left them in a heap on her bedroom floor while she jumped into the shower and enjoyed the hot water coursing over her body, cleaning and refreshing her and giving her a renewed sense of optimism and hope.

She was even more energized to fulfill her ambition of becoming an epidemiologist. Everything she'd learned in Q'ehazi—their philosophical ideas and the practical application of their medical knowledge—Charli wished to bring back and utilize in her own world.

She had always had a desire to contribute to the world and a strong sense that society needed to be improved. She once believed that her intelligence was inherited from her father. Now when her mother claimed she was "just like her father," both in looks and personality, the words had a new and bittersweet meaning. While the biological father she had recently discovered did not have such a commendable past, the fact that he was part Cherokee—and passed his Native American blood to her—possibly explained why she had always felt different, as well as linking her to the Q'ehazi people, who were also descendants of native tribes from these lands. But Charli still felt close to Chuck Speranza, the man who had raised her and instilled in her a desire to make the world a better place.

When her mother arrived home from her night shift the following day, Charli was in much better spirits and felt surer of how to explain things to her mother so as to not give away any secret information about Q'ehazi while at the same time maintaining her innocence of any wrongdoing and being almost completely honest.

Angela was also in a better mood than usual when she arrived home. She kissed her daughter on the head and made herself a cup of coffee, then asked Charli to meet her in the living room when she was ready.

Charli smiled when she caught Angela watching one of her favorite TV shows, a romantic period drama.

"It's okay. I can turn this off," said Angela when her daughter entered. "Come sit." She patted the seat next to her on the couch, and Charli dutifully followed instructions.

"How are you, Mom?"

"Oh, you know. Tired, but okay. How about you?"

"Good," Charli replied noncommittally.

Angela gave her daughter a brief hug and was happy to notice that Charli didn't pull away but accepted the gesture of affection gratefully.

"You know, I worry about you sometimes."

"I know," Charli said.

Angela waited for her daughter to explain why she had disappeared the day before, then prompted her, "What has been going on?"

"It was Sean," admitted Charli.

"Sean?" Angela was genuinely surprised.

"They had to take him to the hospital."

"The hospital?! So that's where he is!" Things were becoming clearer now. *But why is Charli mixed up in it? She's never exactly been one of Sean's fans,* Angela wondered.

"He was suffering pretty bad."

"What's the matter? Is it something serious?"

"Pretty serious, I guess, yeah. He said he was having an asthma attack."

"What? He never even told me he had asthma."

"He was coughing up a storm. He was in a pretty bad way. I had to do something, so I called 911."

"Of course. It's a good thing you could help. I guess it's good that you were able to pay him back. After all, he found you after your accident and helped get you to the hospital; now you did the same for him."

Charli mused, "Yeah, I guess you're right, Mom. I hadn't thought about that."

"Where is he? Should I call the hospital?"

"They might let you visit him. I don't know what's happened since he's been there."

Angela patted her daughter on the shoulder. "You just impressed me tonight. My grown-up little girl; perhaps you'll be a doctor after all." She gave her daughter another hug, even more affectionate this time.

"It's not a regular doctor, Mom. It's an epidemiologist—"

"Yes, yes, I know. I always forget what you call it."

"Mom." Charli sucked in her breath while she pondered how to broach this topic with her mother. "I want to talk to you about Sean anyway."

"About Sean?" Angela sat back in her seat and folded her arms across her chest. "What is it, dear?"

"I know you think he's a good guy and all, and I guess he's not quite as bad as I thought, but I still don't think he's the guy you should be seeing—not forever, I mean."

"Sweetie, there's a lot of good in Sean. I think if you got to know him better, you could see that."

"Actually, I know Sean better than you think." Charli looked away momentarily.

Angela pursed her lips. Then she placed a hand on Charli's shoulder. "Honey, I know I don't have the best track record when it comes to guys—apart from your father, of course." Her daughter turned back to her. "I hope you won't make the same mistakes I did. I hope I've raised you to be brave and strong and to have self-esteem so that you never choose losers. But when it comes to my choices, I guess I just have to make them myself."

Charli suddenly felt moved to hug her mother close. She realized in that moment that it didn't matter what choices her mother made; Charli was free to live the life she chose, and that was all she was responsible for. She felt grateful that she could confide her, even if her mother didn't share those feelings or always understand where Charli was coming from. The fact that she could listen and validate Charli by taking her seriously was worth everything else.

Charli had often opined to her friends about how terrible it was to only have a mother and not a father, especially as she'd been "daddy's girl" up until he died and much closer to him both in looks and disposition. But now she realized how lucky she was. Charli had friends who'd suffered abuse at the hands of their parents, and she had never had to deal with anything like that. She'd had to be independent and strong and courageous and to take care of herself many times. But that had given her as much as it had taken from her. Perhaps, if she ever attained the state of grace, it would be because of the strength and wisdom she'd gained from the challenges she'd faced and overcome.

Charli decided in that moment that it was time to forgive her mother for the mistakes she'd made. Every human being made mistakes, and she recalled the old proverb "To err is human, to forgive divine." She'd already partly forgiven Sean, having seen the vulnerability and weakness under his mask of strength and power. And now it was time to forgive her mother, a woman who might be weak and make terrible choices sometimes but whose heart was in the right place and who was trying to do the best she could for her daughter.

There was one more thing Charli wanted to know, needed to know. "Is there anything you would leave him for, Mom? Something so terrible . . . ?" She let the question hang between them for a few seconds before her mother replied.

Angela didn't want to admit to Charli the spontaneous memories that had been flooding back since starting therapy: the shame, the embarrassment, the humiliation she'd been through, the lack of confidence in her own lived experience because of how her mother had invalidated her and stopped her speaking out.

Yet all of these things were present in her mind as she responded to Charli's question, knowing that the one thing she wanted was for her daughter to have a different experience than she'd had. Even if she couldn't protect Charli from all the bad things that could happen in the world, she could at least aim to be a role model for her daughter and forge a new path that would make it possible for Charli to defend herself. If Sean ever laid a hand on Charli like her own father had done to her, how could she ever forgive herself?

"If he ever laid a hand on you."

"But if he lays a hand on you, though, that's okay?"

"No, of course not."

"But he's done that, hasn't he? I've seen him do that." Charli couldn't stop her voice from rising as the injustice of it all rose up in her.

Angela started to say something, then pursed her lips, stopping herself.

Charli, emboldened by her mother's silence, continued: "I mean, you say you want me to respect myself, and I do. But what about you? Shouldn't you respect yourself first?" When Charli looked at her mother closely, she saw that her eyes were full of unshed tears. With a rush of affection, she hugged her mother closely as she whispered fiercely: "Swear you'll leave him if he hits you again. Say it, for me. Please!"

Slowly and silently, with the tears fresh on her cheeks, Angela nodded, and Charli's heart felt lighter than it had in months.

◉ ◉ ◉

Angela had been in hospitals before—mainly while visiting her elderly father-in-law or her mother when she'd been sick with hepatitis one time—and she still found them anxiety provoking and almost as scary as courtrooms. But she forced herself to visit

Sean, and she intended to demonstrate that there were no hard feelings about anything that had happened. Now that he needed her and was sick, she would take care of him.

The hospital visit was made even more challenging by having to wear a mask and gloves and "stay six feet away from the patient at all times." Even though Angela was aware of the new COVID restrictions, she had not been so directly exposed to the virus before. Like Charli, Angela had not immediately made the connection between Sean's illness and COVID, and she was shocked when the hospital staff told her he was being monitored closely to avoid transfer to their one remaining ICU bed, and she'd have to take precautions to stop further transmission of the disease.

When she saw Sean lying in the bed, unconscious of her arrival and weak and fragile, Angela's compassion increased. She felt guilty for thinking about leaving him, as though she had somehow betrayed his trust by speaking badly of him to her daughter, and she wanted to make it up to him. *I will be better*, she said to herself, *more understanding and patient.* Maybe with her tender love and affection, he would decide to drink less and therefore his moods would be less volatile.

She was not allowed to sit by his bedside and stroke his hand as she had wished, but still she could envision happier days ahead with Sean and Charli and everyone getting along, just like the family she longed to regain, and a tender smile spread across her face.

The smile disappeared slowly as another woman marched into the room with a small boy. Both were also masked, and it was therefore difficult to see the woman's expression clearly, but her body language conveyed surprise to find another visitor in the room with Sean. The woman wore uncomfortable-looking high heels, and a short skirt, which seemed incongruous in that sterile hospital setting. Angela noticed all these things and with a woman's intuition became instantly aware that this woman was more than just a friend to Sean.

"Who are you?" the woman demanded in a voice strained with tension.

"Angela," she responded simply, not knowing what else to say.

"I guess you're his new girlfriend, huh?" The woman's eyes over the mask showed skepticism. "Huh, that asshole."

"What?" Angela was surprised that the woman would use such language in front of her young child, but the boy seemed unaffected.

"This is what he always does. Disappears on me—and Dylan here." She indicated the boy, who looked mournful and shamefaced. "And shacks up with some new chick without even telling anyone."

Angela felt her stomach drop but tried hard not to show it. "And I could ask who you are."

The woman gave a harsh bark of laughter. "Yeah, you could," she responded. "I'm Sean's wife, Bobbie, and this is his son. I guess he never told you about us, right?"

Angela was so shocked that she could only shake her head in reply.

"He owes me child support, which is why I'm here. Not to pay the bastard a courtesy call." The woman shoved the child forward. "Go on, Dylan. Say hello to your dad. Even though it looks like he won't recognize you anyway." The boy complied reluctantly with his mother's demands, moving a few inches closer to the bed before darting a sheepish glance at Angela.

Angela started to gather her things with trembling hands.

"I'd better go," she said in a quiet voice.

"Yeah, I guess you better had," agreed the woman with a smirk in her voice.

Once out of the room, Angela breathed a metaphorical sigh of relief that surprised even her. She was relieved not to have to deal with that confrontational woman any longer, and she was very relieved that she had been prevented from acting on the impulse to make more of an effort with Sean. Now she knew for a fact that Charli's suspicions about him had been correct, and with this new information, she was better able to let go of him forever, let go of her unrealistic and toxic dreams, and face the reality that she was raising Charli on her own.

With a calm fortitude that was uncharacteristic, Angela drove home and packed up all of Sean's things, trying not to think too much about events that had transpired, as that would throw her off her goal of merely accomplishing this task. Then she picked up the phone and called the only other person she knew who was close to Sean, his friend Martin. In a firm but quiet voice, Angela told Martin that he could come and collect Sean's things from her front porch (since she was now quarantining) and let Sean know that he was no longer welcome in her house.

Martin sounded unshocked by this and agreed to come and collect his friend's clothes and other belongings. Perhaps he felt a little guilty for not having defended Angela before when he'd witnessed violence towards her. In any case, she was grateful that this chapter in her life was now over.

⊙ ⊙ ⊙

When Sean woke up again in the hospital bed, the first thing he felt was annoyance bordering on rage, partly because he hadn't had any alcohol for at least two days, which was a state his body wasn't used to, and partly because he was still harboring significant resentment over a phone conversation he'd had with Martin the last time he'd been awake.

Martin had called to tell him Angela was kicking him out and that Sean was not welcome to stay with Martin for any longer than a few days. Sean's sense of grievance at this betrayal by his "best friend" was overwhelming, and he raised himself on one arm to see if he had the strength to get out of bed.

Sean immediately spotted a face he almost didn't recognize, partly because the man was wearing a mask and partly because it had been so many years since he'd seen him—his brother, Bill.

"How are you, buddy?" Bill leaned into him. His eyes above the mask registered concern, though it was difficult to tell whether he was smiling.

"Okay, I guess." Sean's voice came out raspy, and he cleared his throat. "What are you doing here?" Realizing how this might sound, he added, "I mean, it's good to see you, brother."

"I came up from Florida a week ago, but they didn't let me see you till you got out of ICU."

"I was in ICU?" Sean looked around the room. He knew he'd been in the hospital for a while, but in intensive care? He tried to move his arms and legs a little. Everything felt old and creaky. He hated feeling so feeble. "Oh man, I feel about ninety-two right now."

Bill laughed briefly. "Now you know what it's like to be old," he teased, reasserting his status as older brother.

"How did you know I was here?" This was the last visitor he'd expected. Angela, maybe, or Martin, perhaps Bobbie making good on her threats to come after him for money after he'd left her and the kid, but not Bill.

"The hospital called me. I'm your nearest relative, apparently. You'll have to tell me what happened with Bobbie. At any rate, the hospital told me you were in a bad way. I'll have to quarantine after this visit, but I figured it was worth it, to see my only brother."

"Did you talk to . . . anybody else?"

"Nope. I don't know who your friends are these days, do I?"

"I guess not," Sean replied a little mournfully, reflecting on the fact that his brother had come through for him in the end, better than anybody else he thought was his friend. "Do you know how long I've got to stay here?"

"Well, you don't look all that great to me, but the doctor said the hospital was going to release you tomorrow. Seems like your insurance has run out, even if you wanted to stay."

"Shit!" Sean realized the full implications of his brother's words. Where did he have to go back to? Since he'd been shacking up with Angela, he'd let go of the expensive apartment that cost him too much money. He knew Bobbie would no longer have anything to do with him, and he didn't really have any other friends in the area to crash with now that Martin had told him he couldn't stay there long term.

He felt tired, more tired than he'd ever felt before, as if he'd been fighting something his whole life; he wanted to put down the sword and just accept that the world wasn't the place he wanted it to be.

"Hey, brother." Bill's voice interrupted Sean's reverie. "You can come home with me."

"You're out of rehab?"

Bill scoffed. "Jesus! I wrote to you about it, and texted and called but never got a reply. I got out of rehab a year ago now. I've been doing really well. Got myself an apartment and a job, been seeing a nice woman. Really turned my life around. I was hoping maybe somebody might be proud of me. My little brother, at least, since you're all I've got left now." Bill had gotten up and was pacing around the small hospital room.

"I *am* proud of you. That's great!" Sean remembered how emotional Bill could get. It was partly the reason Sean had moved away, wanting to avoid all the drama. Nevertheless, Bill was always loyal, always heartfelt, and always there for him, even if Sean had repudiated his efforts to reach out.

"Why didn't you answer my letter? Or my phone calls? Jeez, that was heartless, man!"

"Look, I'm sorry, I— You know what I'm like."

"Yeah, right."

"I started dating this lady."

"Bobbie told me you'd left your apartment. Nobody even knew where you'd gone."

"I wanted to start over."

"You're always starting over, Sean. And it never seems to change anything."

Sean sighed. "I know. You're right."

Bill had not expected this answer and was bracing himself for an argument. He considered that maybe Sean's sickness made him less combative than usual. His tone softened. "I wanted to reach out. I wanted to let you know that we could be close again."

Sean grabbed his hand. "Thanks, brother. I mean it."

"Come home with me. Where else can you go anyway?"

"Where are you?"

"In Florida. Back at the old place."

"You mean . . . ?"

"Yeah, back in Jacksonville. Got an apartment close to work."

"What are you doing?"

"Just construction again. But the real estate market's hopping down there. You'd be amazed."

"Even in the pandemic?"

"Even *more* in the pandemic. People still gotta live somewhere, right?"

"Wow."

"And working in construction ain't bad. You're outside, you can do your own thing, the hours are flexible."

"Have you got room for me?"

"Sure. It's a two-bed. Apartments are cheap. Not like this fancy-dancy place."

Sean laughed. "I know, Weaverton, right?"

"You don't belong here, kid. Come home. I'll take care of you."

All of a sudden, Sean felt a wetness around his eyes. It was such an unfamiliar feeling that at first he wondered what was happening to him. Ever since his dad had hit him and told him, "I'll give you something to cry about," Sean had never let anybody see him cry. Something had definitely changed inside him now, but he didn't know how or why.

"Jeez, bro, I thought *I* was supposed to be the emotional one," Bill said, leaning over and offering Sean a tissue.

"Must be the meds I'm on," Sean quipped in muffled tones as he wiped his eyes and nose. "Seriously, though, I appreciate this. I really do."

The brothers hugged, as much as they could with Sean lying prone in a hospital bed and Bill masked up. It was the closest thing they'd gotten to a reconciliation. Sean realized, for the first time in a very long time, the value of family.

But resentment stirred towards the people who had let him down: his so-called friend Martin; the people he'd met while living in North Carolina who had professed to like him; and, most of all, Angela, who had suddenly and unfairly—in his opinion—rejected him when he needed her the most.

He vowed that as soon as he got settled in with his brother, he'd find a way to contact her again and let her know that he was not the sort of guy that could be tampered with; a vision of Arnold Schwarzenegger declaring "I'll be back" entered his mind, and he imagined saying those words to her in a threatening voice and her cowering in response. The vision made him smile.

CHAPTER SEVENTEEN

Two weeks later—when they thought they had finally put bad news behind them, what with the removal of Sean from their lives and Angela being freed from quarantine—Charli and her mother got the phone call they had been dreading for a long time. It was from the nursing home where Grandpa Speranza had been placed in hospice care a month earlier. Charli was grateful that she and her mother had the opportunity to say goodbye, even if only over Zoom, since the doctors were convinced his time was near. It was hard to hide her devastation at the amount of loss piling up.

"Not this too!" she couldn't help whisper-screaming as her mother told her the news. A pain in her heart constricted her breathing. How could she manage without Q'ehazi, without Abbe, without Aurora, without Joslyn, and now without Nonno? Charli tried to push the pain away long enough to put on a brave face. She didn't even cry as the video call connected and she saw the once strong and now frail body lying on his hospital bed, surrounded by tubes and monitors that signaled his impending passing.

After a few minutes, Angela intuited that her daughter needed to say goodbye to her grandfather alone, so she crept out of the room, mumbling something about making coffee. Now that Charli was alone with her grandfather, she longed to stroke his hand. She settled for looking deeply into his wise old eyes as he gazed back at her. His voice was feeble and cracked, but his eyes still held a fierce strength, and his tone was insistent: "Little one, Tesoro, remember I will always be with you in spirit."

"Yes, I know, Nonno," replied Charli, even though she didn't really believe his words.

"No need to be sad. Your life will be full and long. I'm proud of you." He lifted a fragile, wrinkled hand, and she imagined him gently patting her on the arm.

The words flew out of her mouth without forethought: "Something happened to me, Nonno. Something miraculous."

Nonno didn't seem surprised but regarded her calmly. "What was that, sweetheart?"

Charli leaned into the microphone and almost whispered, "I found this other world. It exists alongside this one."

Perhaps because he was so close to death that anything seemed possible, Nonno accepted this without demur or question, simply asking: "Is it a beautiful world?"

"Oh yes!" Charli exclaimed, wanting to tell her grandfather all about Q'ehazi but lacking the words to describe just how beautiful it was.

"This world is beautiful too, you know. You just have to look closely." The corners of the old man's mouth curved into a faint smile.

"Sure, I know." Charli didn't want to admit that she disagreed.

"Whatever world you're in, being good to others is what is important." The words came out slowly and with some difficulty, but Nonno was determined to pass along this information.

"Yes, yes, I know, Grandpa." Tears filled the corners of Charli's eyes as she recognized that these might be the last words she heard from him, and she wiped them away quickly, hoping he hadn't seen. "I'm doing my best. Actually, I think I learned a lot. You know, I used to hate Sean—mom's boyfriend—but then I realized he's just a guy and he's not all bad, and I helped him."

"That's good, Tesoro. You did the right thing."

"Really?" Charli was genuinely surprised. "But I thought you hated Sean too."

Nonno gave a brief chuckle. "Well, he's not my favorite person, that's for sure. But I don't hate him, no. I didn't think he's the best choice for your mom to replace your dad. But that's her decision to make."

"Right," Charli agreed.

"No matter what another person is like, you can always make the choice to be a good person. That's the main thing."

Charli felt overcome with emotion as she reflected on what a good person her grandfather was, and how wise he was, almost as wise as Sovereign Aurora. Now that she was about to lose both of these important people in her life, her eyes filled with tears again, and this time she couldn't stop them flowing.

Now her grandfather said something she didn't understand in the moment, but later on, it became clear to her: "When I go, you will know. I'll always be with you."

At that moment, Angela came back into the room with a mug of coffee, and the two women sat by the computer for another hour or so, until they could see that he had drifted off to sleep.

◉ ◉ ◉

Charli went to bed that night feeling drained from all the crying she'd been doing. Her mother had allowed her privacy, knowing that the girl needed to grieve alone.

At around seven the next morning, Charli was awakened by the distant sound of a rooster crowing on the farm about a mile away. She felt uncharacteristically alert, and she got immediately out of bed and drew the curtains, pleased to see a beautiful, early-summer day just beginning, with the sun peeking over the horizon. Charli rarely got up earlier than she absolutely had to, but this morning she felt the urge to fling on some clothes and head out into the back garden. She took her cell phone with her, just in case of an urgent call or message.

Once outside, Charli stood for a few moments, taking in the beautiful scene: the curve of the mountains and their varying shades of blue and green; the sounds of the birds with their different calls and songs; the fresh smell of the earth. Everything was vivid to her senses, as it had been in Q'ehazi when she'd first visited that world. Charli turned her head at a sound to her side, and she saw a beautiful bluebird sitting on a branch. He lifted his head and sang a full-throated song that seemed aimed just at her. At that moment, Charli felt a rush of something like bliss that passed through her in a wave. She opened the phone camera and took a picture of the little bird, silently thanking it for providing her with such a great photo opportunity. Then she wandered back into the house to make coffee.

Angela was already in the kitchen preparing breakfast. About ten minutes later, when the landline rang, Angela answered, and what she heard made all the color drain from her face. Once she hung up, Charli intuitively knew what she had to say. "Your grandfather passed."

Charli's lip began to tremble, and she went to her mother and hugged her. "When did it happen?"

"Just now. Well, about ten minutes ago."

The two women commiserated and gradually were able to function well enough to start taking care of the practical business surrounding the death of Angela's father-in-law.

Because she was so taken up with these necessities, it wasn't until later that day that Charli realized something miraculous had happened. She had gone out into the garden and taken the photograph of the bluebird about ten minutes before the phone call. Nonno must have passed at the exact moment she was taking the photograph. Her grandfather loved taking photographs; Charli remembered how thrilled he'd been when she gave him a digital camera. He'd always loved birds and was particularly fond of bluebirds. He had told her, "When I go, you will know," and now she realized the implication of those words. She now knew that his spirit had passed through her on his way to the other side, or wherever he had gone.

Charli felt overjoyed that she'd been able to feel her grandfather's spirit in this way. Perhaps that also meant she could find a way to communicate with the people in Q'ehazi, since they all were able to communicate without speaking aloud. Maybe her own abilities to connect on this level were becoming enhanced. She wasn't sure, but she was incredibly grateful for this final gift her grandfather had given her, and for the message that his soul persisted, and he would always be with her in some form.

◉ ◉ ◉

Several months later, as Angela cleaned out Charli's closet in preparation for her daughter's return to in-person classes at school for the fall semester, she discovered the pair of shoes Charli had been wearing the last time she went to Q'ehazi—flung haphazardly into the back of the closet and forgotten about. Angela wrinkled her nose in disgust at the amount of soil and dirt embedded in the underside of the shoes. There was even a green shoot protruding from one of them; something had started to grow in there.

Ordinarily, she would have cleaned the shoes herself, but she felt that her daughter really needed to start taking responsibility for her own items, especially in this case, where her carelessness and laziness had caused the whole closet to smell musty and dirty. She harangued her daughter and ordered her to clean up her room—and especially the dirty shoes—immediately.

Charli was at first annoyed with her mother for being so peremptory, but she followed instructions, not wishing for a confrontation. She found the offending footwear lying on a plastic bag on the floor in her bedroom. With a small thrill of discovery, Charli noticed the green shoot, and her excitement only grew as she took the shoe into the light to examine it.

Yes! It was one of the seeds she had dropped on the ground inside Q'ehazi. *It must be!* Because it had been locked away inside her dark closet and out of the toxic air, it had actually sprouted on the side of her shoe and was now about an inch tall. Very, very carefully, Charli extricated the tiny shoot from her shoe and, finding a small plant pot in the shed, transplanted the seedling and filled the pot with soil, hoping fervently that the seedling would be able to grow outside its native atmosphere.

Since the shawl was destroyed, Charli had brought back the glass bottle and kept it in her room, both as a memento and a reminder of her adventure. Now she took the bottle out of the cupboard where it had been stored for the past few months, dusted it off, removed the lid, and placed it upside down on top of the tiny seedling in its tiny pot, forming a protective shield. As the seed grew and outgrew its pot and its barrier, Charli planned to create a small greenhouse or enclosure that would help the plant survive until it had grown into a fully formed tree such as the ones she had seen in Q'ehazi.

Later that day, Charli took a drive in the new car she had diligently earned over the summer by working at a local café where they served customers outside. She headed up the Blue Ridge Parkway to witness the beautiful fall colors creeping across the mountainside.

She reflected on many things as she gazed out over an abundance of red, yellow, and green, lost in her thoughts. She thought about how her grandfather had told her he would always be with her in spirit, and how he had passed through her on his way to the other side; she mused on the fact that she had already experienced similar instances where she could "feel" her friends in

Q'ehazi communicating with her psychically, in the same way they had "spoken" to her in Q'ehazi itself.

Charli contemplated the beauty of her world, and how it had always been here and was at times unsurpassed by the beauty she'd seen in the Q'ehazi world—once she learned how to really see and appreciate it. She thought of how she felt good about having helped Sean, even though neither her mother nor she had heard from him since he'd left for Florida to live with his brother. She thought about how her relationship with her mother had improved ever since she had made the effort to understand and empathize with her mother's needs.

Charli remembered Joslyn telling her about the Q'ehazi seeds, and how they usually took around ten years to grow into a tree that could form its own seeds. She remembered how he had tended to the man who visited his clinic with leaves from the very same plant. And she thought of what a miracle it was that one of the seeds had been saved—just one, but that was all she needed. Once the seed grew into a tree and was planted in the ground, she could harvest new seeds that not only would help her get back into Q'ehazi but also might help people in her world to overcome diseases.

She recognized everything that her visit to Q'ehazi had given her and was grateful. And in ten years' time, when she was a full-fledged adult with some achievements of her own, perhaps she would be ready to go back to Q'ehazi. Maybe by then she would have achieved the coveted "state of grace" that enabled her to live there forever. Or maybe she would change her own world, even if only in some small way, to make it better and more like the Q'ehazi world she loved so much.

Perhaps this was only a utopian dream. Well, if it was, she wished to stay in it forever. Better than the dystopian nightmare forming across the globe. It seemed like everybody around her, in her world, had lost faith in everything—in institutions, the government, other people, and even the nature of truth itself. Charli was lucky to glimpse another way of being, a way that seemed to flow effortlessly, where everything seemed right and honest and true. Could her world be this way as well, if certain changes were made? Charli didn't know. But she did know that she had the will and the youth and the energy to try.

In any case, Charli could see the world of possibilities opening up for her as she stood in the Blue Ridge Mountains, taking in all the beauty at the age of sixteen and a half, with her whole life ahead of her, visualizing what the future could hold.

APPENDICES

APPENDIX 1

The Qehazi Game:
The Game Where Everybody Wins

WHAT THE GAME TEACHES THE PLAYERS

- To the Q'ehazi people, the notion of competition means using the energy of each other's performance to enhance one's own; it does not imply that we should crush our opponents or try to win at any cost.

- When we choose to gain at the expense of another person, we are not operating at optimum efficiency. The Q'ehazi believe that survival of the individual at the expense of the whole threatens the survival of the whole—which incidentally includes the individual.

- Symbiosis, which is the assembly of individuals based on mutually beneficial relationships, is a major driving force behind evolution.

- Life did not take over the globe by combat but by networking.

- The old way: I win, you lose. You win, I lose. The new way: Transcendence happens when the problem is solved by avoiding it entirely. Compromise, and each person wins by agreeing to lose a little. Transcendence produces a resolution above and beyond the problem.

- There is a value to interdependence, and everybody has an important role to play. Some analogies and metaphors are as follows: a machine where all parts need to work in order for the machine to operate; a play where all players are necessary, from the bit parts to the leading roles; if a boat is crossing the ocean and encounters a storm, everybody needs to pull together in order to make it.

- Money is not the most valuable commodity to acquire. The gold stars or karma cards are most valuable because they demonstrate what you have truly achieved in the life of the game. You only acquire these things by giving away things or performing good deeds to help others.

GAME FORMAT PLAYED WITH CARDS

- Each card has a standard logo, a large *Q*, on one side and is part of a beautiful picture on the other side, with a small space for text.

- The aim is to put down all the cards in the rectangle format.

- The cards make the "board." There's one set of cards that you lay down to make the board in a sort of interlocking jigsaw. On the underside, they are part of one large picture, and each card also has some text that gets revealed when you turn over the card.

- Players move around the spiral by throwing dice, and when they land on a card, they overturn it to reveal the message. They pick up and keep that card, so gradually the spiral disappears to be replaced by the rectangle, which makes up the finished picture.

- When you pick up a card, you sprinkle some of your colored seeds in that space; this is how you "give back." So, the person who takes the most cards also gives the most, in the form of seeds.

- The game has sixty-four cards and does not take very long to play: no more than two hours for up to four players. It can also be playable by young children because it's fairly simple in format.

- Each player plays one of the four primary colors and holds the seeds and the origami figure of that color. Players make their own origami figures from the tissue paper. Use these as player markers.

- The object is to plant as many seeds as possible. There is a finite amount of seeds, so it is advisable to maintain a balance between too many and too few seeds every time you play. You can't win if you have any seeds left; you must have planted all your seeds.

- The cards are standard sized and come in a plastic bag within a drawstring cloth bag. There is also the instruction booklet; tissue paper in four colors for making up the origami player counters; a set of dice; and colored dots in four primary colors, which are the "seeds."

- Shuffle the cards first and lay them randomly from the center outwards to form a spiral shape. The middle card has a heart design. Because there are eight cards to a standard sheet of cards, it takes eight sheets to make each game.

- Players have to keep picking up the cards until all the cards are gone from the spiral. If you land in a space with no card, you cannot pick up anything. If you run out of seeds, you may borrow seeds from another player, but this will make it more difficult for you to be the winner.

- Everybody wins because everybody has planted some seeds throughout the game and has contributed towards making up the board.

- The sixty-four cards get laid out into a rectangle by all the players, constructing a beautiful picture. Cards are numbered and in pairs of crisis/opportunity, where two players must match their two cards in order to add them to the final design. So, it's a truly collaborative game. The game only ends when the design is complete and all the cards have been overturned from the first spiral and laid down in the final design.

- The winner could be either the person who happens to lay down the final card or the person who has sprinkled the most colored seeds on the spiral.

- The captions with CRISIS and OPPORTUNITY are written in small letters at the bottom of each card so they're not too obtrusive to the final design, which is best viewed from a distance.

- The winner gets to do something nice for the other players— that's their prize (similar concept to when it's your birthday and you are the one who buys everybody else a drink or a meal).

- When you pick up a card, you read it out so the others know and have the opportunity to match one of their cards with yours.

- Cards must be played in pairs only. You have to help each other in order for everybody to win and the game to end.

Some examples for the cards appear below. Regular players of the game are typically expected to make up their own situations and cards before playing. That way, their own lifestyles can be taken into account, and they engage their own creative process towards constructing the game.

Eventually, there should be thirty-two challenge cards and thirty-two matching opportunity cards. Here are some potential challenge and opportunity captions:

1. You develop a rare skin condition. C

2. You discover a cure for a rare skin condition. O

3. You get lost while wandering in the wilderness. C

4. While wandering in the wilderness, you discover a beautiful fountain. O

5. You lose touch with a dear friend. C

6. Your dear friend from long ago finds and contacts you. O

7. You break your leg and are laid up for six months. C

8. While laid up for six months, you complete an artistic project. O

9. You forget something very important. C

10. You remember something very important. O

11. Your car breaks down and needs major repairs. C

12. You barter your services to an auto mechanic. O

13. You are unemployed and looking for a job. C

14. Your volunteer work leads to a great career opening. O

15. You are lonely and looking for love. C

16. You meet a wonderful potential partner through a friend. O

17. You are bored with life and stuck in a rut. C

18. You are invited to travel somewhere exciting. O

19. You have split up with your boyfriend/girlfriend and are feeling blue. C

20. Someone invites you out dancing and you discover a new passion. O

21. You can't seem to stop eating too much. C

22. You get sick and lose a lot of weight. O

23. You love playing tennis but keep losing. C

24. By practicing regularly, you improve your tennis game significantly. O

APPENDIX II

THE Q·EHAZI STORY

The long history of an oral tradition that preserves the stories of the Q'ehazi people means that we are able to trace back our ancestry to almost the dawn of civilization. We know with relative certainty that a few people from one tribe migrated from the far south to the islands close to the equator around the time of Jesus's birth. These were the Arawaks, who settled and lived in harmony for many centuries, mostly deriving their living from fishing and harvesting small crops of the abundant tropical fruits, such as coconuts, mangoes, plantain, breadfruit, etc.

In the early 1500s, however, the warlike Caribs invaded these islands, and many of the peaceful Arawaks were slaughtered. A small band managed to escape and headed north, where they settled on the shores of the northerly continent we now know as Pacifica, which stretched from the Atlantic coast in the east to the Pacific coast in the west and was a vast and untapped land, at that time inhabited by many diverse native tribes.

These Arawaks settled and formed a new life in these more northerly climes. As they were on the coast, they continued using their skills at fishing and harvesting crops, although the food they planted changed to vegetables such as corn, sweet potatoes, and yams. The most important thing the Arawaks brought with them was the seed of their culture, which was one of peace and harmony and a respect for all living things. Gradually, as they merged with the peoples of the area they now inhabited, they began to adopt new customs while maintaining some of their own.

With this, they formed a new peoples, and they called themselves the Q'ehazi, which is an old Arawak term meaning "peace" or "harmony." They lived in what they called a *maca bana,* which is their word for "tree dwelling." The Q'ehazi also began using a local herb called pukatl, which came from a local tree. This herb enabled them not only to survive disease and maintain optimum levels of emotional stability but also to calm any visitors or interlopers who attempted to conquer them or corrupt their way of life. The use of this herb on a regular basis, coupled with a societal system that valued community over individualism, taught a respect for all nature, and managed and controlled both procreation and child-rearing, forming the basis for the successful and gradual growth of the Q'ehazi people into what we are today—a flourishing and thriving society and economy where all members are able to live a harmonious and happy life.

One of the main challenges the Q'ehazi faced early on was a small band of English would-be colonists who arrived on a ship, led by Sir Walter Raleigh, in 1563. For some months, the future of the Q'ehazi tribe—at that time relatively new to the area and lacking in substance or population—hung in the balance, as the incoming settlers could have provided either a threat or a benefit to them. But ultimately, the two groups recognized that they both would profit from living together in harmony, rather than one group attempting to control the other.

The Europeans brought with them skills related to metal production, writing and mathematics, and systems of government; the natives possessed skills related to their lifestyle, such as fishing and harvesting crops and the mining of gems, as well as information about their local plants that were good for eating, growing, and harvesting; also their medicinal herbs, which healed all sorts of ailments; the local animals and flora and fauna; and their type of religion, which was really a form of nature deity. The people intermarried and became as one. After several generations, they were indistinguishable.

This new and more developed tribe successfully infiltrated and influenced all of the other tribes, eventually "taking over" the entire continent—but with their ideas, and not by force. Their ideas were so powerful and persuasive that others wished to follow them. Life was good for the Q'ehazi, and others wished to live as well as we did. When warring tribes attacked, the Q'ehazi people turned them around with love and peaceful means. "Love always wins over hate and fear" is one of our favorite mottoes.

In the 1700s, other travelers heard about the success of the Q'ehazi society and started coming to Pacifica's shores—not only from Europe and Asia but also from Africa. The Q'ehazi people welcomed everyone, no matter their ethnicity or color, so long as they were committed to maintaining the peaceful and harmonious society they had entered. These travelers were given absolute citizenship in exchange for helping build infrastructure and contributing in whatever way they could. They also had total rights to intermarry with the Q'ehazi people and create an even stronger blend of racial characteristics.

All of the cultures weaved together, and the best parts of them were absorbed into the Q'ehazi society so that it became like a strong and colorful blend of cloth. The Q'ehazi had a way of representing this visually and passed this down through the generations: a sacred ceremonial shawl woven of many colors was worn by many women in Q'ehazi society as a symbol of their recognition of the rich cultural tapestry they had inherited.

The Q'ehazi culture believes it is stronger when it adapts. The original mission is never forgotten, which incorporates ideas such as "all human beings are created equal," and which are contained in the original Q'ehazi manifesto, written in the 1600s and adhered to ever since. (This original document is kept in a safe place and can be viewed by modern-day descendants and visitors.)

In the twenty-first century, this is the history on which the Q'ehazi rests.

Q·EHAZI CULTURE AND SOCIETY

Our modern Q'ehazi people are a blend of many races and ethnicities. Some of us have dark skin, and some have pale skin. Many women choose not to have children, as they have multiple opportunities to express themselves in other ways. For the women who do wish to become mothers, parents are encouraged to raise only enough to replace themselves. We believe that things like intelligence, empathy, and moral character are the most important attributes a person can demonstrate. We believe in quality over quantity.

Our current sovereign is regarded with great respect because of the quality of her character and her personality, which has shaped her into a state of grace. It takes a huge amount of hard work and dedication to become a sovereign, so it's not a job everyone is suited to or even wants to have. There is power, but there is also great responsibility and a lot of hard work. The sovereign is a lot more than just a figurehead.

The sovereign often acts as a mediator/therapist/doctor, and people go to her with their problems. The sovereign makes herself available to people for many hours each day, and she works very hard. If she's not available, she has surrogates, called "elders," she has trained who also talk to people about their problems. All Q'ehazi people love, trust, and revere the sovereign. We do not have separate tribes with separate customs, because we are all are governed by the sovereign.

The Q'ehazi use things like herbs and dreams to help us solve problems. We all become involved in our own health in a very proactive and preventive manner. Our people are taught to listen to their own bodies. Meditation and dream analysis are an important part of everyday life. Children practice meditation from an early age. Our peaceful nature is encouraged in this manner. There is an institute for dreams analysis, and it is a morning ritual to discuss dreams from the night before and obtain whatever messages they impart.

Aspects of society such as justice, mental health, and physical health are all linked and dealt with in much the same way. It is recognized that mental health problems can lead to both physical health problems and behavioral problems that lead to acting out negatively and breaking laws. So, there is an inextricable link between all three of these things. They are also tied to good parenting. The whole village gets involved with parenting; it is not left up to just one or two parents, who may or may not do a decent job of raising the child. The child is imbued with all of the values of the society, right from the start. Religion is also tied to the above; if a child has a good concept of right and wrong, good and bad, it will tend to not have behavioral problems that can instigate emotional problems, and vice versa. A strong belief system helps the child to develop a conscience and also a faith that good will prevail.

Stories act as inspiration for good behavior. In the stories, the good person always wins out, and love always conquers hate in the end. There's a big emphasis on live performance and artistic and creative self-expression. Everybody does something creative.

Some people spend their whole lives as storytellers (actors, writers, singers, etc.), and their work is valued as much as those who work in the fields harvesting food, etc. Every type of work is valued equally, as it is all work. If a person does not wish to work, it is up to the elders to figure out why, not punish them. Work is regarded as something good and sacred that everybody should wish to do, so long as they are doing the job they are best at.

For the news of the day, Q'ehazi people use a town-crier system, where one person is designated to tell the latest stories every day from the main square. Most individual communication is done through extrasensory perception, by tuning into the other person's thoughts. However, when there is a large group of people gathered together, words are spoken aloud. Our accent, it is said, is derived from a unique blend of Old English from Geoffrey Chaucer's time and the original dialect of the natives that inhabited these lands for thousands of years.

Our clothes tend to be very functional, colorful, and comfortable, as well as attractive, though there is no value placed upon things like "style" or "fashion."

The Q'ehazi people all play the game where everybody wins (outlined in appendix I).

In some ways, our society operates similarly to a tribal one. The Q'ehazi are very aligned with nature. We talk to trees, plants, mountains, rocks, and animals. All of the trees have names and are often grouped into families. Most people grow their own vegetables on small farms, and there is a complex barter system where everybody gets everything they need. People also raise chickens, pigs, cows, and fish, etc.

However, we embrace technology and have developed complex systems that work for us. Electricity is all powered by solar and wind energy. Q'ehazi people use computers and phones to access information and to communicate. We have already visited several other planets and have a flourishing space research program.

We have learned how to control the weather so that both the crops and the people are always satisfied. The temperature ranges from sixty to eighty degrees year-round. It is mostly sunny with a few high clouds, and it rains every day from 3 to 3:30 p.m., quite heavily, and then is over. There is plenty of water for the plants, and people know to stay sheltered during the rainstorm.

We therefore don't need to construct many buildings. We have small treehouses for our daily needs, and we sleep in hammocks in the trees. Most of our possessions are owned communally anyway, so there's no need for personal property. We live in small villages of around 150 people. For larger gatherings, we have longhouses, which also house large extended families within the village.

Transport is all done on a conveyor-belt system that travels at a steady speed of 25 mph so it's easy to get on or off via ramps. There are seats along one side, or you can walk along the conveyor belt if you wish to get to your destination faster. The conveyor belt stops running at night.

The computers, etc., are also communal. There are special places where you can access the internet. On the whole, it's a very communal society, but if somebody wishes to be alone, they can go off into the wilderness by themselves.

SYSTEM OF GOVERNMENT

In the Q'ehazi world, you have to attain a state of grace to hold any position of power. You can attain this state in a number of ways. You can demonstrate that you are a good person through acts of good such as volunteering and helping others. And/or you can make great works of art, such as through painting, writing, acting, singing, music, dance. Other forms of art and creativity are recognized as well, such as cooking, gardening, and building.

The system we live under is commonly called not government but rather "leadership." It is a privilege to be a public servant in this way; you are not paid for it (there's no money), and you don't have a lot of power, but you do command respect. Nevertheless, it's a tough job, and many people don't want the responsibility. You have to work hard, attending meetings with the people and listening to them and applying decisions in a fair and just way. You don't have materially more than others; you are considered a "thought leader," as Christ's disciples were thought leaders who gave up all their worldly goods and aspirations. These leaders combine justice and religion. They carry out the wishes of the people, and they are beholden to them. People may wish to give their leaders material objects as a sign of their gratitude, but nothing is expected on a material level.

The sovereign is not born a sovereign; he or she has to attain that position. Every sovereign chooses the next leader who will take over from them. It might be their child, or it might not.

They might not choose anybody until they're really old, because sometimes you don't attain the state of grace until you have been through a few trials.

A person chosen as the next leader must also overcome many tests and trials and prove themselves fit and worthy. Although the sovereign nominates the next leader, their decision must be validated by the people. If the people truly object, the sovereign must choose a different successor (although this has never happened so far).

Each village or community holds regular meetings where everybody is allowed to participate.

Most of the Q'ehazi living on Pacifica are happy with the way things are and content to live in this way. If a person feels a large amount of discontent with the system, they are theoretically free to leave to start their own society; however, that has never happened so far.

THE JUSTICE SYSTEM

If somebody has done "wrong" to another person, the sovereign or another elder of the village will intervene and mediate between them. There are no formal laws; the person mediating the case will judge situations on a case-by-case basis. He/she will operate from a place of love to find the solution that will benefit everybody equally. Often, an outdoor fairness test will be held to determine the community's opinions in order to make the wisest judgment.

PROCREATION AND POPULATION

Many generations ago, the Q'ehazi people realized that if they could control their population growth, they could improve the quality of their people. Widespread use of the pukatl herb has the side effect of significantly lowering the aggression commonly associated with testosterone, especially in males. Everybody can have as much sex as they want, but it has been separated from the goal of procreation. Everybody uses birth control. All children are brought up by the community. A mother carries her baby in her womb for nine months, but the baby does not technically belong to her once it is born; it belongs to the whole community.

At around the age of fifteen years, every Q'ehazi person has a "naming ceremony" in which they are allowed to select their name and to change their gender, if they choose. Up until that time, all names are generic ones, such as "middle child" or "oldest sister," although some people develop family nicknames. It is believed that by the age of ten, every person will have enough sense of who they are and who they wish to be to choose their own name. If they are particularly creative, they can also create a new name and spelling! As to genders, we have three possible genders in Q'ehazi (based around the idea from the Germanic languages of male, female, and neuter), so you can be either male (his, him, he); female (hers, her, she); or twin souls (zhers, zher, zhe). Thus, there is no sense of any gender being superior to the others, and homosexuality and heterosexuality are equally accepted.

All our Q'ehazi people are empaths, both men and women. Therefore, we are all very sensitive. We don't welcome loud music or noises or ugly sights and sounds. We are kind and gentle with each other and we value kindness and compassion above all. All skin colors are welcomed equally. Nobody is considered inherently more intelligent.

Q'EHAZI PROFESSIONS

Healers; mechanics; growers; caretakers; artists; organizers; administrators; scientists; maintainers; servers; transporters; philosophers; musicians.

ORGANIZATION OF SOCIETY

All Q'ehazi people live in villages comprising about 150 people. The population never grows because people only have enough babies to replace themselves. Until the child is sixteen, all the villagers participate in caring for and teaching it. Most people know who their father and mother are, but it's not considered very important. A person typically forms a special bond with their "primary caretaker," whether or not they're related by blood.

You might be born in a certain village, but later in life, if you wish, you can transfer to a different village. Some villages are named after vocations and some by location, such as the Village by the Creek or the Village on Top of White Mountain. Q'ehazi people tend to stay in their own village most of the time, as there's not much need to travel. The villages barter between each other based on what they produce, e.g., the Village of the Farmers may send produce to the Village of the Healers, and in exchange some healer may visit the Village of the Farmers and tend to the sick. The villages are divided into professions and interest areas, and then in directions, so the Village of Teachers West, East, South, and North, for example.

Around thirty million total people live in Pacifica, with about twenty villages in each directional area of a province—so, a total of eighty villages in every province comprising a 100-mile radius, meaning around 12,000 people. In each directional area of the overall continent, there are around 800,000 people and seventy provinces. Each province has a name, and each area has a name. Usually, names represent land or water features such as mountains or rivers. The continent is divided geographically into around thirty of these areas, and their names represent their geographical location, e.g., the Northern Mountainous Area, or the Northeast Coastal Area.

This type of land distribution and definition was originated by the English settlers who blended with the natives in the sixteenth century. Before that, the tribes had existed independently of each other.

ENTERTAINMENT AND SPORTS

The Q'ehazi people do enjoy a wide variety of sporting activities, but they tend to be noncompetitive and show objective rather than relative prowess of the participant.

ARTS

There is a very strong emphasis on the arts and sports, for everybody. Every single person has at least one artistic form of self-expression or one sport they play and are good at. Artists and sports people are all seen as incredibly valuable in our society. That means that every single artist and sports person has a role to play and is able to do what they love best and what they're good at and be valued for it. Playful skill is a basic human trait that is good for the whole person and the whole body of mankind.

WARS AND FIGHTING

When our Q'ehazi people "fight," we don't want to kill or hurt anybody, so we shoot at them with arrows dipped in a concoction of the pukatl medicinal herb that makes the person fall asleep. We then take them to our village and persuade them to join us rather than fight us. The pukatl herb has healing qualities to take away pain and suffering, is full of endorphins and serotonin, and reduces testosterone considerably, thus reducing aggression, especially in males.

This is how the Q'ehazi tribe gradually absorbs the tribes and peoples who visit our land. Everybody affected by this herb has more empathy and tolerance and kindness towards their fellow human beings and all of nature.

MENTAL HEALTH

Everybody in Q'ehazi has access to free therapy whenever they want it. In fact, the Q'ehazi people are mandated to do therapy so that we can develop insight and self-awareness and keep on the right path.

JOINING THE Q'EHAZI

If you want to join the Q'ehazi, you can, but you must undergo various tests in order to demonstrate that you can attain a state of grace.

BUSINESS

Businesses are all run as cooperatives. Nobody "owns" a business, just like nobody "owns" a child, but everybody in the business contributes to managing it.

MONEY

There is no such thing as money, so in order to be in the Q'ehazi society, you have to be productive in some way. You have to contribute; you have to serve; and the ones who contribute and serve the most are the ones who are the most "successful" and who end up being the leaders, by default.

TAXES

There are no taxes; however, there are different "funds" that people can support, such as a fund for space travel; a fund for education; a fund for defense. There is no money involved, but people can give time and whatever resources they possess, such as voluntary work or food.

Q'EHAZI BELIEFS:
TRADITIONAL AND SPIRITUAL

It is the Q'ehazi belief that if you are not spiritually connected to the earth, it is likely that you will not survive long. Everything has a spirit. Humans are here on earth only a few winters; then they go to the spirit world.

There is a need for understanding, not for vengeance, a need for reparation, not retaliation. The Q'ehazi people believe in hugging strangers because once you've had that kind of physical touch with somebody, it's much harder to think of them as the enemy. We treat both strangers and members of the community with sincere warmth. Society, not a transcendent being, gives human beings their humanity, and humanity comes from conforming to or being part of society. Humanity is a quality we owe to each other. We create each other and need to sustain this creation. And if we belong to each other, we participate in our creations.

Our philosophy encourages community equality, promoting the distribution of abundance. We believe that everyone has different skills and strengths; people are not isolated, and through mutual support, they can help each other to complete themselves.

Our notion of redemption relates to how people deal with errant, deviant, and dissident members of the community. Men and women are born formless like a lump of clay. It is up to the community, as a whole, to use the fire of experience and the wheel of social control to mold them into a pot that may contribute to society.

The Q'ehazi Manifesto talks about the spiritual and ethical beliefs of the people: that every person is created equal, no matter their gender or skin color; that the highest aim of every person is to do good and to attain a state of grace; that the health of the community as a whole is as important as the health of the individual (because it creates the health of the individual, and two are interdependent); that all living beings are to be valued; that it is important to live in harmony with the rest of nature.

Mother Earth must be respected and honored as a living being, and all beings in nature honored and left alone in their natural habitat. Their energy must be allowed to resonate freely throughout the universe for healing to come to the world.

We are all one, just like cells in a body make up the whole body, and when some cells are sick, the whole body is sick. In exactly the same way, the whole of humanity, the whole of the world, cannot be healthy unless every single being within it is healthy.

The Q'ehazi realize that we are all here together in order to live a meaningful existence. Q'ehazi take care of our own bodies, minds, and spirits because we have healthy self-esteem. Because we have meaningful and pleasant lives, we never need to abuse drugs and alcohol and medications. Every single person is a valuable treasure to be taken care of and nurtured, body, mind, and soul.

The Q'ehazi people are born with an obligation to give back and pay forward. Status is acquired by giving things away. Thus, we have a ceremony in which the goal is to give away as much as possible. We maintain balance by repaying favors and doing good for others and for the earth. Balance is essential for human survival. The future of our environment is our responsibility. How we transport ourselves and how we heat and light our homes is a major factor in protecting our earth, and we optimize our health by eating food free of poisons that we grow ourselves.

The three basics of the Q'ehazi calling are as follows:

The giving of gifts: the gifts of the people in our neighborhood are boundless.

The power of association: we join our gifts together, and they become amplified, magnified, productive, and celebrated.

Hospitality: we welcome strangers because we value their gifts and need to share our own. Our doors are open.

APPENDIX III

Your Turn

Now it's your turn to contribute to the Q'ehazi story.

This book is the first of a trilogy, and the book is only partly a story. It's also partly a creation of a new potential world. Our current world appears to be breaking down before our eyes.

Can you imagine a better world? If we can visualize it together, perhaps we can collectively manifest it.

You can set up Q'ehazi groups where you discuss how a more ideal world would look, and what it would take to get there.

You can come up with your own ideas on how to create a perfect world, and we can continue to modify and add to the vision in future Q'ehazi books.

You can have fun using your own creativity and wisdom to imagine how the world could be better.

You can contact the author here:
info@yourworldbeyond.com

Visit the website here:
www.yourworldbeyond.com

Now that you've read the book, get updates on further books in the trilogy and stay a part of the community!

CPSIA information can be obtained
at www.ICGtesting.com
Printed in the USA
BVHW040921070623
665497BV00008B/684

9 781646 639373